Grandfather Poplar

Grandfather Poplar

by Diana Henderson

Diana Henderson

ISBN: 978-1-944662-40-0

Illustration by W.R. Heustis © 2015
Cover Design by Diana Henderson © 2015

Dedication

To my parents, grandparents, and ancestors who instilled a love
for nature that lives forever in my heart and to every tree I have
ever known and loved.

Acknowledgments

Thank you to my parents and grandparents who showed me how to cherish the land and live in harmony with nature. Thank you for giving us a yard filled with trees and a forest in which to roam.

Thank you to Worth Dewey Henderson, my late father, for being the consummate storyteller and to Doris Henderson, my mother, for awakening and encouraging my love of books and writing.

Thank you to my patient, loving, talented husband Drew Becker for giving me the time to write this book and for serving as its editor and publisher.

Thank you to Orson Scott Card, Hugo and Nebula award-winning author, for the wonderful critique and input when this novel was just a short story.

Great appreciation also goes to Dennis Sixkiller, longtime host of the radio show Cherokee Voices, Cherokee Sounds, and Marc W. Case, author of *Simply Cherokee*, for your help with the Cherokee language.

I also want to acknowledge my readers who, like me, love the trees and walk softly on the earth.

Contents

Discover more:

Visit the website at www.GrandfatherPoplar.com

Facebook page: facebook.com/GrandfatherPoplar/

Chapter 1:
An Unexpected Encounter

A sound as loud as a nearby crack of lightning pulled her consciousness back from the nightmare. It was one of those dreams that felt more real than what happens in this world, and she was relieved to awaken from its devastating landscape. Although her heart was thumping madly, the rest of her body felt as if it were made of lead. It took a few moments to discern whether the world around her was real or some subconscious scene.

If indeed the sound had been a lightning strike, Melissa needed to check her forest friends. The trees were always her first thought, because they were her truest companions, her secret home. From the tallest poplar to the sturdiest oak, each one held her heart and called her kindred.

The red digits on her clock read 3:12. She rose in lumbering movements of half-sleep still trying to shake off the dream. Everything seemed quiet now. As she came to the window, she looked for signs of a storm, but only still, cool air greeted her. The October sky was filled with a panorama of stars and all was silent beneath its canopy of velvet serenity.

"Was it just something from the dream," she whispered to herself. No, she was sure that the sound had come from this world. Although she had school in the morning, her inner voice kept prompting her to discover the source of the booming crash.

Melissa quickly dressed in some sweats, her favorite hiking boots and a jacket. She considered waking her parents to see if they had heard the noise, but, as she crept past their room, snoring from both of them made it clear they had not. She decided not to rouse them out of a deep sleep. Her father so often had insomnia that she knew he needed the rest. Besides, she had made many excursions into the woods during the wee hours to breathe in the sunrise atop her favorite ridge beside her beloved yellow poplar, the grandfather of all the forest. At this hour, she knew she would return before anyone got up for the day; so off she went, stealthily closing the door behind her.

How she loved the night air this time of year, she thought as her breath expanded its warm fog into the atmosphere. She felt the peaceful blanket that the star-filled sky created for the Earth wrap her senses in its serenity. This time, though, she didn't take the time to drift into that peace. Perhaps it was simply the lingering effect of the nightmare, but she felt a sense of urgency that propelled her quickly into the forest.

The trees were sleeping now as was most of the world around her. She touched a few of her friends along the path, but they were clearly in that state of nightly quietude that most of the forest residents sank into after sundown.

She wanted to shake the memory of the dream, and so she placed all her attention on the task at hand. Find the source of the crash that called her into consciousness. As she walked through the slumbering woodland, it seemed that somehow she knew exactly where she was meant to go, and she found her footsteps growing swifter. Despite the darkness of the moonless sky, her eyes adjusted to the seeming pitch of night.

Everything remained still as she came to the clearing in the woods where the creek meandered slowly and quietly. She stopped just at the edge of the trees. Melissa had been told that she had the sight of an owl, and, even in the dimness beneath the starry sky, she could see a beautiful white-tailed deer, probably a doe by her size, standing by the brook. Bending her slender head down to the water, the doe drank in silence.

Melissa imagined herself as motionless as the trees around her. She determined to make no sound, to do nothing to disturb this precious scene. Internally she repeated, "I am a tree, only a tree. You have nothing to fear from me." Breathing so quietly that even she herself could not hear her respiration, she sent love and gratitude to the deer for sharing her beauty and gracefulness.

Melissa heard nothing except the slightest wind rustling a few precarious autumn leaves ready to depart their perch and waft to the ground. Silence. Calm. Then came a sound—so small— nothing more than a twig breaking beneath the weight of an unannounced stranger. The deer caught the scent and bounded away into the forest so close that Melissa could have reached out and touched her as she fled.

Yet, Melissa stood rigid, making no sound, for she saw the reason behind the deer's retreat. As she looked at the mountain lion from her post at the edge of the forest, the oddest thoughts passed through her mind. It sounds like a house cat on serious steroids, she thought. No, no, like a baby wailing somewhere in another room. That's it. As though acknowledging something that was not her own, she noted that her heart was beating outside her chest.

"Quiet now, quiet now. Silence even your thoughts," she heard an inner voice say. "You are a tree, a part of the forest, nothing more. You are invisible."

As the voice within her spoke—such a familiar voice, she thought—she experienced the strongest sensation of someone having placed a blanket of calm all around her. Her mind became stillness. Her body seemed to merge with the ethers as if she were made of smoke or starlight or the cool fresh air that surely continued to move in and out through her lungs but now ever so slowly and softly. She grew as silent as the sleeping forest.

Then the strangest thing happened. The mountain lion gazed in her direction, made a mewling chirp and ran swiftly back in the direction from which it had come.

Melissa's knees suddenly felt as if they were made of water. The mantle of calm evaporated and her body started to tremble. As quietly as possible, she knelt and then simply fell to the ground. She looked around for the source of the wisdom and peace she had received in that moment of terror. For so many years she had communicated with the trees, and they always helped her find the place of stillness within, so she was certain that one of her tree friends must have awakened and shared his gentle sense of security with her. Yet, they all appeared to be still in their own nighttime blanket of splendid sleep.

As Melissa sat on the ground, she began to find her inner strength again. She reached into her jacket pocket, where she liked to keep a snack for those times when hiking left her hungry. Thankfully, she found a granola bar that she wolfed down in three bites. Feeling more herself, she pondered whether to return home or keep going on her errand in search of the source of the sound.

Something told her that she needed to continue. She turned to follow the creek in the opposite direction from the path taken by the mountain lion. This was the way she originally intended to go in any case. She didn't have far to walk before she saw why she was called here.

"Oh, Lonnie," she said. The tall loblolly pine whom she had named Lonnie was hit by lightning two summers past, and all those in his forest clan knew that his injuries were likely fatal. Melissa had hoped fervently that he would recover. He had withstood the pain of his sap boiling after the strike, and his body was severely damaged. Yet, he had chosen to remain amidst his companions near the stream for as long as he could.

By the time she arrived, Lonnie's sweet spirit had departed. When he fell, his long, slender trunk created a bridge across the creek. His two sister trees, who had stood beside him for many decades, were the only wakeful companions near where his once tall frame had climbed toward the sun.

"Lily, Lolly, I'm so sorry," Melissa said, caressing their scaly gray-brown bark. She felt a sense of loss fill her heart but held it at bay in hopes of bringing them comfort.

"He was ready to go, dear walker friend," the sister trees said in unison. "He only stayed so long to be sure we would recover from the blast that barely touched us in comparison. Precious brother," said Lily.

"Lonnie was such a kind tree," Melissa said. In truth, this was a massive understatement. The rugged pine had refused to allow his fellow trees to feel his pain after the lightning strike. He held it all within himself. Every tree could feel and know their companions. Yet, Lonnie had chosen to place a buffer of pine resin-strong protection around his pain. Although Melissa didn't visit Lonnie often or know him well, for this and many other things, she would remember him always.

"It's all right," said Lolly. "No more pain now. He's gone to be with our ancestors. He'll be happy in the arms of the Mother of us all. We're at peace and so is he."

Melissa hugged Lily and Lolly and filled her heart with all the love she could to send to their very core.

She knew that her tree friends experienced such losses differently from humans. They would live on and pay homage to his memory by thriving and spreading the tales of their brother tree who was so strong he outlasted the lightning. She would join them in honoring this once brave and loyal loblolly.

Melissa wasn't sure how long she had been away. Thankfully, the sky showed no sign of impending morning; so perhaps if she hurried back home she would find a little rest—this time free of nightmares—before the clock or her mother beckoned her back to wakefulness.

Walking home with less urgency, she let her mind attune to the sleeping giant of the forest. In times like these, she sensed more than the unique spirit of each tree here. It was as if the whole forest were one great consciousness that stretched for miles and miles and held everything in its comforting embrace. If she could sleep in that presence, she felt sure that her rest would be as deep and dreamless as the Earth itself.

After stealing through the house on tiptoe, Melissa climbed into bed weary to her deepest core. But her sleep was not dreamless.

Chapter 2: Communing with the Trees

Melissa had felt ragged all day after her excursion in the night. The threads of her nightmare wove silken webs through her brain like the spiders' handiwork that gleamed in the forest when touched by dew or sunlight. The difference was that these strands were anything but beautiful. Yet, they clung just as surely to the parts of her consciousness that sought to escape the images from the realm of sleep.

It was only a dream, Melissa kept telling herself over and over. It's just that it felt so real. She had had this terrible feeling one other time not that long ago. Her favorite neighbor who had become like family to Melissa died during the wee hours some months back. The night "Grandma" Reynolds passed, Melissa dreamed that she was by the old woman's bedside and saw her soul leave her body. She awakened that morning crying and aching to her bones. It wasn't long before the call came confirming that her beloved neighbor had died.

She felt much the same this morning. Last night's dream left her with that feeling of pain etched into every muscle.

She tried to tell herself that these were just the remnants of fear after facing down a mountain lion. But the nightmare that even in this moment threatened to rewind itself into her conscious thoughts shrouded the corners of her mind in a cloud of apprehension.

Melissa pressed her back against the cool, rough bark of the slippery elm as she pretended to listen to her younger brother Kevin, who seemed at times more like some bizarre alien life form than a blood relation. As she watched him stab the caterpillar with a stick, Melissa fought to keep from visibly wincing. The pain signal emanating from this small fuzzy creature sent waves of screaming sensation into every fiber of her body.

A shiver ran down her back as an inner storm began to thunder inside her. A dream image of a dead forest, only stumps remaining bubbled up beneath the surface of her consciousness.

"Grossed you out, didn't I?" Kevin said, leering in her direction.

He pushed the stick that held the oozing caterpillar toward her. She couldn't help herself. Wriggling her back against the tree, she wrenched her face and turned away. But she knew the shudder inside stemmed from more than this small dying insect.

"You really don't get it, do you, Kevin? Everything in this world has its purpose. That woolly bear caterpillar doesn't hurt anything. She only eats the weeds. She lets us know what kind of winter is coming by the length of her stripes. Plus, she was going to be a beautiful tiger moth come the spring. And you killed her for nothing more than your twisted amusement."

Melissa's voice trembled with emotion and her eyes watered, but she could see that her younger brother was feeling a little less triumphant now.

Melissa felt Slippery Sally's voice echo through her spine and heard the elm tree's words in her mind. She pressed her back harder against Sally's craggy bark so she could listen better.

"Are you sure this beast is related to you? It acts more like the spawn of a beaver," Slippery Sally said. "And you know how much we trees love those nasty, devouring little rodents."

Sally laughed her silky smooth chuckle, and Melissa's cloudy mood began to dissolve like a morning fog lifting slowly beneath the rising sun. She fought smiling, but Slippery Sally's zinging energy zoomed through her with a feeling of what she liked to think of as electric waterfalls.

"What are you grinning about, metal mouth?" Kevin asked. "You look like some kind of nut case. Next thing I know, you'll be talking to the stupid trees again."

Melissa closed her lips but still smiled knowingly.

"Melissa, I do wish he hadn't heard you talking to 'Old Buzzard Breath,'" Sally grumbled, referring to Grandfather Poplar. Sally's voice hummed in Melissa's head like an itch she could never quite scratch. "Now, this brother of yours won't leave us *alone*.

"Of course, this squirrel brain could *never* hear our voices. He's too busy listening to his own," Sally added. "I hope he doesn't bother you too much. Maybe I could drown him in a puddle of falling leaves."

Melissa gazed up into the spreading branches high above her. Most of Sally's foliage was a dull yellow this time of year. A few of the brown leaves wafted gently to the ground around her and her brother. Melissa picked up one of the fallen ones and caressed its saw-toothed edges with her fingertips. Kevin, who fumed—no doubt because she hadn't reacted to his remarks—brushed a leaf from his sweatshirt.

"Just you don't forget," he said, "if you don't keep cleaning my room, I'll tell Mom and Dad how you talk to trees. 'Course, they'll probably think you were talking to yourself, but, hey, that's just as bad. So you're doomed any way you look at it, maggot breath."

He looked smug. Kevin had been blackmailing her ever since he caught her talking to Grandfather Poplar in late August. She'd been cleaning his room for almost two months, and he was such a total slob—constantly leaving dirty dishes on the floor and then covering them up with his slimy clothes. Things were always growing in Kevin's room, and they weren't houseplants.

"Don't worry, Kevin. I haven't forgotten yet, have I? And if I ever did, I'm sure the smell of your grungy socks and underwear would remind me. Whew! How can one person have such incredible B.O.?"

This brought an end to his perfect grin—the straight, white teeth that always reminded Melissa of her mouthful of braces.

"Well, I'm going back to the house. Oh, and Mom said my room had to be clean before dinner," he gloated. Again the self-satisfied showing of teeth.

"Yes, oh master, oh one who grins like the jackal and laughs like the hyena," she said. As he sneered and turned to walk away, she added, "And let us not forget farts like the elephant, oh exalted one."

Kevin quickly retorted with a frog to her thigh—his favorite comeback when she teased him. Another bruise to join the others—quickly fading tattoos on her pale skin. Melissa thought momentarily about retaliation, but, although Kevin was four years younger and a thousand years more immature, he was as big as she and maybe a little stronger.

"What's the matter? Scared to fight me? Know I'll beat you good, eh, Sissy Melissa?"

"I won't resort to your barbaric level," she replied in an even tone.

Kevin paused long enough to consider a worthy comeback, but instead he shuffled away toward the house, and Melissa was left alone with her thoughts and her friends—maybe the only real friends she had in the whole world—the trees.

A momentary flash of last night's dream suddenly forced its way into the foreground of her thoughts, but she fought it back so swiftly that her friend Sally didn't seem to notice.

"Someone needs to teach that grub some manners," Sally said with her soothing inner voice that slid along the corridors of Melissa's mind.

"I know, Sally. Believe me, I know. I can't do much about it except try to be who I am and let go of whatever he throws at me."

"Well, at least that's one walker who got up and walked away," Billy Black Gum chimed in. As the wind touched Billy's leaves, there was a flurry of color. Each October, he wore dazzling reds and garnets mixed with the last remaining deep greens of summer.

"I do hope you won't be walking off too soon, Melissa," he said.

Until he spoke, Melissa hadn't realized that her foot was leaning against an outgrowth of one of Billy's roots. She had to be touching the trees in order to hear their voices. She reached over and caressed his trunk.

"Sorry to inflict my aphid-infested brother's presence on you, Billy."

Sally and Billy's leaves rustled with laughter.

"I think I need to visit Grandfather Poplar," Melissa said.

"I know he's not your favorite tree in the forest, but to me he shines like the sun."

"Grandfather Sun might not take kindly to the comparison to that cantankerous old poplar," Sally said. "That old sack of root rot's so full of bile that even the woodpeckers wouldn't chance a nip in his bark."

"In this vast forest, couldn't you find a more pleasant poplar," Billy asked.

"You other trees are too rough on him, you know. You just have to understand him. Be nice to him. Bring out his good side a little."

"That's a novel approach," Billy offered, "but it would never work. Besides, if your advice is so good, why don't you use it on your brother?"

"Believe me, I've tried, but he is, after all, a much lower life form than a tree," Melissa answered, and gave both of her friends a little pat on the bark in parting.

As she walked away, images from her nightmare persisted in their assault. It was just a dream. Stop replaying it. Grandfather Poplar will set me straight, she thought. I need to be free of this.

Pushing those inner visions away, she walked toward the center of the woods careful to watch her feet to be sure she didn't trample on the young saplings that climbed toward the light beneath the limbs of their parent trees. She paused for a moment to touch "hi" to her friends along the way—Penelope Pinnoak, Dagmar Dogwood, Beatrice Beechtree, Sammy Sweetgum, Randy Red Maple and the rest. The human names she'd offered them seemed to suit her friends, whose real names were not translatable and couldn't be spoken by a walker, as they referred to humans.

Melissa climbed the steep hill to the summit where Grandpop, the nickname she gave her long-time friend and tree teacher, raised his limbs toward the sky. This time of year he was covered in gold, and she had to catch her breath as much from his beauty as from the uphill trek. A shadow passed above him and Melissa heard the familiar screech of one of the pair of red-tailed hawks that nested high in Grandfather Poplar's limbs.

"You'd think those pea-brained birds would know you by now," Grandfather Poplar said as soon as Melissa's hand reached bark.

She gazed toward the treetops where the hawks soared. If she closed her eyes and lifted her psyche beyond her physical form, she could connect with them and feel the heady sense of flight riding one current of wind to the next.

"What's the matter, Grandpop, allergic to birds?" Melissa teased. "Or are you just jealous? You'd probably fly away from most human beings too if you weren't rooted firmly to the ground."

"Hmmph." He rustled his disapproval.

"You know why I like to tease you," Melissa asked. "Because you're so good at taking a joke. Well, that and the fact that nobody else has the nerve to do it. You're the oldest, the biggest and the orneriest tree in the forest, and somebody's got to teach you not to take yourself so seriously."

"I've never met a polite walker in my life nor one who could *teach* me anything. In case you've forgotten, I numbered 144 rings last spring. That makes me one of the oldest of my kin and a lot wiser than any 14-year-old paper-making, wood-burning plant-eater that walks on two feet."

Ignoring the insult, Melissa caressed his knotty brownish-gray bark. "Your modesty always amazes me, Grandpop, but I love you anyway," she said with a grin. "Truth is I can't quite imagine being so *old*, but I'm sure I'd be just as proud and as grumpy about it as you are."

It had taken Melissa years to gather the guts to tease Grandfather Poplar. The great yellow poplar first spoke to her when she was only six, and at the time his voice frightened her so much that she screamed, jumped up and ran full force down the hill. When she tripped over a rock and fell, she glanced around for her pursuer and saw no one—just the trees above her and the brook below. She heard nothing but a few distant songbirds and the breeze rustling through bright green spring leaves. She'd gone home that day with skinned knees and elbows and a bump on her head. Although she failed to mention hearing a voice, her mother had forbidden her to play alone in the woods again. Not that she needed the warning. The scare had been enough—at least for a while.

During that next week, she kept repeating the words over and over to herself: "Stop digging at my trunk, little worm." Who would have said such a strange thing? Melissa's natural curiosity finally triumphed over fear. She returned to reenact the moment, but this time she waited to find the owner of the voice. Thus, the world of trees had opened to Melissa—simply because she'd used a sharp rock to burrow into the bark at the base of a tree. She had wanted only to see if there were sap in it as her first-grade teacher said. She thought the biggest tree would have the most sap. Besides, she was drawn to this one because of its funny crooked trunk—like something out of Chutes and Ladders. But she got more than she bargained for that day.

Melissa could tell from the lengthy silence that Grandfather Poplar was sulking and required a little coaxing to return to his usual good-natured though crabby self.

"Yessir, Grandpop, you may be getting old, but you're just as pretty as when we met eight years ago. I remember your leaves looked like thousands of green butterflies perched on your gray limbs, and your green and orange flowers made me think somebody had planted tulips in a tree."

"How many times have I told you not to call me 'pretty'? When you get to be my age, it's not respectable to be referred to with such a silly human word."

Melissa detected the ease of gruffness in his inner voice and knew she'd gotten to him.

"You're right, I guess. 'Beautiful' would be a better word—especially at this time of year. That gold autumn overcoat gets me every time."

"I know exactly what you're doing, little sapling," he said, using his affectionate nickname for her. "I just let you get away with it sometimes because I'm such a good-natured old fool."

"Now, Grandpop, don't go putting yourself down. You're just as big a crabapple as you were yesterday and the day before and the day before and the —"

"As I told you, Melissa, you can't fool me with all these compliments," he said with a chuckle that rattled Melissa as if she were leaning against a big bass drum.

Melissa sometimes wondered what Grandfather Poplar's voice would be like if it were spoken aloud rather than felt through the reverberation of touch and thought. The voices of the trees seemed to echo through her skin along a path to her brain. Each tree voice was different—Sally's as smooth and rich as warm butter, Susie Sugar Maple's a thick and syrupy drawl, and Grandpop's so deep, gravelly and powerful that she could only touch him lightly or she might be blasted by the resounding bass that boomed inside her mind. Melissa still wasn't sure if these voices, accents and intonations belonged to the trees, or if her imagination filled in the gaps and made each tree sound as she thought it should. Anthropomorphizing, that's what her teachers would say—giving human qualities to inanimate objects. But Melissa knew the truth—that trees were just about the most animated creatures she'd ever met. Each one spoke to her in a distinctive way and had a unique personality—Grandpop's being a little too different for almost every other tree's tastes.

"Grandpop, I hate to bring this up when you're in such a good mood, but —"

"Why on Earth are you doing it then? I'll never understand why a walker would start a sentence that way."

"Well, I guess it's sort of a polite warning that we're going to say something you don't want to hear. Anyway, I was wondering if you couldn't try to be a little friendlier to the other trees in the forest. A human really shouldn't be your only friend, you know."

Grandfather Poplar was silent for a long moment.

"And maybe trees shouldn't be your only friends, little sapling," he answered in an unusually kind and quiet manner. "I suppose we're just two leaves growing out of the same shoot, Melissa. Neither of us can stomach much conversation with our own kind."

Melissa had expected the usual argument, the typical remarks about the many lesser trees in the woods, about how he was too wise to be understood by their sort. But she didn't count on having her own words turned against her.

"I get what you're saying, Grandpop. It's just that I don't fit in. My parents tell me I should make more friends, but they don't know what it's like. I *feel* everything too much, and I'm just useless when it comes to talking to *people*."

"Well, if you're that awful, I don't know why I should waste time speaking to you," Grandfather Poplar interrupted. "Yes, I can see I picked the wrong Kincaid when I let you hear my voice. I should have chosen your brother—what's his name—Devon, Evan? No doubt he would have been much more entertaining. You sound like a hive of hornets building one of their wretched nests on my limbs and are obviously every bit as mindless as a worker bee, a drone. I think I'll start calling you Drone, that is, if I decide to talk to you at all."

This was the very kind of wicked wit that his fellow trees failed to appreciate. But Melissa felt his love beneath the bluster.

"Bzzzzzz. Bzzzzzzzzzz. Bzzzzzzzzzzzz," she replied.

"Owning the part, I see," Grandpop said with a tone somewhere between a growl and a guffaw.

Melissa laughed at herself and at Grandpop's phony gruffness. In her mind, the storm-etched yellow poplar was replaced by a wrinkled, gray-haired bespectacled man—the grandfather she'd never known. His voice was deep and reverberating, and everyone listened when he talked. That's how she imagined her father's father, who died when she was only two. Her mother's parents lived all the way across the country in Seattle and were nothing more than a faint presence in her life.

Grandfather Poplar was the closest thing Melissa had to a real grandfather, and she had an adopted grandmother as well but not among the trees. Grandma Reynolds had owned the land across the creek until she died a few months ago at age 87.

Her brown, leathery skin always reminded Melissa of bark, and the wisdom of her stories was not unlike the lore of her forest companions. Most people wanted nothing to do with the old lady but Melissa loved her. Besides, visiting her gave Melissa a great excuse for trekking through the woods onto the Reynolds' land, and she got to share passing conversations with her tree friends all along the way.

The thought of Grandma Reynolds brought Melissa back to the dream she had on the night her friend died, which in turn prompted more awareness of last night's achingly painful excursion into the nether realms of the unconscious.

"Grandpop," she said but stopped herself from continuing. How could she tell him about such a horrible dream? Surely it was just some crazy combination of tamales for dinner and too many bad TV shows. She pushed the thought aside.

"Grandpop, did you ever talk to Mrs. Reynolds?"

"I never needed to, little one. She treated us well; she nourished and cared for many in the plant world. Unlike most walkers, including yourself, she never needed a reprimand."

"But that can't be the *only* reason you would ever talk to a person."

"Not the only one but probably the best. I don't make a habit of letting walkers into our world. I can't stop other trees from doing it, but for the most part it's a mistake," Grandfather Poplar said seriously. "Still, it's lucky for us that most of you have terrible memories and short attention spans. The children who seem able to hear us soon grow too bored to listen, and eventually they forget it ever really happened."

"But you're not sorry you talked to me, are you?" she asked, a little hurt by his remarks.

"I can't say I haven't thought better of it a time or two, but you're different from most, Melissa. You never got bored or stopped listening," he said reassuringly. "I do hope you realize the depth of sarcasm in my remark about your remarkably uncurious brother. I would never have spoken to such an odious droning tree frog."

"Yeah, I may only be a walker, but even I know *that*. Speaking of my creepy brother, you know about my little problem with Kevin blackmailing me? What do you think I should do about it?"

"As far as I can see, there's only one solution: Lock him in a dark place, and deprive him of all water, nourishment and sunlight until he shrivels up."

"Come on, Grandpop, be serious. I'm getting pretty tired of cleaning the uncleanable. The bad thing is his room is dirty the very next day, so it starts all over again. If 'Squirrel Breath' weren't such a rodent, I'd just forget about it. But you've seen and heard him...."

"Well, little one, you have three real choices: Continue to meet his demands, take your chances and let him tell your parents that you converse with trees, or be honest with them yourself. Mind you, I still like my original plan best."

"Out of those three, I really have only *one* option, and speaking of which, I'd better get going. I have a scum-covered, rat-infested stink hole to clean, disinfect and deodorize before dinner. I'll probably come back to see you tomorrow afternoon if I can shake the brother from the bottomless pit."

Melissa hugged Grandfather Poplar's trunk, which was far too wide for her arms to encompass even by a quarter.

"Come soon, little sapling," he replied, and she thought she heard what in a human would have been a sigh as she pulled away to go.

Melissa stopped at the bottom of the hill before crossing the rocks in the stream. She lovingly stroked the deep golden leaf she'd found beneath Grandpop's trunk. Gazing up toward him, she held her breath as she watched the golden-orange rays of the setting sun mingle among his branches and play upon his leaves.

"Bye, Grandpop," she called, and the wind blew his limbs gently as if in answer.

Melissa stepped gingerly over the stones that made her path across the creek. They too were her friends. With Grandpop's help she had learned to sense and sometimes even see the nature spirits of the stones, the water, the plants. At dusk and dawn when the twilight danced upon the water of the stream, she could sit at the foot of Grandfather Poplar and catch glimpses of those spirits—little glowing lights brighter than fireflies—as they capered on the hillside below and at the water's edge.

The creek was low this year because of the dry summer they'd had, but the water still sparkled in rainbow hues as the waning sunlight touched it. A hundred yards or so beyond the brook, a small faded orange flag attached to a post marked the property line between Mrs. Reynolds' place, where Grandfather Poplar resided, and her family's land. Melissa's father had shown her the edges of their property when she was very young. He triggered her interest in the outdoors by telling her about all the different trees and plants, but that was a long time ago; he was much too busy these days. So on her own Melissa explored the woods on both sides of the line.

Over the years, she'd learned to recognize most of the forest inhabitants—not just the trees but the birds, mushrooms, ferns, insects, even the weeds—especially the dreaded poison ivy, oak and sumac. She knew these woods better than any place in the world. When she needed to escape from a dull class or the pressures of school, she simply recalled them in perfect, vivid detail. The smell of deep rich forest soil, of decaying leaves; the scent of spring blooms; the gentle sound of water flowing over rocks; of dead leaves crackling beneath her feet; of squirrels chattering, high limbs creaking under them as they swooped from treetop to treetop; the feel of coolness beneath the elms and oaks on a warm summer day; the touch of bark, gnarled or smooth against her cheek or her fingertips; and always the colors—from the chartreuse of spring to the emerald of summer, from the jeweled flashes of autumn to the crystalline grays of winter—Melissa loved every facet of this world, her world.

As she walked back through the woods, Melissa heard the birds begin their early evening chatter. But the closer she got to home, the more she became aware of the unwelcome intrusion of humankind. In the distance, she could hear the cars passing on the newly-widened road in front of her house. Her family had a big front yard, and the house was far enough from the street that most people wouldn't be bothered. But after Melissa talked with the trees, after she listened with her heart and heard with her whole being, the noises outside her were magnified into the pitch of a scream. Even the quiet sounds of the woods were amplified, but these simply reassured her. Yet, she still got chills up her spine as the onslaught of noise pollution bombarded her ears. It felt like the real world was scratching its fingernails on the blackboard of her psyche.

Before going into the house, she took one last look back at the woods that were her truest home. She shook her head as images from her nightmare blazed briefly in her mind. Just a dream, she thought. Nothing but a dream.

Chapter 3:
A Family Nightmare

As usual, Melissa managed to get Kevin's room neat before their parents arrived home from work. She didn't have time to start dinner though, so her Mom wasn't exactly thrilled. After all, she couldn't take credit for cleaning her brother's room. That had to be their little secret.

She was used to the nagging. That went on almost every day after her mother came home from work at Drexell's Department Store, where she managed the cosmetic department. Perhaps all the noxious perfume odors at Dreadful's, as Melissa not so affectionately referred to the store, assaulted her mother's senses and gradually ate away her natural kindness. Maybe because she had to smile at people all day long, her face was too tired to smile at home.

Whatever the case, Melissa never envied her mother except for her appearance. She knew how to wear makeup so that she looked like a natural beauty, which wasn't far from the truth. Melissa had always wanted to look just like her mom, but she didn't believe for a minute that it would ever happen—no matter how many times her mother read *The Ugly Duckling* to her when she was a kid.

"Melissa, is the table set for dinner," her mother yelled from the bedroom. "I just called your father to get him to bring something home."

Melissa walked to the kitchen door. "Yeah, I've set a place for you and Daddy, but I've got homework to finish; so I'll just grab something later. And Kevin's already stuffing his face with leftovers in front of the TV."

Her mother came out in her bathrobe and proceeded to stalk down the hall toward the den with Melissa following at a safe distance.

"Kevin, drop that slice of pizza right back onto your plate," she demanded. "Your father wants us all to eat dinner together tonight. It's about time we started acting like civilized people in this house."

As much as Melissa relished seeing Kevin reprimanded for a change, she wasn't thrilled with the idea of a family dinner. That usually meant the four of them arguing or sitting in silence around the kitchen table or, worse yet, having to discuss something serious with her parents. But when her mother took this tone, there was no escape.

Kevin too knew when he was beaten. An angry look pinching his face, he turned off the TV and took his plate back to the kitchen, grumbling under his breath the whole way. A little later their father made his entrance, set down his briefcase and a bucket of KFC and took the quickest route to the bathroom just like every other night of the week.

But Melissa soon realized that this wasn't just another night. Her parents had made a decision that was going to affect her life; she just wasn't sure how much yet. Melissa was taking a bite of her biscuit when her father made the announcement.

"Your mother and I have decided to sell off some of the land. We'll keep a few acres around the house so we won't be losing any of the yard, but everything past the first acre or so of the woods is part of the deal. The developers who just bought Old Lady Reynolds' place made us an offer that was too good to turn down."

"Does that mean I can't go down to the creek anymore," Kevin interrupted. "And what happens to my tree house?"

"Sorry, Kev. The tree house will have to come down. You can build another one in the trees closer to home. As for going down to the creek, you can still do that for now, but pretty soon they'll start grading the land and then *neither* of you will be able to make your little trips into the woods." He looked pointedly at Melissa.

Melissa's head was spinning. She hardly knew what to say. She glanced glumly at Kevin, who obviously wasn't too thrilled with the idea himself. When he noticed her dismay, a gloating grin spread across his lips.

"I bet you'll really hate that, won't you, Melissa? You won't be able to—what do you call it—oh yeah, *commune* with the trees anymore, huh?"

Melissa barely heard Kevin. She fixed her gaze on her father, the man who had shown her how to love the forest. "Dad, I don't understand why you want to sell that land," she said, trying to control the turmoil within her. "It's beautiful; it's the best part about living here. How can you take that away from us?"

"The decision's already been made, Melissa," her mother replied in an icy tone. "I know you just love to go off tromping into the woods, but that's really not a very smart thing to be doing in this day and age. Besides, you need to get involved in some kind of social activity. You spend far too much time by yourself. It isn't healthy."

"Your Mom's right, you know. It was different when Old Lady Reynolds was alive. Nobody ever came near her place except you. You must've been the only kid in the county that wasn't scared stiff of the old crone. So you were surrounded by 110 empty acres. But now that's all changing, and like it or not, you'll have to change with it. To tell you the truth, one of the main reasons we decided to sell was to keep you out of those woods now that they're not going to be such a safe, serene place anymore."

"But Daddy, how could you?" she pleaded, tears stinging her eyes. She wouldn't let them see her cry.

Melissa's chair scraped loudly against the wooden floor as she rose, pushing the seat back with the motion of her body. She felt like throwing her plate across the room, but instead she simply stormed out and ran upstairs.

After she had a chance to cool down, Melissa walked to the window and looked outside into the dim reaches of the woods. She was always thankful during difficult times that her room faced the back of the house so that she could get a glimpse of the one place in the world where she belonged. She opened the window and breathed deeply blowing the smoke of warm breath into cool autumn air. She gazed out at the trees in the sleeping forest. All the days of her life they had inspired her with the renewal of spring, shaded her in summer, filled her with awe in autumn, and warmed her heart in the depths of winter. Her truest companions, her friends, her family.

"I won't let them do this," she whispered. "They can't keep me from you. I'll still find a way to visit you, and that's a promise."

Melissa didn't finish her homework that night. She couldn't keep her mind on algebra; the numbers and the symbols kept transforming into trees. She knew her teachers would be surprised when the reliable one didn't have the answers in tomorrow's class, but that didn't seem to matter much now.

Her mother attempted to coax her out of her locked room once and even sent Kevin to try and do the same, but Melissa didn't want to hear it. She turned off the light and went to bed early. As she lay there, she contemplated ways she could sneak around and spend time with the trees. Just before she fell asleep, she had the nagging thought that she was forgetting something very important, but it wouldn't come to her. The last thing that floated through her consciousness as she drifted into the darkness of slumber were her father's words: "grading the land."

Chapter 4:
The Oncoming Storm

Melissa awakened trembling and soaked with sweat. She'd left the window cracked last night, and now the cold air stung her moist forehead. It was still early. It would be well over an hour before the golden-orange streaks of dawn began to paint the sky with the gilded brushstrokes of glowing sunrise. For now, the canopy of stars remained visible, and the forest lingered in the luxury of slumber.

All night Melissa had been wracked by frightening dreams, but none had quite awakened her until this last powerful nightmare galloped into her mind with thundering hooves that shook her still. The dream had pounded certain knowledge into her brain: THE TREES! Her friends were in terrible peril.

She got up and closed the window. Holding her breath, she looked outside. Everything appeared just as it had the night before. Still, Melissa could feel the danger like a dark and nameless creature gnawing at her heart and mind.

She quickly and quietly dressed in her jeans, warm sweater, wool socks and her most noiseless pair of sneakers. After throwing on a light coat, she opened the door to her room and crept down the stairs. At 6:00 in the morning, the house was soundless. No one would be up for 45 minutes. Melissa walked through the kitchen and out the back door into the bracing October air.

In the darkness of the woods, most people would have trod fearfully, but Melissa could have found her way even without the gift of her night vision.

She made her way carefully so as not to disturb the drowsy inhabitants of the woods. When at last she reached the edge of their land, she almost leapt across the whole creek, stepping only once upon a stone near the far edge; then she bounded up the steep hill and reached Grandfather Poplar a little out of breath but with no loss for words. She leaned heavily against him.

"Grandpop, are you awake? I've got to talk to you," she said. "You and the other trees here are in a lot of danger. I don't know what to do. They just told us last night, and now it's too late. I'm so scared...."

"Slow down, little one. Yes, I'm awake before the sun today," he said calmly. "And I know why you're here."

But how? Melissa could communicate with the trees only when she touched them. Surely he hadn't somehow reached her mind in the night. Had her dreams been so powerful that she projected them over such a distance?

"How could you know?"

"There's nothing mysterious. I've seen it coming, that's all. I almost told you yesterday, but I didn't want to spoil an otherwise beautiful afternoon."

"Grandpop, are you sure we're talking about the same thing? Mrs. Reynolds' property has been sold, and my parents sold most of our land too. Some developers are going to build houses here. Don't you know what that means? It means they're going to cut down trees, Grandpop. They're going to cut down TREES! Not one or two but hundreds." Tears poured down her face.

"I know, little sapling. I know. And I'm mad as a hornet battling a spider and as bloodthirsty as old Red-tail after a juicy mouse, but I'm a tree, Melissa—not a hornet nor a hawk. I can't fly away, and I can't sting anybody. I can't tear their eyes out with my talons or peck them with my beak. And I'm not a walker; so I can't fight them with their own weapons or get up and walk away. None of us can. You walkers have been chopping us down and plowing us under since you learned how to walk on two feet. That's the way of things. Our lives are nothing to your people."

His words stampeded her mind with such force and intensity that she had to withdraw from his touch, her whole being shaken. Melissa couldn't speak for quite a while; she had no idea how long. Finally, she calmed herself enough to reach out to Grandfather Poplar once more, but this time her touch was light—just her fingertips—so that maybe the voice and the intense feeling wouldn't overwhelm her.

"All right, Grandpop, please listen to me and speak a little more gently this time," she said, taking a deep breath. "I still don't understand how you knew this was going to happen. Please tell me. I'm so confused."

"That's a fair request, little sapling," he said with a much gentler tone. "You know we trees communicate with each other. Of course, I don't listen to their endless chatter most of the time.... So few of these saplings have anything worthwhile to say.... But even I couldn't avoid the thunderous and feverish communication of late. But much worse has been the silencing of voices—more and more each day.

"You see, the destruction has already begun," he continued, "at the far edge of our old friend's land. She would never have permitted such a thing, but your kind die so soon. You're not a very sturdy lot—just a very ruinous one.

"I've listened to the gasps, the screams and then the silence. I've followed the paths these huge, yellow hard-shelled gnawers make...."

"Bulldozers? You mean they already have bulldozers," Melissa asked. "Why haven't I heard them or seen them? *Why* is this happening?"

"You know more about 'why' than I do, but you haven't seen them because they're still a good distance away. But I can feel their shaking of the Earth and sense Her cries. I can feel the death and the terror of the winged and four-legged creatures and the quiet ebbing of my own kind."

As he said these words, Melissa understood that he'd been bearing this anguish without sharing it with her, that there had been a wall up around his deepest heart that her mind hadn't penetrated. Now that he let her see it, she was able to sense this boundary between them, a secret place barred to her knowing in her communication with him. It was sort of like the wall she had to put up when she went into the world and was around a lot of people—so many feelings and so much pain. She had learned almost instinctively to place a barrier around her heart and mind as much as she could. She let it down only when she was with the trees.

"Grandpop, does everyone know—all the trees in the forest? About the bulldozers and the death?"

"No, Melissa, I've managed to contain the news on this side of the traveling water. Before this morning, I believed that those on the other side—on your family's land—would be safe. I asked the others here for silence, and those whose roots extend beneath the water to the other side are old enough and wise enough to see the need. After all, what can we do? What can any of us do?

"Of course, everyone will know the truth soon enough. Through the thoughts of the others, I've watched the walkers carving their roads with their chewers and their cutters. One will almost surely come here to this hillside, and then we'll all know what truth there is to tell in this world."

Grandfather Poplar's sadness became palpable and amplified her own a hundredfold. At least a layer of the shielding he'd built inside his being had been razed. Through linking with him, she envisioned the bulldozers pushing over and tearing out trees, the chainsaws cutting deep into their trunks. She felt the silent screams of the tall oaks, hickories, poplars and pines—all the forest plants—as well as the animals, whose homes had been uprooted and destroyed. In the midst of all this, she heard a distant wailing like the weeping of a mother losing her beloved child. She grew lost in those sobs that seemed to echo from the center of the Earth and felt as if she were being swallowed by some vast consciousness.

It was too much. Melissa pulled away from Grandpop until she could take slow, easy breaths again. Then she renewed her whisper of a touch against his trunk.

"But maybe they'll leave you, Grandpop. I mean, you're special with your huge, twisted trunk, and you're the biggest tree around here, so they might not want to cut you down."

Melissa felt pretty hopeless, but he had enough distress without adding her fears.

"Besides, I'm not going to let them. Somehow I'll find a way to stop them. I just don't know how yet. The fact that you're the oldest tree for miles around ought to count for something."

"And you remember how I got to be the oldest. At what cost to the ones I loved."

"Yes, Grandpop," she said softly. "I remember. That was the first story you ever told me and maybe the one that made me love you. I wish you'd tell it to me again—just to take me away from the present for a while."

Truthfully, Melissa had heard that story a few more times than she really needed to, but today she wanted to hear it again, this tale of survival against the odds.

"Today is the one day when it's too hard to tell, Melissa. Too close."

"Then I guess I'll just have to tell it to myself."

"Then recount it to yourself when you're alone," he boomed. "I don't want to hear it today any more than I want to relate it. Too much loss," he said more softly, a sense of resignation evident in his voice.

"Okay, Grandpop. I guess I'd better go anyway—before I'm missed. I've been here as long as I can. But, Grandpop, do something for me. Help me think of some way to stop this. *Please.*"

"If I knew that, I would be as wise as I claim to be," he said with what might pass for a chuckle.

Melissa knew he was trying to make her feel better.

"You're a lot wiser than I am anyway, Grandpop. So please think about it. Okay?"

"I will, little sapling," he said. "Come again—*soon*," he added with the strain of urgency in his deep inner voice.

Tears still in her eyes, Melissa hugged him hard. As she ran back down the hill and made her way home, her heart felt ripped apart and her senses ragged. Her thoughts remained on that hillside.

When she reached the house, Melissa approached the back entrance carefully to make sure no one was in the kitchen yet.

Her hands shook as she reached for the door but not because she was afraid of being caught. She trembled partly because of her inner turmoil and worry but mostly because her communication with Grandfather Poplar had been so intense. Her nerves were always raw after a prolonged in-depth conversation with the trees, but this time the aftereffects almost overcame her.

She was just inside the door when her mother walked into the room wearing her faded pink robe and slippers.

"Where have you been at this hour, young lady," her mother asked with a tone that said she already knew the answer.

Her mother's face looked hard and pale in the harsh fluorescent overhead light of the kitchen. The tiny wrinkles around her mouth and eyes showed more than usual. Melissa just stood there staring at her—unable to answer the seemingly simple question.

"I... I, uh—"

"I thought we just told you last night that you weren't to go back to the woods anymore, and now I catch you coming from there when it's not even light. What were you thinking, Melissa Jane?"

Melissa knew she was in trouble, but at this moment she didn't have the strength to care or to come up with excuses.

"I'm sorry if I scared you, Mom. It just hit me during the night that the woods won't be here much longer," Melissa said, her voice breaking as the pain welled up again. "And I just had to see them. Losing the forest might not matter much to you and Dad, but it does to me."

Her mother's face softened somewhat.

"Well, you still shouldn't have gone. I really don't understand your attachment to those woods, and I can't fathom why an attractive girl your age would want to spend so much time alone."

"No, I guess you couldn't. But I feel at home there. And now I guess I won't feel at home anywhere," Melissa blurted out.

Her mother's forehead quickly pinched into a frown. Melissa knew her words had hurt, but it was too late to take them back.

"What about this house, Melissa," her mother said. "Your father and I work hard to give you a good home with everything you need, and you and your brother don't even appreciate it. No, I really can't understand that. Of that you can be sure."

Her mother paused for a moment.

"Oh, I suppose it's useless talking to you. Just go get ready for school. And from now on stay out of those woods."

Melissa walked meekly past her mother toward the hallway.

"Do you hear me, Melissa Jane?"

"I hear," was all Melissa could say. She couldn't and wouldn't stay away from her friends now, but she had no desire to continue the argument. The way she felt it was lucky she could stand there and listen to her mother at all. She trudged up the stairs with leaden feet and went to her room to change for school.

Chapter 5: Sleepwalking through School

Melissa didn't pay much attention in class that day. Her biology teacher called on her and caught her daydreaming twice during first period. She loved Mr. Brown's biology class. This was his first year teaching, and his enthusiasm for the subject, especially the botany section they were working on now, made him, or rather his class, even more appealing to Melissa. But today even the study of plants couldn't hold her attention. As the bell rang and she was walking out, Mr. Brown stopped her at the door.

"Was class so boring today, Melissa? I start to get a little worried when my best student can't keep her mind on the lesson."

"I'm really sorry," Melissa said, doing her best to keep at bay the embarrassment that threatened to wash her cheeks and throat in red. Too late. She could already feel the heat climbing up from her chest.

"I just didn't get much sleep last night, Mr. Brown. I'll pay better attention tomorrow. Promise."

With those words she turned away and hurried down the hall. The excuse she had given was at least true as far as it went, and she couldn't share the rest of her truth with anyone—not even her favorite teacher, whose deep brown eyes peering into hers made her a little weak in the knees on her best days.

Second period algebra didn't go much better, and by the time P.E. rolled around, Melissa could pretty well predict how it would pass. If only she could have just run laps around the track all period. That might have relieved some of her unbearable worry and allowed her to forget at least for a while. But this week they happened to be playing field hockey, a sport that required a certain amount of skill and attention. Of course, she tried to remain focused, but she kept having visions of bulldozers, and the sound of chainsaws buzzed in her brain.

Melissa's team had made a goal—no thanks to her, of course. She spent her time trying to catch up to the ball without tripping over anyone—without much luck—and avoiding frowns from Ms. Matthews, her gym teacher, who didn't hold great love for Melissa even at her best.

"Why don't you watch where you're going," asked an angry Tracy Beaman as Melissa backed over her.

Melissa offered her a hand to help her up off the ground.

"Forget it. I don't need help from a clumsy idiot like you," Tracy said. "If you can't play any better than this, you might as well stand on the sidelines."

"I'm sorry. I guess I wasn't paying enough attention to where I was going."

"I don't know which you need more—new feet, new brains or more metal in your mouth so you can tune in better to that planet you're from," Tracy sneered turning her back to Melissa and running to catch up with the team.

On any other day, Tracy's words would have cut Melissa deeply, but today a kind of numbness enveloped her. Maybe for the first time in her life, she genuinely believed that adage about "sticks and stones." The trees had a similar saying that Grandpop had recited to her on many occasions: "Beaver teeth and woodpecker beak may gnaw my bark, creatures that burrow may leave their mark, and lightning, it may strike me, but neither whispering winds nor sapling song nor hooting owl nor buzzing drone knows words as strong as tree."

Melissa pulled herself together and hurried to the other end of the field, where Ms. Matthews had called a foul on someone. Otherwise, her gym teacher would be breathing down Melissa's neck by now, and the last thing she needed was more unwanted attention.

By the time Ms. Matthews blew the whistle for showers, Melissa had skinned an elbow, scraped her left knee and managed to get a huge swollen bruise on her thigh that landed right next to the one Kevin had given her the previous day. Considering she'd fallen twice and gotten whacked with a stick once, that wasn't too bad.

Melissa lagged behind when the class went inside and ended up being one of the last girls to get a shower. As she went into the shower room, she saw Tracy laughing with a couple of her friends. When Melissa came out sopping wet holding her white towel firmly around her, Tracy and her friends were already dressed and started to snicker again as she passed. No doubt Tracy had shared the *hilarious* remarks she'd made on the field.

A twinge of pain got through the numbness, and the familiar feeling of "outsider" washed over Melissa. It was like an old, filthy blanket that she'd had since childhood, a tattered, worn and scratchy rag with the words, "I don't fit in" emblazoned on it. Maybe someday she'd be able to throw away that feeling, that tired old blanket, but now the only time she didn't wear it was when she talked with the trees.

At lunch she sat with Cheryl as usual. Melissa didn't have many friends, and Cheryl was the only one of them who had third lunch, which fell in the last part of fourth period. Even with Cheryl, she never quite discarded the feeling that she didn't belong.

"How's it going, Melissa," Cheryl asked as she sat down.

"Not so great."

"Yeah, I heard about what happened in P.E. third period. That Tracy Beaman is such a cow. I don't know why she thinks she's so great. Who died and made her queen of Oakcrest High School anyway?"

"Beats me." Melissa didn't feel much like carrying on a conversation. She had more important things on her mind.

"By the way, what was up with you in biology class? It's not like the teacher's pet to nod off when *Mr. Brown* puts a question to you. Of course, I could understand if you were daydreaming about Buncombe County's sexiest biology teacher," Cheryl teased.

"If you ask me, Cheryl, you're the undisputed champion when it comes to thinking about guys. Some of us have other things on our minds."

"Yeah, *sure*. Anyway, I don't know what you have on your mind, but it sure is doing a number on you. You know, you don't look so good today, Melissa."

"Gee, thanks for brightening my day."

"Sorry," Cheryl said. "It's just that, well, no offense, but you're even more pale than usual. I just thought maybe you were sick or something."

"Sick of school maybe," Melissa said, forcing a grin. "Truth is I'm just tired. I didn't get any sleep last night."

"How come?"

"Let's talk about something else. Okay?"

Cheryl looked a little hurt that Melissa wouldn't confide in her, but she changed the subject. During the rest of lunch, Melissa got to hear all about the many charms of Ricky McManness, Cheryl's latest hope for true love. But Melissa's thoughts remained deep in the forest. She wracked her brain for a plan, but none of her ideas seemed at all plausible. She was still too upset to think clearly.

The rest of the day was relatively uneventful. On the bus ride home that afternoon, Melissa gazed out the window as they drove through Cherry Point development just a few miles from where she lived. A lot of families had moved in there in the last two years, and the bus had to make frequent stops.

Usually, Melissa paid little attention to the neat little houses all in a row—one very much like another—or to the bare yards in various stages of being landscaped. The main thing she'd noticed as the development took shape was the lack of trees. All but a few of the old ones had been removed; small saplings took their place, offering no shade and no wisdom. The houses were nice enough, but the development seemed a severe and sterile place without any strong, sturdy trees. Melissa wondered if any of the kids who lived in these houses missed having trees. Would any of them understand how she felt now?

Finally, the bus reached the outskirts of the development and turned onto High Ridge Road. The houses became fewer and farther between, and the yards were filled with old oaks and maples and beautiful golden poplars. The autumn colors washed over Melissa's being like warm sunshine. She was on her way home now—back to the world of trees. But today she couldn't take pleasure in their beauty without feeling a deep and heavy burden of sadness and concern. Her cause seemed hopeless.

She could only pray that Grandfather Poplar had come up with some plan.

Melissa hardly noticed when Kevin sat down beside her.

"Hiya, metal mouth," he said with his obnoxious grin. "Lost in space as usual, I see."

"Yeah, I really must have been deep in thought not to get a whiff of your unmistakable odor coming my way."

"Yeah, well at least I don't have constant halitosis and railroad teeth covered with slimy bits of lunch," he said.

Kevin had a sixth sense about just what got to her the most. Melissa knew she'd brushed her teeth after lunch, but that didn't stop her from running her tongue along the edges of her braces just in case. The only time she ever stopped being self-conscious about her crooked teeth and her mouthful of braces was when she was with Grandpop and her other "toothless" friends.

"So did you just come up here to bug me or what," Melissa asked.

"I just thought I'd remind you about what Mom and Dad said. You don't get to go play with your little tree friends today. Remember?"

"What's it to you anyway, Kevin? Afraid you've lost your free housekeeper? I may not like what's going on, but at least I have that one consolation: Mr. Slug has to clean his own room from now on."

"Well, just you remember, dog face, I'll be watching you, and I'll tell Mom and Dad if I see you sniffing your ugly nose around those woods."

"In case you've forgotten, Dad said we couldn't go there anymore *after* they start grading the land near us. From what I can see that hasn't happened yet, so I guess I'm free to go where I please for the time being," Melissa added triumphantly.

"I guess we'll just see what Mom has to say about that, huh?"

Melissa knew very well what Mom had to say.

"Unless you want to make a deal," Kevin said with that oh-so-sweet hyena's grin. He knew he had her just where he wanted her.

"Okay, what's the deal? I guess I have to keep cleaning your room?"

"Uh-uh. You clean my room, take out the garbage on my days, and take my turn at the dishes."

"You can't really believe I'd do all that?"

But he had that look on his face, and she knew that her kid brother had beaten her again.

"Come on, Kev. Cut me a little slack, why don't you? I'm your sister, not your worst enemy."

As the bus pulled to a creaking halt at their driveway, Kevin just smiled wickedly, picked up his books and strolled to the door. Melissa followed him off and caught up to him.

"Well? What do you say, Kevin?"

"Well, Sissy Melissy, the way I see it, since you *are* my sister you probably won't mind helping me out with my chores anyway, huh?" He grinned again, turned his back and tromped into the house.

Melissa wanted to go to the woods as soon as she got home, but she had to straighten the den and clean the kitchen first. She needed to make sure that everything was just right when her parents got home so they wouldn't know where she'd been.

It had been a warm afternoon, but the autumn chill was already beginning as the shadows lengthened and the woods grew dimmer in the late afternoon sun. Melissa pulled up the hood on her sweater to keep warm.

Her route through the woods took many paths, and she had friends along each of them. Today, she needed to be cheered up before she went to see Grandpop; so she stopped to visit Randy Red Maple. He was always full of laughter and charm, which made him one of the most popular trees in the forest. Randy could tell a "woody," the trees' version of a joke, better than anyone, and he was one of the most beautiful trees in the woodlands as well. This time of year his leaves were washed in brilliant hues of scarlet, orange and gold, and on him the color seemed to last longer and shine brighter than any of the other red maples.

In the late afternoon sun, Randy looked like his usual dazzling self. Melissa gave him a big hug, wrapping her arms most of the way around his coarse trunk.

"Well, if it isn't the lovely Melissa, the only walker with the heart of a tree. I'm tingling to the tip of my roots to see you, my little friend with feet. You don't visit me nearly enough, you know. You must owe me at least 500 hugs by now."

"Oh, Randy, you're such a flirt that you even flirt with walkers," Melissa said.

"Now, Melissa, you shouldn't say such things. You know if you rub my bark the wrong way, you'll end up a sap," he said with a chuckle. "I've never 'flirted' in my life. I'm just sweet, that's all—not so syrupy as my cousin Susie Sugar Maple but every bit as delectable—if I do say so myself."

"Like I said, you're a flirt, Randy Red Maple, with about as much modesty as that red-headed woodpecker you remind me of."

"You don't need to insult me," Randy retorted. "Imagine, comparing me to one of those tree-pecking creatures. What a little twig you are sometimes, Melissa," he added with a good-natured laugh.

"Yeah, well, I guess I get a little sap-happy when I'm around you, Randy."

"Oh, that was a bad one. Worse than one of mine.... But you didn't come to me today to trade bad puns, did you, Melissa?" He paused. "I haven't felt you in so long, and now you come to me with some secret purpose, some shadow on your mind."

Melissa had seldom heard such seriousness in Randy's voice. She had to be so careful with the trees. They could detect the slightest change in mood or expression and sometimes read her thoughts more than she wanted. At times it seemed to Melissa that the trees could peer into her very soul. What was most remarkable to her was that they still accepted and loved her even though they knew all her flaws.

Now, for Randy's own sense of well-being and for the sake of a promise to Grandpop, she had to choose her words carefully.

"Randy, you're always so good at picking up my moods even when I try to disguise them," Melissa said. "The truth is I had a lousy day at school, my wretched brother is being his usual annoying self, and, worst of all, my parents are on my back about spending too much time in the woods. I guess I just needed a little cheering up today."

She had spoken only the truth, since trees could spot a lie way faster than they could clean the air of carbon dioxide. She hoped this much truth would be enough for Randy.

"Are you sure that's all that's bothering you? You wouldn't leave me out on a limb, would you," he asked more lightheartedly.

"Not for all the sap in a forest full of sugar maples," she said from the heart.

"You said that with a bit too much feeling, my little walking tree. One might think you were nuts, seeds and acorns over me," Randy said with a gentle flutter of sparkling color as his leaves rippled in the breeze.

"You're such a show-off," Melissa said. "Of course, I love you, Randy. Just don't let it go to your crown." Again, she had to fight to keep her tone light. "I've got to get going now. I promised Grandfather Poplar I'd visit him today."

"How is the old buzzard brain anyway? I haven't heard a word from the other side of the creek for some days."

"Oh, Randy, you know those are hawks, not buzzards, that roost in his crown. Anyway, you know Grandpop, he's just as wise as ever," she said with a grin.

"Wise-cracking you mean. Well, give him my sappiest greetings. And visit me again soon, little twig."

Melissa hugged Randy "good-bye" and hurried through the woods along the old familiar path. She stood at the foot of Grandpop's hill watching the red-tailed hawk soar above his branches and wondering what she would say to her old friend. For eight autumns she had stood in just this spot to catch a glimpse of afternoon sunlight flashing on golden leaves, but never had she felt such awe or sadness when she beheld this tree's noble beauty. And he was regal—even with his bent and twisted trunk. To Melissa, he was perfect. Reluctantly, she cast her eyes to the ground and made her way up the steep slope.

When she reached Grandfather Poplar, she sat down at his base and leaned against him gently.

"Feeling tired today, little one," he asked quietly.

"Yeah, I guess I am. How about you, Grandpop?" She tried to sound cheerful.

"Feeling every one of my 144 rings today, Melissa."

"I know exactly what you mean. I went to see Randy Red Maple and even he couldn't brighten my day."

"And how could you expect to get anything more than utter nonsense from that brainless chattering mockingbird anyway?"

"Well, he's pretty witty for a brainless chattering mockingbird, and I like his company—*almost* as well as yours," Melissa said with a grin. "By the way, before you ask, the answer is 'no;' I didn't tell him anything about our crisis. It was hard, but I kept my word," she added more seriously.

"I never doubted you," he said, and the sadness brought a thickness to his voice.

Melissa felt hopeless.

"Grandpop, I still haven't thought of anything we can do to stop this massacre of trees. Please tell me you've come up with a solution. I'm getting more worried by the minute."

"I know you are, Melissa, and I've thought long and hard, but there's nothing for us to do but learn to accept the truth of things. I won't lose my life happily, but I will give it up as surely as you will someday. All creatures eventually depart this realm and others are born. That's the way of things. Surely I've taught you that in all these years, or was I just talking to the air?"

"Grandpop, you know very well I understand how Nature works, but this just isn't right."

"As for your first statement, you nor I understand the doings of the Mother Earth, but this isn't Nature, Melissa. This is Man. Make no mistake about that. The Mother weeps for her lost children, little one. She makes the choice for us to be born, to grow and then to die. Now She has no choices."

"You almost never talk like that, Grandpop. I didn't think I'd ever hear you reciting the beliefs of the trees' Mother Earth philosophy."

"I don't always say what lies at my deepest core, but every tree knows the wisdom of the Earth Mother, to whom we owe our lives. It's human wisdom we're not so sure about."

His voice echoed within her with a sense of finality and lost hope. She could hardly speak.

"I'm sorry, Grandpop; I'm so sorry," Melissa said, silent tears streaming down her cheeks. "If only I could change things—if I had the power or strength to make a difference...."

"Little sapling, you can't change the way of the world for all your fervor of heart. All you can do is remember us and go on with your life just as we do when a brother grows old and weak and falls in the forest or when a tiny sapling fails in its struggle for light and life. Each of us becomes part of the forest, of the Earth and of each other when the Mother takes us. But where we go or what becomes of us when the walkers end our days, well, I suppose you know better than I. At least you'll be here to remember."

Suddenly Melissa couldn't bear her feelings in silence anymore. All the anger, the sense of injustice flashed from her heart in one blow.

"Oh yeah, I'll remember. I'll remember that you just stood there and died without a fight. That you just gave up and didn't even try to help me come up with a solution. That you accepted this ridiculous fate with no more than a pretty speech about the ways of Mother Earth. That's what I'll remember!"

Had she the power of Grandpop's tree voice, the huge poplar might well have fallen to the ground from the weight of the fury she flung with those words. But no sooner had she spoken than her rage was replaced with remorse.

"What am I saying?! Please, Grandpop, I'm sorry. I must have lost my mind for a minute or something. Please forgive me."

She expected anger and silence, but Grandfather Poplar surprised her once again.

"Maybe you're right, Melissa. Perhaps I haven't been seeing the forest for the trees, as you're so fond of telling me. It's true that I can't physically do anything to stop this from happening, but I still have a powerful mind. Perhaps I can at least use that."

"Grandpop, you're brilliant!" It hit her like lightning on a treetop. "All I have to do is find someone who *can* do something and bring them here to listen. Then you can explain to that person why the trees must be saved. It's perfect."

"Hold on, Melissa," Grandpop interrupted. "It's not that simple. Don't you realize by now how rare you are? Very few walkers have the ability to hear our voices. I know of not a one who has ever been able to hear us long past childhood. Your minds become too muddled after that, and your belief in such possibilities becomes almost nonexistent. Walkers reach a certain age and their minds just close up tight."

"But surely there must be somebody who's still open enough to hear your voices, Grandpop. I just have to find that person."

"You've set yourself an impossible task, I'm afraid, little sapling. We'll just have to think of another solution. And I promise I'll try to discover one. I'll send out word to the others of my kind in the colder country and in the direction of the setting sun. Maybe far from here, there's a tree who has found a new way of dealing with the madness that looms before us. At any rate, I'll keep trying, little one. I won't give up until the chainsaw is nipping at my malformed trunk."

"Thanks, Grandpop. I feel so much better than I did when I came. But I'm not giving up on my first idea either. I'll keep trying to think of other solutions, but in the meantime, I'll be looking for that special grownup out there."

"Well, you're no more stubborn than any other walker, I suppose," he added in his typical gruff tone. "Just remember that I told you what a waste of time and energy this search would be."

"Yes, Grandpop, your words of wisdom are always appreciated," she said. It was the first time all day that she'd felt like teasing him. But now she had at least a little hope.

The position of the sun told Melissa that it was time to hurry back home; so she pressed her cheek to Grandpop's bark and wished him luck in his quest for answers.

"I love you, Grandpop," she added, caressing the gnarled bark with her palm.

"Of course you do," he hummed into her head. "Come tomorrow, little sapling."

Chapter 6:
The New Boy

As exhausted as she was, Melissa lay awake in bed for hours that night wracking her brain to find a savior for her friends. She watched the red numbers of her clock radio blink 1:00, 2:00, 3:00 before she finally drifted off. When the radio alarm blared out a really old Nirvana tune at 6:45 AM, her mind definitely felt like it had been "dowsed in mud" and "soaked in bleach."

Unfortunately, she didn't receive any miraculous answers during her sleep. She was no closer to a solution than she had been in the middle of the night.

In whom could she possibly confide? Her parents were obviously out of the question, and her grandparents were too far away to help. She really hadn't been close to any adult since Cora Reynolds' death.

If only she were still alive. Somehow Melissa knew Mrs. Reynolds would understand. She took such care with her fruit trees while she was able. Melissa recalled climbing carefully to the top of the tall black cherry tree and feasting on the juicy and delicious cherries before the birds got them all, and she collected the peaches and pears for Mrs. Reynolds to can on those sweltering summer days. The elderly woman would drip sweat as she completed the task, but the fruits of her summer labors tasted sweet and delicious when winter left the trees bare and barren.

Mrs. Reynolds had shown Melissa how to nurture the trees for the time when she could not. She loved to sit in that creaky old rocker on her back porch "just enjoying the scenery" as she used to say. The two of them spent hours looking out at the tall oaks in the yard as they stretched giant limbs toward the sky. Some days they sat there until the sun fell behind the woods in the distance, spreading its pink and pale orange fingers of light between the trees as the sky faded to lavender then purple and at last darkest blue. At times, Mrs. Reynolds went on at length about the days she and her husband Jack had planted gardens enough to feed the county. But sometimes they found silence and the beauty around them enough to share.

What irony. Mrs. Reynolds was the only one who might truly comprehend this situation, but it was her death that brought it about. As long as she lived, her land remained a sanctuary to birds, raccoons, deer, squirrels, groundhogs and all the animals of the woods, and, of course, to the trees. But now Melissa's only adult friend was gone, and she alone stood between the "progress" of humans and the world of plants and animals she'd come to know and love. She would be their champion now. She had no other choice.

Melissa finally rolled out of bed at 7:00 and hurried to the bathroom to get ready for school. When she looked in the mirror, she wasn't surprised by the dark circles under her eyes.

"If I looked bad yesterday, how about today," she murmured. The mirror was never exactly her friend even though she spent a lot of time wishing it were, but today she couldn't let that apparition staring back at her deter her from her quest.

A bizarre idea was beginning to filter into her conscious brain. It was scarier than she wanted to admit but it might work. And if it didn't, well, she was used to making an idiot of herself, but this was just about the most bone-chillingly dreadful prospect she'd ever encountered. Still, *he* just might be the one, the only one who could help, and if there was a chance....

Melissa steeled herself against the thought of failure and embarrassment and quickly got dressed for school. All through homeroom, she pondered what she would say. Playing the scene in her head 10 or 20 different ways, she couldn't come up with a single scenario that didn't seem completely insane.

"Oh, well, not long to wait now," she said to herself as she walked into her biology class. Mr. Brown stood near the door talking intently with Mrs. Pinnix, another teacher in the science department. Melissa took her seat behind Rachel Johnson and tried not to stare at Mr. Brown. Of course, she was seldom successful in that regard. She noticed the way he tilted his head while he explained something. His dark wavy hair curled a little at his ears, and his brown eyes always appeared to burn with some secret intensity.

If there were one person who could understand, surely it was he. With his love for plants and his understanding of the importance of environmental issues, he had to be the one. He would hear their voices. He would see that they were *alive*.

Still, the thought of speaking to him filled her with fearful anticipation. An odd excitement coupled with a sense of doom whirled inside her. How could she talk to him—pour her heart out to him—when he might all too easily see the real reason she chose him as her confidante? What was the real reason, she asked herself now. And all through class the battle raged within her until the bell rang and the moment of truth came.

Her feet felt weighted as she plodded toward his desk. He sat looking down as he straightened the papers he'd just collected from the class. Melissa stood in front of his desk and cleared her throat.

He smiled broadly and genuinely as he looked up and into her eyes.

"Hi, Melissa. I'm glad you stopped after class because I wanted to talk with you. You seemed more than a little distracted again today. Is there anything I can do to help? After two days in a row, I really am beginning to think that you've suddenly become bored with biology."

"Oh no, I mean, that would never happen," she said, her voice shaking a little. "I love your class. It's just that, well, I have a problem and I think maybe you could help."

"By all means, tell me. I'll do my best."

This is where the hard part came, and to make things worse people were already beginning to filter in for his second period class.

"I can't get into it now or I'll be late for algebra." Melissa's throat was so dry she could hardly get out the words. "Would it be all right if I stopped by after school for a minute or two?"

"Of course, Melissa, you know my door is always open. I'll be here." With that, he stood and headed for the hallway and Melissa did the same.

"I'll see you then," she said as she walked out the door.

As she hurried to her next class, she felt weak-kneed and breathless. *Six more periods of anxiety ahead*, she thought.

At third lunch, Melissa again took a seat beside Cheryl. Her friend wasn't beautiful in the usual sense of the word, but there was something about her, a kind of inner confidence. Cheryl genuinely didn't care much what people thought about her—except maybe Ricky McManness or her heart throb of the moment. She was just herself pretty much all the time. She said what she thought and didn't hide herself from the world. This quality made Cheryl particularly appealing to Melissa, because she could sense in others their true feelings unless she closed herself off to it as she desperately tried to do most of the time. With Cheryl, she felt a greater sense of ease knowing that her outside demeanor matched her inside disposition.

Still, even with Cheryl, she never shared her whole self. She knew that she was different and had to keep her secret world safe within her.

"I saw you talking to Mr. Brown again, teacher's pet!"

"Yeah, well, I needed to discuss a project with him," Melissa said with a laugh. "That's all."

Cheryl grinned. "Okay, okay. I get it. No need to tell me more. A crush is a crush; that's all I'm saying."

When Melissa remained silent, Cheryl didn't press the issue further. She knew how to take a hint.

"Melissa, have you met the new boy? He was in my homeroom this morning. His name is Arthur *Fox*, and he is one too! I think he has third lunch. Let me see if I can point him out...."

Cheryl scanned the filled room. The school had over 1270 students; so there could be over 400 people eating during each of the three lunch shifts.

"There he is," Cheryl pointed.

Melissa grabbed her arm and pulled it down. "Do you have to be so obvious," Melissa asked.

But Melissa had to admit that her gaze was drawn to this newcomer, and she could see the reason for Cheryl's attraction. Like her favorite teacher, he had dark hair and eyes. But, unlike her Mr. Brown, Arthur Fox's sleek mane fell just below his shoulders, and his skin was a light bronze. He looked like he might be part

Cherokee, as Melissa was, or perhaps from one of the other First Nations. Of course, she was only one-eighth Cherokee and the rest was Scots-Irish. Her pale but ruddy skin and blue eyes, even her chestnut-colored hair revealed only the larger part of her heritage. Although she would never admit it to Kevin, she envied at least a little her brown-eyed, dark-haired brother, whose skin actually tanned in the summer.

Melissa felt a strong kinship with her Cherokee ancestry. Since she was a child, she'd had dreams of a Cherokee boy walking through the woods behind her house to greet her. As she grew older, so did her dream companion, whom she knew as Adahy. In the dreams, he called her Amadahy. He would gently take her hand and lead her through the forest. At the outskirts of the woods, they walked through a shimmering, almost invisible, wall that appeared a bit like a wave of heat off pavement on the hottest summer days. Adahy guided her to the stream, which looked much larger in this dreamscape; there along the water's edge a small village stood. When she surveyed the scene, she always felt as if she had come home, and so real did it seem that with each awakening from this dream Melissa felt disappointment that she lay in her bed in the present.

Stranger still was what happened one day close to dusk as she sat lost in reverie leaning against Grandfather Poplar's sturdy trunk. She had almost fallen asleep but was brought back to wakefulness by the sound of someone humming softly and gently seemingly close by.

When she opened her eyes, she beheld the same scene. There before her just down the slope, the village and its dwellers stood—the children running, women washing their clay pots in the stream, old men sitting around a fire and Adahy—older than he was in her dreams—for all the world appearing to stare straight at her. She blinked and rubbed her eyes, but the vision remained—a snapshot from another time long ago—that faded a moment later as Adahy smiled up at her and then turned away.

Melissa hadn't realized she was staring into space in the direction of the new boy until he looked up from his lunch and saw her. A wide grin crossed his lips, which Melissa answered with a timid smile and then looked quickly around the room at something, anything else. She felt a kind of shiver run up her spine as well as prickly bumps on her arms, and for a moment sensed a hand on her shoulder. But when she looked around, no one was there. She looked back at Arthur Fox and found him still gazing at her with the same grin.

No doubt the redness was beginning to blossom on her chest and neck in its rising stream toward her cheeks, so she turned back to Cheryl, who was eying her with a blatant smile.

"Well, what do you know.... An actual guy our age that has Melissa flustered! I thought I'd never see the day. Next thing you know you'll be acting like a real girl."

"Uh...I was just having a cellular memory moment," Melissa said.

"Huh? It's a good thing I'm your friend 'cause you sure do say some weird things. And we both know you were having an Arthur Fox moment." Cheryl giggled and patted her friend on the arm. "It's nice to know I'm not the only one."

Melissa smiled back at her in spite of herself. Determined not to gaze in the direction of Arthur Fox again, the rest of lunch passed uneventfully.

Chapter 7: Seeking Mr. Brown's Help

Melissa found Mr. Brown at his desk once again—this time grading papers. He raised his head as she walked into the room and a smile graced his lips.

"Hi, Melissa. Thanks for stopping by."

Melissa walked over to stand beside him. She squirmed a bit under his gaze as he asked her how he could help.

"I just learned that a huge amount of wooded land near my home is about to be plowed under for a development," she said, getting right to the point. "There are some beautiful trees there including one that's rare and very special, and I wondered if you would be willing to help me save him, I mean, the tree, or better yet find some way to stop this development."

There....She'd done it. She said just what was needed and nothing more, nothing that would sound crazy—except for the slip in calling Grandpop "him."

"Well, that sounds like something that's right up my alley. I'm not a card-carrying member of the Sierra Club for nothing," he said with a grin.

"You say there's an unusual tree in those woods. What makes it so special," he asked.

What makes him special? If only she could tell her teacher that. He's wise and cantankerous; he's loving and gentle even though he rarely shows it. He listens to her like nobody else. This magical and grizzled poplar is her *grandfather*. But she could say none of these things.

"Well, he's the biggest poplar in the woods, maybe the largest anywhere around here, and he has the most interesting crooked trunk."

"I can see you're really attached to this tree—even calling it *he*," Mr. Brown smiled.

She had said it without thinking. Even having rehearsed the speech in her mind, she couldn't escape the need to refer to Grandpop as a conscious being, which he most assuredly was.

"Uh, yeah, I am attached. I've sat in front of that tree daydreaming, reading, doing homework, just *being* for the last eight years; so there's nothing more important than saving it," she said, remembering to use the less personal pronoun.

"Well, then, let's see what we can do. The first thing I'll need to do, if it's possible, is to inspect the specimen. If this tree really is unique, maybe we can gain support from my friends in the local ecology network and work on getting publicity and public support.

"Of course, it sounds as if we would be trespassing to go on the land that's being developed, and I'm not sure how comfortable I am doing that; I do still have to be a role model," he said with a look that said this wasn't actually uppermost in his mind.

"So I'll have to see if I can get permission to look at the property. I could always be a prospective home buyer," he smiled. "Who knows, I may be in the market for a new home in the future."

"Thanks, Mr. Brown. I'd really appreciate anything you could do," she said. "And if there's any way we could save all the trees or stop them from going through with the development, it sure would be great," she added.

"The only thing is…I hate to say it, Melissa, but there's usually very little that can be done to stop developments from going through as long as they've already filed the appropriate papers with the county and all the i's have been dotted. Is that the case here?"

"Yeah, I think it must be since they've already started grading the land."

"Then truth is it may be kind of a lost cause. But we can look into it at least."

Her heart sank a little. Mr. Brown didn't sound encouraging. He probably wasn't the one.

"We've got to do something," Melissa said, revealing the urgency in her tone.

"Believe me, I understand," said Mr. Brown. "What passes for progress in the world is a mystery. We'll see what we can do. Chin up." He pressed his hand on her shoulder as he stood looking at the clock on the wall. "Don't want you to miss your bus," he added.

Melissa excused herself quickly and ran for the parking lot to catch the bus before it left. On her ride home, she replayed the conversation over and over in her mind. She wasn't sure what she expected from her plea to her favorite teacher. Deep down she had hoped he would come to the rescue like some knight in shining armor—no doubt with a forest of trees as his crest of honor. She wished that he had displayed passionate concern toward the trees that matched her own. But at least he might be willing to help save Grandpop, and that was something.

I guess it really is up to me, Melissa thought, as the bus pulled to a stop in front of her driveway. Gazing toward the woods, she couldn't help feeling that she'd already let down her friends.

Chapter 8:
He Who Dwells in the Forest

After a solemn visit with Grandfather Poplar and an evening with her family, Melissa longed for the solace of sleep. She only managed a few replays of the day—the meeting with Mr. Brown, the odd sensation of connection when she saw Arthur Fox, the time spent with Grandpop—before slumber cascaded into her consciousness. Her dreams were always vivid in full color and often seemed more real than her waking life, and tonight was no different.

In sleep, she journeyed again to the forest. Adahy, her long-time dream companion, greeted her at the border of the woods as always. She thought it made sense that she so often found him here in her dreams since he once told her that his name meant "lives in the woods."

Tonight Adahy led her to an encampment not far from the Cherokee village of her dream life. There she beheld a large camp fire with a group of people sitting around it. Adahy motioned her to a place in the circle. There was only one other female in the group, a plump woman who looked like she might be in her 60s.

With kindness in her eyes, she stared at Melissa, who had the strongest urge to call her Grandmother. But she remained silent and looked back at Adahy.

"Amadahy, we have called you to council tonight so that some of your friends may be saved," he said to her. It never felt odd that he called her by this name but rather like her own name in the real world was an ill fit.

As she looked around the circle, Melissa could see all eyes fixed on her. Some of the men appeared ancient, wizened, as though they could easily have lived more than a century. As she returned her gaze to Adahy, she could have sworn that his face changed with each flicker of the firelight—at one moment appearing as a youth, at another as a man in his prime, the following instant as an aged man with silver hair and then back to the view with which she was most familiar. It was as if she could see his journey from childhood to the grave written upon his face.

"It's time to come into your power, Amadahy," he said to her. "Time to remember that you are my daughter, the water that flows through the forest born of the one who dwells in the woodland."

She had no understanding of what he meant. How could she be his daughter? Except in those mysterious flashes as the shadows interplaying with light from the flames danced over his face, he appeared her own age. Perhaps he was saying simply that she was his descendant. Yes, that must be it.

"You were born of the Mother as well," said the bronze skinned woman, who, though aged, also appeared strangely ageless. "And the connection to the Mother flows through your whole being. Now we invite you to remember," she too added.

"Tonight we celebrate the rain dance," Adahy said. "Because time is needed in your world in order to save your friends."

Although Melissa saw no drum, she heard the beating echo in her mind. All the elders around the circle closed their eyes; so Melissa did the same. She could feel the heat of the fire rising. Her body felt heavy against the ground and yet connected to it—almost as if she were growing roots into the Earth herself as her tree friends did. A fleeting thought asked how she could feel these sensations in this sleep state. But she knew by now the lucid dreams seemed as tangible as life itself.

Melissa—ah, but she wasn't really Melissa...she was Amadahy... felt herself surrounded and filled with a great light—brighter and more luminous than the fire at the center of their circle. She sank into that light. At its core, there was a warm, enveloping darkness, sweet and nurturing like a mother's womb. She was aware of the others in the circle, her kindred, her soul family, and felt a deep sense of oneness with them, with the Earth, with the plants and animals, the people, the elements and beyond that with the planets, the sun, the moon, the stars. She saw herself as an infinitesimal pinprick within a vast sea of Light.

Suddenly she opened her eyes. The circle of nine still sat, but beyond them she could detect other figures dancing in a ring just beyond the edge of the firelight. She felt the rhythm of the drumbeat stirring within her, calling her to the dance. Along with the other eight in the circle, she stood instinctively. They sang and danced, each step a perfect interplay of all their spirits, each tone they chanted connecting them more firmly to one another and to the Earth beneath them.

After a time there was no distinction, no separation, until at last the drum beat stopped, and Melissa returned to her physical world. In that realm between sleep and waking, she thought she heard Adahy's voice say, "I will be here to guide you."

Melissa awakened to the sound of pouring rain pounding on the rooftop.

"The rain," she whispered, and understanding filtered into her consciousness like the dim gray light of a rainy morning. "They won't be able to grade the land in the rain."

Chapter 9:
The Uncanny Fox

After homeroom, Cheryl caught up to Arthur Fox as he headed toward his algebra class, which, as she noticed yesterday, was just two doors down the hall from where she and Melissa had biology. Since they walked in the same direction, she decided this would be a good opportunity to see what he was like.

"Hi," she said. "I'm Cheryl Harris. I sit a few seats behind you in homeroom. You're Arthur, right?"

"Yeah, right. Arthur Fox. Nice to meet you."

"Actually, I noticed you yesterday in the cafeteria with your friend."

"Hmmm, yeah, I wondered if Melissa might have caught your eye," she said, trying to discern his tone and see what he thought about her best friend.

As if he were reading her mind, the next thing he said was, "She's an interesting person, isn't she? What's her name?"

"You have no idea," Cheryl said with a smile. "Anyway, her name is Melissa Kincaid."

Interesting most assuredly was the right word, Cheryl thought. Melissa clearly kept much of herself hidden from Cheryl, but a little mystery wasn't such a bad thing. Cheryl kind of liked that Melissa wasn't a total chatterbox like some of her other friends although she wouldn't have minded being clued in to some of her secrets. Still, the parts of herself Melissa allowed Cheryl to see were to say the least intriguing.

Yet, Cheryl wondered how this new guy could get any insight into her friend with just a glance and a smile across the cafeteria.

"I could see she has spirit," Arthur said, again as if in answer to her inner query. This was a little uncanny, Cheryl thought.

"Is she your best friend," Arthur asked.

"Yeah, we've known each other since second grade."

As Arthur stopped at his locker, he turned toward her and looked Cheryl directly in the eye. "What do you like best about her," he asked with a look of sincere interest.

Cheryl didn't have to consider her answer. "I think maybe the best thing about Melissa is she's a good listener, and I know I can trust her."

Somehow this new boy brought out the absolute honest truth from her, Cheryl noted. One thing was for sure, he must have liked what he saw in the cafeteria, because all he wanted to do was ask about Melissa. She smiled a little knowing grin inside and out.

Closing his locker and adding the heavy algebra book to his stack of texts, Arthur said, "You must be a very good friend to answer so quickly.... You feel more than you let on, don't you, Cheryl Harris?"

He was looking into her eyes like someone who could see right through her. A shiver ran down Cheryl's spine. She always tried to be lighthearted and give off an easy-going, laid-back vibe; so people thought that was what she was really like. But this Arthur Fox must be psychic or something. Good looking *and* deep, she thought.

She felt a little twinge that he wasn't more interested in her, but she already had someone in mind for herself anyway, and the image of Ricky in his JV football jersey flashed into her mind.

They walked down the hall the rest of the way in silence. This guy was perfect for her friend, she decided. Two of kind—strange and interesting. This was a match she was definitely going to make.

When third lunch rolled around, Cheryl got in line in front of her friend to grab the usual rubber pizza and bland salad. She fought to hide the glimmer of mischief as she planned their *accidental* meeting with Arthur Fox. Her idea was to clumsily drop something on her tray as they walked by Arthur's table, or better yet, run into him if he was up walking to his seat. It was all too easy.

Cheryl noticed that Melissa appeared tired again. She said she'd gotten lots of sleep, but she looked a little beaten up. Cheryl considered that this might not be the optimal time to introduce her to Arthur given the dark circles under her friend's eyes. Besides, Melissa seemed different today. There was some inner quiet about her that Cheryl had noticed during their biology class. Oh well, it could wait until tomorrow.

But apparently the universe didn't think so. As Cheryl turned around after paying for lunch, she bumped right into Arthur. Melissa, who was just getting her change from a $10 bill, looked completely caught off guard, and Cheryl actually felt embarrassed since the plan happened without her intention.

"Gee, Arthur, sorry about that! Didn't mean to just about knock you over," Cheryl said, recovering her composure.

Arthur seemed completely unrattled. "No worries," he said as he effortlessly readjusted his tray. "So this is your friend Melissa."

Cheryl coaxed her forward. She definitely looked a little like a deer caught in the headlights.

"Yeah, Melissa, I don't think I had a chance to mention that I'd bumped into Arthur—no pun intended—between homeroom and first period. Anyway, Arthur, yeah, this is Melissa. Melissa... Arthur."

Melissa sometimes stammered a bit when she got flustered; so Cheryl caught herself holding her breath a little. But her friend actually managed to get a few words out without anything more than a major blush. Stranger still, it was as if neither of them could completely look away from each other.

Arthur finally glanced at Cheryl for a moment and said, "You didn't have to run me down so I could meet your friend." He grinned widely at her and then returned his gaze to Melissa.

"I've wanted to meet you since you caught my eye yesterday about this time," he said.

Cheryl thought Melissa's blush grew a little redder. She expected her to fumble for words now for certain, but Cheryl was surprised again.

"I wanted to meet you too," she said.

Chapter 10:
A Time of Remembering

Melissa felt drawn to Arthur Fox in a way she never had experienced. It was as if she had known him forever. She truly wanted to pay attention to every word he said as he chatted with Cheryl and her at lunch. But instead her thoughts waffled back and forth between the plight of her tree friends and the dream images that haunted her from the night before. She knew she had transformed somehow from the girl she was a day ago. She couldn't put it into words even if she were inclined to share this inner shift.

"You're not listening at all, are you?" Arthur said, peering into her eyes across the table.

She wished she could say, "Yes, of course I'm listening," but she felt as if her lips would only speak truth today—especially to Arthur.

"You caught me," she said.

"Don't feel bad, Arthur," Cheryl said. "She phases out on me all the time. It doesn't mean she doesn't like you," Cheryl added with a sly grin. "Besides, she listens when it counts."

"It's okay. I do a little bit of phasing out myself," he said. "Especially when I have important stuff on my mind."

He looked more seriously at Melissa. "I think maybe you have something a little weightier to deal with than why we moved here and what I think of Oakcrest High School."

As she glanced from Arthur to Cheryl and back, Melissa realized they were waiting for her to speak. Her normal reaction would be to change the subject and draw attention away from herself. But normal seemed to have flown out the window with the first breath of dawn.

"You're right," she said, almost as if her mouth had a mind of its own. She went on to explain that all the woods around her home had been sold. She told them that the land and the trees meant more to her than just about anything in her life.

"They're going to take it all and obliterate all the trees. I can't sleep or eat for thinking about losing everything I love," she said on the edge of tears.

"God, I didn't know," Cheryl said. "I'm really sorry."

Melissa had acquainted Cheryl with the beauty of the forest by her home when they were young. At age seven or eight, she even introduced Cheryl to many of her tree friends, although no doubt her friend had simply thought it was a child's game they were playing. Still, Cheryl had some inkling of how much Melissa cherished her time among the poplars, oaks, birches, maples and all the others.

"My Dad said last night that it was the same developers who built Cherry Point, and you know what that means…. They just took down everything." Melissa couldn't bring herself to continue. She pushed away her virtually uneaten tray of food and looked down.

Arthur reached his hand across the table and placed it on top of hers. She hadn't expected the gesture from someone she just met. Raising her eyes, she gazed toward him.

"The tree spirits will live on," he said. "They will live on."

She pulled her hands beneath the table and looked away. She wasn't sure if their spirits continued. She wanted *them* to live, to thrive, to touch the sky with their graceful limbs, to hold the birds' nests in their embrace, to nourish the land with their leaves, to nurture the world with their presence and, most of all, to remain her cherished friends, whose wise counsel, bright spirits and laughter filled her heart and her life with joy.

Melissa grabbed her things and marched to the tray return section of the cafeteria. She hadn't meant to leave so abruptly. Turning at the exit, she looked back at Arthur, who followed her with his eyes. Cheryl's brow pinched in a frown. With an inward shrug, Melissa turned and headed to class.

The remainder of the school day was spent in contemplation, which her teachers doubtlessly mistook for daydreaming. Gazing out the window into the streaming rain, she allowed the grayness and the liquid echo of the flowing water to engulf her. Safe. Let the rain wash her worries away.

At the end of the day, she went to see Mr. Brown again and found she wasn't the only student who wanted to talk with him that afternoon. Arthur Fox appeared to scan her face as she entered the room. Seemingly unperturbed by her earlier behavior, Arthur smiled genuinely as she walked to the desk.

"Hi, Mr. Brown," she said. "Hi, Arthur." Both of them right in front of Melissa was almost more than she could handle. But determination and tenacity anchored in every cell of her body at the moment. She stood her ground as if supported by the full strength of the Earth.

"I hope I'm not interrupting," Melissa said trying to be patient.

"You go ahead. I can wait," Arthur replied.

"Um...I wanted to speak with you alone, Mr. Brown, but since Arthur knows about the situation, I'll go ahead and make this quick. I only have a little while before the bus leaves."

She spent the next 10 minutes discussing strategy to help save the trees. Surprisingly, Arthur contributed a lot to the conversation and seemed almost as avid about the subject as she was. Equally unexpected, Mr. Brown had already contacted his local chapter of the Sierra Club, WENOCA, and they had made plans to attend the next County Commissioners' meeting to lodge a protest of the developer's wasteful policy of destroying woodlands.

"One of our members is on the newspaper staff, so she's looking into public appeals. I'll be calling the development company later today to see about 'inspecting the land for my future home site,'" Mr. Brown said with a grin.

Melissa offered her sincerest thanks to her favorite teacher. He asked her to talk with him again before or after school the next day. Feeling a little less burdened and slightly hopeful, Melissa left the room. She was surprised that Arthur followed her out since he never had the opportunity to talk with Mr. Brown about his own reason for being there. They walked in silence toward the exit to the bus parking lot.

Just before they went outside, Arthur pulled her aside and placed his palm gently on her forearm. She inhaled with a slight gasp and then breathed more deeply. A flush of warmth rose in her chest.

"I'm different too," Arthur said, his brown eyes voicelessly articulating a hint of secret worlds as they peered deeply into hers. "I understand your gifts," he whispered. "I think maybe I need to take you to visit my ulisi, my grandmother. We'll talk about it tomorrow," he said. "The buses are pulling out. We'd better run for it."

With that, he opened the door wide and the two of them dashed out into the cold October rain.

* * *

Melissa felt impatient to share her news with Grandpop that day. She waited for the rain to slacken but the fierce downpour continued without ease. All the better, she thought. Can't move bulldozers in the mud.

She bundled up in layers of sweaters beneath her blue slicker and ran into the rain, its hard drops pelting her face in the wind. An umbrella would only have slowed her progress; so she raced unfettered through the woods. Balancing her weight against the wind, her feet clung to the slippery rocks in the stream as she crossed. Its waters had elevated considerably since the previous day and rushed along lapping at the stones and splashing against her already soaked jeans. On the other side, her feet sank into the muddy soil as she trudged up the hillside to the haven of Grandfather Poplar's limbs.

"I thought the rain might keep you away," he uttered, his voice coursing through its familiar channel to her brain. "Walkers tend to be afraid of the weeping skies," he added with a trace of humor. "But not my brave little sapling."

Much like the rain that streamed down at a rapid pace, a flurry of thoughts and images poured out of Melissa's mind in her communication with Grandfather Poplar. The last 24 hours left an abundance of tales to relate. She shared the promising information from her biology teacher, her strange encounter with the new boy whose intense sense of knowing instilled a feeling of wonder in her and whose Cherokee roots awakened questions about her own heritage. He also reminded her of her dream companion, Adahy, who was as close to her in those sleeping hours as her tree friends were in waking.

Grandfather Poplar listened intently to all that she told him. When she detailed the dream sequence and talked about the council and the rain dance, he seemed especially still, a profound inner quiet blanketing even the sound of the rainfall.

As Melissa leaned heavily against his trunk, slick with rain, she felt herself sinking into his thoughts. She experienced the world as a tree—sensing everything—from the water that flowed underneath the hillside, roots stretching to its life-giving essence, to the wind whipping against his bark and the motion of limbs moving with each gust of air. Immersing her consciousness even more deeply into his, she could see echoes of a world that no longer existed, the memories of Grandpop's parent and grandparent trees, his long-gone ancestors, extending farther and farther back through time. She flowed into this as if falling backward through a chasm with no end.

In free fall, her, or was it his, mind paused upon a scene of dancers around a blazing campfire. At their center, a circle of nine people sat in some silent reverie amid the sound of drumbeat and rattle. The resonance of a dream reverberating through time.

Shaken, Melissa pulled herself back to reality. She was sopping wet, and her breath felt frosty in the chilling air.

"Where was I," she asked.

"In a place not so different from your dream," he murmured. "The Mother recalls every rain dance, every footfall, every battle for life. Through her I remember too. And, you, little one, are starting to remember."

Melissa still didn't understand all this, but somewhere, deep within that unconscious part of herself, dawn was breaking. She could feel it edging up just beyond the horizon of her waking mind.

"Was it real, Grandpop," she asked quietly. "I mean…it seemed so *real*. And then the rain this morning…."

"Melissa, you *know* it was," he answered. "When you turn around sometimes, you catch a glimpse of something or someone out of the corner of your eye, don't you?"

She nodded inwardly.

"You're getting a flash of the unseen worlds," he said. "The worlds you've perceived at times when you and I shared thought and mind. When you were very small, you saw them without my help. I know this because I look far deeper into you than you yourself.

"It continues to amaze me that walkers fail to view what's right in front of them," he said with genuine wonder mixed with a bit of irony. "Your dream friend stands beside you even now."

She looked around quickly and had that familiar impression of someone there just outside the periphery of her vision.

"Look more deeply," he said. "I'll help you."

Untouched by the rain, Adahy stood to her left smiling, his ageless aspect gazing down at her with infinite compassion. His stance held the air of confident strength and inner knowing. Then the vision evaporated.

"You're getting it," said Grandpop. "But for now you'd better get out of this downpour since, as a walker, your body is fragile."

Melissa knew he was all too right. She felt the chill sink into her flesh like a deep frost settling into the earth. "I'll come back tomorrow—rain or shine," she said.

"It will be rain," remarked Grandpop. "Earth Mother says she and the elementals can give us one more day of falling water.

"We're depending on you, young walker," he added as she rose to leave.

"I'll keep up the fight, Grandpop. You can count on me."

Melissa hurried home racing against the darkening skies. She left her slicker at the door along with her drenched Nikes and rushed upstairs to dry her hair before the arrival of her parents.

Chapter 11:
Shedding the Old Skin

Melissa remained quiet through most of dinner that night. Lately her mother had insisted on sitting at the table together to eat even though Melissa would have preferred to be anywhere but with her family right now. Although a small hope channeled through her today, internal chaos still reigned, and she raged inwardly that they had sold the land where she had roamed and played since childhood. She felt that the most essential part of her home had been stolen. Spending the time during their meal in sullen contemplation, she only spoke when asked a direct question.

"Anything interesting happen at school today," her father said trying to coax her out of her gloomy mood.

She wanted to shriek at him that he obviously didn't care but instead held her tongue. In the midst of her anger, she had to wonder what would possess him to sell the land that he once loved. She recalled the long walks they took in her early years when Kevin was very young. Carrying one or more of the Audubon Society's Field Guides—to trees, birds, insects, mushrooms and other creatures of the woodland—her father and she had trekked through hillside and valley exploring all their acreage, drinking in its beauty and learning its secrets. Always a quick study, Melissa knew all the forest dwellers by name in no time and delighted when he quizzed her on the varieties of plants and animals they encountered along the way.

She held on to the faintest hope that somehow all that still mattered to him—more than the clients of his advertising firm, more than the promotions he'd had in those years since, more than all the things that robbed his attention and led him away from the man who shared those nature walks with her a decade ago.

"Actually, I had a very interesting day," she announced matter-of-factly. Out of the corner of her eye, she saw Kevin put down his fork and stop chewing to see what she would say.

"I'm planning to protest Cherry Hill Development Company's annihilation of trees. You might not mind them destroying all the life forms on our land like they did in Cherry Point, but I do, and I'm going to do something about it!"

She instantly felt better for having released a little of the venom she'd been swallowing. Usually she would have felt immediately guilty but not this time. The trees meant too much to her to shy away from confrontation now.

"I can see you're serious about this," her father said sounding mildly interested.

"Oh, Robert, don't encourage her," said her mother.

"No, no. I want to hear this out. Just what do you plan to do, Melissa," he asked, a look of earnest curiosity on his face.

"Well, I'm going to try to organize some kind of protest and get some publicity." She didn't want to tell them who was helping her since she feared Mr. Brown might get into trouble.

"You know, that's not a bad idea," her father said to her surprise. "I have to admit I hated to let the land go when I thought about how much might be lost as a result. But the money would pay for both your college educations and leave enough for your mother and me to move in closer to town when you to leave in a few years."

"Besides," her mother added, "As I said, we were hoping you might take an interest in something other than being alone in the woods." Her mother's lovely face looked haggard as her brow furrowed in a frown. "It's not *normal*," she said.

"What's so great about normal," Melissa asked, empowered by a surge of honest emotion. "Does *normal* bring you happiness? Does normal make you better? Maybe normal just makes you dull and lifeless. And *maybe* I don't want to be normal."

In that moment Melissa sensed the tired old blanket falling away. All the anxiety and longing that had poured into her heart every time she realized what an ill fit she was in this world suddenly disintegrated into dust. The feeling was almost tangible like a snake shedding its dry, ill-fitting armor all in one piece and crawling out with fresh new skin. Melissa felt naked without that bit of invisible tattered cloth, the shield of shame that hid her so well from those around her.

Of course, she experienced no immediate need to tell all her secrets. No temptation to share the fact that she communicated with trees. She simply felt the real Melissa beginning to emerge. And that was enough.

After dinner her exhausted body traipsed upstairs to finish her homework and go to bed early. Every sinew in her felt the weariness brought on by the cold, wet afternoon, the dinner conversation and the events of the day, not to mention the weight of worry over the fate of her friends.

She had just plodded through her algebra assignment with a half-conscious brain when the sound of the phone ringing downstairs filtered in through her closed bedroom door.

"Melissa," her mother called up to her.

She dragged her weary limbs to the top of the stairway. "Yeah?"

"It's for you," her mother said. In a lower voice that carried a hint of amazement, she continued, "It's a boy."

"I didn't even know you knew any boys," she muttered. "Anyway, it's getting late; so don't stay on long."

Melissa came down the steps with slightly renewed energy. She couldn't recall any boy phoning her since her friend Gary moved away in sixth grade. It could be only one person, she thought. As she grabbed the hall phone, she took a chance and said, "Hi, Arthur."

"Hi. Good guess," he said. "Hope I caught you before you went to bed. I had to wait for my dad to nod off in front of the TV."

"Sure, no problem. It's still pretty early." Actually, it was only half an hour before lights out, and she barely made it this long tonight, but she was glad to hear Arthur's voice. That sense of connection carried through the phone lines.

"Good," he said. "I figured we were on the same wavelength." She could hear him chuckle slightly on the other end of the line.

"What's funny?"

"Oh, nothing," he replied. "Just the truth in my word choice. You know, some of us seem to operate on the same frequency, like distant radio signals that get picked up by certain receivers if you tune the dial just right. Sounds weird, huh? But I think you know what I mean."

Oddly enough, she understood exactly what he meant. She knew very little about radio waves, receivers or frequencies, but she grasped the deeper meaning in his words.

"I didn't want to wait until tomorrow," he said. I wanted to ask you now. I talked to my grandmother about you. She'll see you this Saturday if you want to go with me. My older sister said she'd drive us. Ulisi lives in a cabin about a half mile off Brushy Mountain Road."

Melissa had ridden along the winding country road when her parents drove her to camp last summer. It was more than half an hour away.

"I'll have to get permission," Melissa said. "But they owe me one right now. So I think I'll be able to go."

"Grandmother's a *wise woman,*" he said, "that is, a medicine woman, like her mother and hers and hers and so on going back a long way. She can help."

That settled it. Melissa had to go. Late as it was, this would have to be put off until the morning when a good night's sleep might give her the insight into how to approach her mother for consent.

"I can hardly wait to meet her," Melissa said genuinely. "We can talk at school tomorrow. It's getting late; so I've gotta run now."

"Sleep on it then," he said. "You'll find a way to come."

The land line clicked off and Melissa put down the phone. Even though Arthur failed to say "good night" or even "see you later," she felt as if he had. In person, he might have communicated it in body language, but on the phone there was nothing except words, or so she'd always thought. But with Arthur she felt as if an entire conversation continued between the sentences. She smiled and returned to her room.

As she fell into the edge of sleep, a soft touch seemed to brush her shoulder as if to tuck her in for the night. But she sensed no one in the room—at least no one in the world of the visible. She felt comforted as she drifted off into the realm of dreams.

Chapter 12: Neurons Firing, Plans Unfolding

Melissa awakened to another dim, dreary morning, the sound of rain still beating against her window. She dressed warmly again and hurried downstairs to face her mother. A sense of anticipation filled her heart intermingling with the turmoil that still reigned.

After many questions from her mother and much cajoling from Melissa, she finally got *tentative* permission to go with Arthur and his sister to their grandmother's home. Her mother insisted on meeting and talking with both of them before they went to be certain they were "reliable." Still, Melissa had a strong sense that everything would proceed as planned.

She wished she could feel that convinced about the safety of her tree friends, but at least the weather would forestall any more grading of the land for now. On the bus ride to school, thoughts of saving the trees, talking more with Arthur and meeting his grandmother raced through her mind—each vying for her focus. But soon the bus pulled up to the school, and Melissa had to draw her attention to the more mundane aspects of the day.

After first period, Mr. Brown stopped her as she walked past his desk.

"Melissa, I have an appointment with the developer to view the property tomorrow morning—if the weather cooperates, that is," Mr. Brown said. "I told him I was interested in a piece of land near the creek if he had one—since that's where your favorite tree is." He smiled at her.

"Thank you *so* much, Mr. Brown," she said from the heart.

"I'll make sure I explain that I need some time to look at the place by myself; then you can meet me at the poplar as we discussed," he added.

Not until that moment did she realize that this was the same morning she was supposed to visit Arthur's grandmother. She was about to say she had to check on a few things before confirming her meeting with Mr. Brown, but she felt as if an unseen hand at the small of her back bolstered her confidence. An inner calm and assurance filtered out her reservations.

"I'll be there," she said. "I can draw a map of the land for you during study hall and bring it by before I leave today so you'll know exactly where to meet me tomorrow. Just let me know what time."

"It's a deal," Mr. Brown said. "Let's say 10:00. I like to sleep in a bit on Saturday mornings."

Melissa left her teacher grateful that he was moving so quickly forward with their plans. Even though she felt more hopeful now, she still found it difficult to focus in math class. The soaking rains made outdoor sports impossible; so Ms. Matthews had the P.E. class doing floor exercises and laps in the gym, which allowed Melissa some respite from her thoughts.

By fourth period Melissa's stomach was grumbling for lunch. As she and Cheryl walked to the cafeteria together, she caught her friend up on plans with both Mr. Brown and Arthur.

"Wow," Cheryl said. "Either you've really changed, or you've sure fooled me all these years. I can't believe it—meetings with two gorgeous guys on the same day," Cheryl teased.

Melissa knew she was blushing but didn't care.

"Oh, come on," she said. "You know I'm just meeting with Mr. Brown because he's helping with the trees."

"Uh-huh. I know.... I know you've had a crush on him since the first day of class!" Cheryl grinned widely. "But I guess maybe you're over that now that you've fallen for someone else."

The cafeteria line edged them forward toward the trays of overcooked spaghetti and lifeless vegetables. "Will you hush?!" Melissa said, squirming and scanning the line to be sure Arthur wasn't in it.

She looked into the huge room with pale yellow walls, its high ceiling echoing the roar of hundreds of voices. In crowds of people, Melissa often felt overwhelmed as waves of thought and emotion crushed against her inner being. If she allowed herself to open to the flood of sensation sent out by such a large group, she would lose herself. Having learned that long ago, Melissa steeled her being against the onslaught as she tuned in to just the single person she sought.

As if he had some invisible radar, Arthur looked up at her the moment her gaze locked onto him. His dark eyes blazed with inner knowing, and he offered her a full wide grin of welcome. Feeling just a little bold, she chose to meet his stare and, completely out of character, actually showed her teeth, enmeshed in metal, as she beamed back at him. Catching herself, she continued to smile with her mouth closed.

Melissa and Cheryl made their way to Arthur's table. He greeted them, as an old friend does, without pretense or reservation. Just the comfort of well-worn neural pathways connecting to one another through familiar thought patterns. Yet, their relationship was actually brand new—carving fresh and unexpected trails through Melissa's internal circuitry, sending out spindly limbs like branches of a sapling aimed toward the sun. She could almost sense the neurons firing in her brain as she talked with Arthur.

"I was wondering about what time you wanted to leave tomorrow, Arthur," Melissa said.

"I had figured on going in the morning, but UliSsi is fine with us coming a little later since you have other plans."

"How did you know I had other plans?"

A look of mischief danced in his eyes. He didn't answer.

Melissa went on to explain about the meeting with Mr. Brown, and Arthur agreed that he and his sister Hannah would wait until 1:00 to arrive at her house.

"I guess you better hope it's not pouring rain tomorrow like yesterday and today," Cheryl said.

Melissa detected a hint of envy from her long-time friend as Arthur discussed the visit this weekend. Any other time she would have asked if she could invite Cheryl, but some inner knowing said this sojourn was for her alone.

"What's the word on getting publicity to stop those evil developers?" Cheryl added. "Did our gorgeous biology teacher say anything about that?"

"Nothing since yesterday," Melissa said squirming ever so slightly.

"Well, maybe I should talk to him and get the scoop. I may not be his *favorite* student like some people," she said, rolling her eyes in Melissa's direction, "but I can be convincing when I need to."

"Amen to that," Melissa said, shifting the topic away from Mr. Brown. "I don't know how many times you've convinced me to do stuff that was totally *not* something I would do." She grinned and nudged her friend's arm.

Melissa recounted the incident in second grade when Cheryl prompted her to put their chewing gum in Jimmy Blalock's shoes at nap time. Cheryl pleaded, "No one will ever suspect you." Melissa had nothing against Jimmy except that he constantly pulled her braids. Still, she went along and, gushing guilt, got pegged instantly for the deed by their stern second grade teacher.

"Well, if you weren't so guilty-looking, you would never have been caught," Cheryl said lightheartedly. "You were always so gooooood with a capital "G" that no one would have thought for a minute it was you."

"That's the problem. I can't stand to do things like that, so I always give off the guilty vibe.... And there was the time you persuaded me to draw that caricature on mean Mrs. Masters' blackboard in fifth grade...."

"Believe me, Arthur, if you'd had this woman as a teacher... Ugh! Melissa and I both had bangs, and she insisted on using bobby pins to pull our hair back every day. Used to tell us we were going to lose our eyesight if we didn't get our hair out of our faces."

Melissa remembered Mrs. Masters all too well. The woman's soul was muddied by years of working at a thankless job and mired in the hatred of those she was supposed to care for and educate. She oozed bitterness. That year was one of the few times Melissa's grades slipped.

"Well, there was one thing we didn't count on when Melissa drew her, let's say, *unflattering* portrait."

"So you got caught again?" Arthur asked.

"You guessed it," Melissa said with a groan.

"Our girl was smart enough not to sign her name, of course, but we never considered that Ms. Master of the Universe might recognize her drawing.

"Oh well, I guess it's time I put my talents to a more worthwhile use," Cheryl said with a grin.

Melissa smiled. Her friend's willingness to support the cause of saving the trees meant more than she could say.

"Anything you could do," Melissa said.

"You know it. I'm here to help."

As Melissa gazed from her oldest friend to her newest, she felt a deep feeling of kinship and gratitude. For the first time in her life, she was starting to feel *almost* as close to people as she did to trees. While she longed for the silent reverberation of thought and complete sense of knowing and acceptance she experienced only with her bark-covered, deep-rooted companions, she knew a part of her *human* self was beginning to emerge. Like a bear after a long winter's hibernation, she stretched slowly into wakefulness.

Chapter 13:
The Heartbeat of the Earth

Later that afternoon as Melissa made her way through the marshy forest, the dark clouds hung low in the sky, rich with moisture as the chilling rains continued to fall. The hood of her raincoat barely kept the wetness from her hair, and drops washed down her cheeks while mist clouded her view. She wiped her face with slick hands as she trudged through the high creek to the banks of Grandfather Poplar's hill.

There were many things to share with Grandpop that afternoon. Although he usually met the efforts of walkers with little enthusiasm, she discerned that he was making the attempt to remain positive.

"Your human teacher sounds like an extraordinary walker," he said. "To take on the cause of the rooted ones and the four legs…Who knows? It's possible he may be the very one you seek."

"He really does care about plants and animals too. He belongs to a lot of groups that work to save the environment. He even talks to our class about it occasionally."

"I confess I'm amazed that there are full-grown walkers who actually do something besides consume," Grandpop said. "I always thought that most walkers only knew how to devour and exterminate." With these thoughts he grew silent.

Melissa sensed a deep sadness in Grandpop, the same grief she felt each time he told her the story of his family, of how he came to be the oldest inhabitant of this forest. It would have been so easy to fall into that sadness, to let it engulf her like the waters of the now flowing stream submerging the stones that normally made her bridge. There was almost a strange comfort in allowing herself to immerse in the expanse of Grandpop's consciousness. But she needed to hold her intention and help him feel more hopeful; so she lessened her grasp on his bark to a light finger hold and felt the sorrow ease a little.

"Grandpop," she whispered the thought. "Please believe me. I *will* find a way to save you."

After a long silence, he spoke to her again, this time just a murmur that rustled wistfully to her mind like leaves in the gentlest of breezes. "I may grumble a lot about the other trees in the forest, their lack of wisdom, their chattering," he said. "But they are my kindred, little one. I don't want to lose them all again. I don't want to be the lone voice in a wasteland of silence."

Melissa was so used to his feigned gruffness, his bellowing and bluster when it came to the other trees, that she felt awestruck by such tenderness in his words and intonation.

"I'll do my best for *all* of you," she answered. "I love you all so much." Tears merged with the raindrops that streamed down her face. In her mind she had a vision of being wrapped in a grandfather's arms, both of them weeping for something precious that was lost forever. She heard the weary cry of Red-tail high above, his shrill and plaintive shriek signaling the need for nourishment and shelter from the sheets of rain, or perhaps he sensed their silent vigil and honored their grief with his own voice.

"Ah, how you walkers think," Grandpop said sounding somewhat brighter. "Old Red-tail is just after something juicy to keep him warm in this downpour."

"I guess you think I'm a regular drama queen," she replied doing her best to seem light-hearted.

"Well, I'm not sure what that is," he responded. "But I imagine since you owned up to it, you probably are."

A small laugh from the giant poplar trickled through her thoughts like a feather lightly tickling the inside of her brain. Her own giggle fell softly into the moist air and evaporated instantly.

"Thanks for making me laugh," she said.

"Your laughter is a song I never tire of hearing," he replied. As she gently touched Grandpop's wet and craggy bark, Melissa felt an inner warmth flow through her as if somehow the great poplar's deep roots drew up the heat from the center of the earth and sent its nurturing energy through her fingertips to her heart.

"Yes," Grandpop said. "Cold bark and chilled skin warmed by the inner furnace, the heart of Mother Earth. As it has always been."

"I don't understand how that works," she said.

"It's simple. Just as my roots gather water and nourishment from the soil, they draw the energy from the heart of the Mother. I've neglected your teaching, child, if I failed in helping you understand that."

"I'm sure the failure is mine," she said with an inner smile.

"Probably right," his tree senses smiled back. "But this much you must remember: When you feel cold or tired, lost or alone, you can ask the Mother to send you her energy, of which she has an endless supply. Imagine that you too have roots and feel yourself sending them down deep into the earth. It's important to be still and quiet your mind before you ask her help, and always, *always* thank her afterward, send her your love and gratitude as payment.

"The trees give their offerings to Earth Mother as a matter of nature. Our leaves when green channel loving breath to her atmosphere, and when those same leaves wither and die, they return to the forest floor to enrich and nurture her soil. We live in perfect flow with her. Even the animals give thanks. Consider the birds whose droppings pass the seeds to the ground and fertilize at the same time. As much as I bemoan our animal companions at times, they do bring their own gifts to the world."

"Grandpop, you must have told me all this before, because I seem to recall it vaguely like something out of a dream."

"Yes, I'm not sure how well you listened to my lessons when you were younger, little sapling," he said with a smile. "But I have the suspicion that I'm not the only one telling you these things."

Melissa thought back. Grandpop was likely right. There was probably a reason these statements reminded her of her dreams. She retreated for a moment to the quietest place inside her mind, and there she saw, felt and sensed Adahy. With a deep in-breath, she opened her eyes and saw him standing beside Grandpop—viewing him this time without the help of her dear tree friend.

"Grandpop, I see him," she whispered.

"I know," he said.

Adahy looked as solid as the trees, but the rain and cold didn't seem to touch him as if he stood outside time and place. He smiled. She didn't hear his voice with her ears, but it echoed in her mind much like those of her tree friends.

"Remember the feeling of connection as you joined us by the council fire, the way the Earth supported you, nurtured you as you sat upon the ground, rooted in her energy and the warmth of her embrace."

As Adahy's eyes looked into hers, she felt that he spoke directly to her soul. "I remember," she mouthed as if lost in a trance.

"Close your eyes," he said to her gently.

She could sense Grandfather Poplar's presence holding her as she leaned heavily against his trunk. With the sound of Adahy's voice in her mind, she felt herself sinking into something close to sleep. Yet, somehow she remained awake. Everything around her was the same. The rain still pummeled against her slicker and dripped down her face, but the sound of it was distant as if she were hearing it from inside a cave, and the sensation of cold and wet grew dimmer as she glided effortlessly along a spiraling path into the Earth. The deeper she went into this silent passage, the more the sense of warmth enveloped her. She felt as if the color green, a bright perfect glow of emerald, was the stuff she was made of. But rather than the cold and hardness of a gemstone, she felt this green was ablaze with warmth and softness.

After she had climbed far down into this place of quiet green light, she sensed Adahy step aside. He remained close but not as present, not uppermost in her consciousness. Then with her inner eye she beheld a beautiful woman cloaked in a gentle green radiance. Her skin was bronze, smooth and ageless, and her eyes burned with a fiery glimmer of green and amber light. At her heart a glowing globe of green and blue seemed to pulsate.

"Dear one, you've come to meet me again." Her voice was larger than Grandfather Poplar's yet as quiet as the murmur of a distant stream. "Touch my heart again. I won't let you get lost."

The woman, whose presence filled the space within Melissa's mind and extended far beyond its boundaries, placed her right hand on Melissa's heart. In the same moment, as if beckoned by something far greater than herself, Melissa's hand reached to the center of the woman's chest, where the pulsing orb was stationed.

"The heartbeat of the Earth," she whispered to Melissa. And then, as once before when connected to Grandfather, she felt herself drawn into a great vastness as if she could reach out and touch the sun, the moon, the planets, and call them kindred. She felt the rivers as her veins pumping into the ocean of her heart through the muscle and sinew of the soil, the great coral reefs, the rock beds and mountainous layers of stone her skeleton, and driving through them all a liquid life force of fiery energy. Were she to stretch, the world would quake.

In a flash Melissa felt the intense and endless consciousness withdraw and the woman stood before her again.

"I come to you in this form so that you will know me as kindred," she said. "I am your home. In the silence, you will find me. In the silence, I AM."

Melissa felt herself climbing slowly into conscious awareness. She opened her eyes. She no longer saw Adahy beside her but still she sensed his presence.

"Grandpop," she said his name aloud, needing for once to hear the sound of a human voice. With the return of her voice came the sensations of her body, completely chilled and soaked in the endless rain. She felt weak and small, unsure her legs would manage to stand much less carry her through the woods to home. Darkness spread its silent wings across the sky as the last dim wave of cloud-filtered sunlight fell behind the mountains.

"I've got to go," she said with some urgency, straining to rise to her feet while still holding on to his slick trunk. "Grandpop, I...I...I'm cold and exhausted and spent. But something else. I'm more myself than I've ever been in my life. And there's some peace that won't ever go away, I think."

"I understand," his voice reassured her. "You are becoming," he said.

No time to ponder his words, Melissa said simply, "Bye for now, Grandpop," with an embrace as strong as she could muster in this moment. She let the mud carry her down to the water, tromped quickly across the stream and with her remaining strength ran headlong for home.

Chapter 14: Grandfather Poplar's Story

As Melissa approached the house, she saw both of her parents' cars in the driveway. How long had she communicated with Mother Earth? Soaked to the skin, bone cold and feeling the effects of the sensory assault brought on by such a deep connection, she felt the need to place an invisible shield around herself as she had instinctively learned to do long ago.

She had no choice but to go inside and face her family. Her mother stood by the kitchen door with the distinct air of a raptor homing in on its prey. Her father sat in silence at the kitchen table, which was set for dinner. Kevin lurked in the hall doorway.

"And just where have you been, young lady?" she screamed more than asked.

Melissa looked her mother directly in the eyes. She felt a change inside herself toward her mother. The ambivalence and wavering between love and resentment had all but disappeared. For the first time it seemed she could see beyond her mother's aspect and into her heart. Her brow was pinched with worry and concern. Behind the mask of fury lived the mother who wanted everything for her child and feared that she was losing her in some nameless way.

Melissa realized that she must look a terrible sight, sopping wet and pale as death no doubt. There were no excuses to give, no creative untruths to proffer.

"You know where I've been," she said softly. "But before you lash into me, please hear me out." Oddly enough, both her parents remained silent—perhaps struck dumb by the serene tone of her voice.

"I have a story to tell you," she said. "Before I start, I want to say I'm sorry for going into the woods without your permission."

Grandfather Poplar had told her the tale so often through the years that she knew it by heart. Even some of the tree language he used—she understood the thoughts and feelings behind them. It was hard to keep from crying now as she related the story to her parents, especially the part about Grandfather Poplar's father. It always made her think of her own father, and the narrative started to feel so much like her own.

"Imagine that I'm an old tree telling you this story," she began. "A tree different from all others with a twisting trunk that winds its way up toward the sky.

"It happened long ago when I was still young, with only 41 rings in my belly," she recited. "My father's limbs touched my own as we stretched toward the sky together side by side. He never begrudged me the sunlight nor the soil as I grew to meet his gaze. I was one of many children, but for me he had parted his limbs to let the shaft of sunlight feed the misshapen sapling that I was...."

She choked back the tears and continued.

"One day the tree cutters came through our forest, hacking and slicing with their axes and saws. Most of my friends and family were taken. I heard the chopping of the axe as my own father was cut to the ground.

"After the men carried my father's body away, I knew that my turn would come soon. I felt the axe draw nearer and nearer, and I began to say good-bye to the sun and the sweet earth, for I knew there was no way I could stop the axe from falling.

"And then came the miracle. All my life I'd been taunted by my brothers for my deformed trunk that did not stand perfect and straight like all the others but was bent and twisted and hideous. Yet, on that day, for the first time in all my years, I thought myself blessed for that deformity. For when the men came to stand by my trunk, one said, 'We don't want this one. Leave it. With such a twisted trunk, it's of no use.'

"There were others left behind—those still too young for the sawmill. But we were few, and I alone of my family was spared except for the tiny seedlings, many of whom had been trampled by the men and by the bodies of their own parents and grandparents as they were dragged away after their deaths.

"As I stood alone in the sunshine, I grew tall and strong and became a father and a grandfather many times over. I've watched the sage brush and then the scrubby pines come and go, and I've seen the forest grow up again around me, and now my friends the Oak and the Maple and the Birch and all my own relatives flourish here on the hillside through the seasons of change.

"I am the oldest of my kind for a far, far distance, or so the birds that come in winter tell me. But I fear I may not be here much longer."

Melissa let out a deep breath and looked at her parents. Her mother had tears in her eyes, and her father sat there staring at her in a peculiar way.

"That's a beautiful story, Melissa. But it doesn't excuse your sojourn into the forest in the pouring rain. You could have caught your death. Get out of that wet raincoat and dry yourself off."

Her mother handed her the dish drying towel that hung from the oven door, and Melissa placed her slicker on the peg by the entry and began to dry her face and hands.

"Where did you hear that story?" her father asked, his eyes seeming to search for some significant answer in her own.

"It doesn't sound like one of yours," her mother said as she pulled a tissue from the box on the counter and instructed Melissa to blow her nose.

"It doesn't matter where I heard it. A friend told it to me. But I believe it's a true story about Gran...about the giant poplar, the hawk tree, on the edge of the Reynolds' land."

"Do you have any proof that it's true," her mother asked.

"There are some things that you don't need proof to believe," she answered.

"It's strange," her father said, "but I seem to remember hearing a story like that about the old tree. I can't quite recall where I heard it—must have been from my grandfather. This place goes back to the turn of the 20th century in my family, you know, Melissa. My grandfather bought it and later sold half of it to the Reynolds and passed the rest on to me in his will. He used to bring me here, and I'm sure he must have been the one to tell me that story about that tree. It had to have been him. Don't know why I can't remember..."

"Dad, what can we do to stop them? Those developers can't just come cut down a 144-year-old tree."

"What? Who told you it was that old," her father asked.

"My friend—the one who told me the story."

There was that strange look on his face again.

"But who? You've got to tell us, Melissa."

"I'm sorry but I can't tell you, Dad. I made a promise to my friend. I can't break my promise."

"It wasn't some stranger, was it, Melissa," her mother asked. "Someone you didn't know."

"No, Mom. It was somebody I've known for a long time."

"It must have been old Mrs. Reynolds then. Was that who it was?"

"I'd rather not say," Melissa answered.

Kevin strolled in from his spot in the hallway. "Maybe the trees told her," he said with a wicked grin.

"Oh Kevin, don't be foolish," their mother said. "Have you finished your homework?"

He walked away looking dejected.

Melissa glanced at her father. A brightness came suddenly to his eyes, and he wore the look of someone who has remembered something important that was long forgotten. A kind of half smile passed his lips.

"I have a plan to save that old poplar," he said. "A tree like that is a local landmark. You know, the Channel 13 news people might want to do a story on it."

Her father promised to call the TV station and the developers and see what could be done. This meant more to Melissa than anything. The father who had taken her on treks through the woods, who had played their naming games for all the trees and rocks and birds, was still alive beneath the business suit and furrowed brow.

Melissa's mother insisted she get out of her wet clothes and dry her hair before dinner. Just when Melissa thought she had escaped unscathed, her mother added as she left the room, "Don't think this means you aren't going to be punished. Pretty stories and precious trees are one thing, but you still did what we told you not to do."

Standing at the hallway door, Melissa turned back toward the kitchen. She prayed her mother would do anything but keep her from the trees.

"I guess we'll have to rethink your trip to visit your friend's grandmother tomorrow.

"I'd tell you that you couldn't go into the woods any more, but apparently that does little good, and your father and I can't be here to keep you from it every second of the day. So this will have to do."

"No, not that, please mom. I'll do whatever else you say. But I really want to meet Arthur's grandmother. You know how much I miss Mrs. Reynolds and how I get along so well with elderly people. And, besides, you said I needed to make some friends."

"Let us consider it for a little while, Melissa," her father said. "If we can come up with something else…Well, we'll see. We'll let you know before it gets too late to call and cancel with your friend."

"Anyway, go get dried off before dinner gets any colder than it is," her mother added.

She said a silent prayer as she went up the stairs. She was glad to step out of the wet clothes and into something warm. But she felt it might be a long while before her blood started to circulate normally again. As exhausted as she was, all she felt like doing was flopping into bed. The thought of dinner with her family brought a sigh to her lips, which the mirror revealed were almost blue from the damp cold. She had to get a definite answer for tomorrow though. After drying her hair, which was softened by the rain water, she steeled herself as much as possible and went back to the kitchen.

There was silence at the table as the tepid mashed potatoes, soggy green beans and catfish dried out from too long in the oven were passed. At last her father spoke.

"Here's what your mother and I decided. Instead of grounding you, we're going to take away TV and video game privileges for two weeks, and no computer time except for school related research," he said with a hint of a smile. "You could say your story swayed us."

"And your Dad and I really do want you to make some friends," her mother added. "So we'll settle things this way *this time.*"

"One more thing," her father said. "It took some doing," he said, glancing with a smile at her mother, "But I think I've convinced your mom that the woods are still safe enough for a while yet. You've just got to promise me, promise us both, that after the workmen get closer to our property, you'll stay far away from them."

Melissa was stunned. She couldn't even manage a reply. This was exactly what she had prayed for.

"Melissa," her father said. "What about that promise?"

"Of course," she said numbly. "You mean until then I can still spend my time in the woods."

"That's what we mean."

Her father looked at her knowingly. He truly must remember their days of fun long ago sharing the joy of sojourns through the forest. She could see it in his eyes. Tears welled in her own.

"We thought that would make you happy," her mother said.

"It makes me happier than anything," Melissa answered in a quiet voice. She lacked the strength to reveal her enthusiasm and joy, but she held it in her heart all night long, through dinner and dish washing and then into the world of her dreams.

Chapter 15: Weaving the Web of Life

There was still a slight drizzle when Melissa awoke Saturday morning at 7:44. She lay in bed half dozing as the birds greeted the dawn. She'd slept for over ten hours. Having managed to stay awake only a short time after dinner, her trip to bed had been much earlier than normal for a Friday night. No TV, no video games, no books. Just the warm comfort of her quilts and blankets on a frigid and damp October evening.

Feeling groggy, almost drugged, from the long sleep, she decided to let the day unfold for a while without her as she lie there listening to the call of the chickadee sounding so much like its name, the clear, repeating tweet of the cardinal, and the other chirps, twitters and warbles of the song birds. Their melodies composed the music of many a daydream on lazy mornings, and now they sang her into a quiet reverie. Here in that peaceful world between sleep and waking, she felt as if a gentle hand brushed her head ever so slightly.

"Good morning, Adahy," she whispered, speaking to her invisible friend as if he were there in the flesh.

"You have an important day ahead," came the reply within her mind.

She smiled to herself and opened her eyes. No one there to see. But there nonetheless.

Closing her eyes again she eased back onto the pillow and fell again into that sense of floating.

"You know I'm here," he said, drifting into focus in her inner vision.

"Yes, I know now," she answered. "Either that or I'm completely crazy as I've always sort of suspected." She smiled inwardly.

Truth was she had never felt saner than these last few days, but she still had a slight nagging question about her rationality. Her mind felt so much more *open* now than ever before. Even in her eight years of communicating with trees, she couldn't recall a time when she had so many visions or such deep connections—not to mention her dream world coming to life before her eyes.

"Sleep a while longer," Adahy's voice continued within her mind. "I have much to teach you," he said, "or rather you have much to remember."

The bird song and light sprinkle on the window grew dimmer as she drifted once again into the embrace of sleep.

At 8:30 the clock radio blared its morning greeting—not nearly so pleasant as the birds. Thankfully, she had managed to set it before sinking into bed last night. Looking out the window, she saw the sun's rays peeking from the edges of a giant fluffy white cloud. The rain had ended after two days just as Grandpop predicted.

She hurried out of bed feeling the excitement of the day ahead. Even in the sunlight, the air was likely to be cool this time of year; so she slid into her warmest socks and a woolen sweater along with her jeans.

Downstairs no one stirred, sleeping in on a Saturday morning as so often was the case. After diving into a big bowl of instant oatmeal with raisins, she thought to leave a scribbled note on the fridge saying she was going to spend some time in the woods.

The ground remained soggy as she made her way along the familiar path. She leaned against several trees along the way, wishing Slippery Sally, Randy Red Maple and her other friends a day of joy in the sun, but didn't stay long enough to go deeply into her connection with them. Uncertain of how much her forest companions knew of what was to come, she needed to allow only the lightest link with them.

Like the other hardwoods along her path, Grandfather Poplar had lost many of his leaves with the heavy rains, but still he stood tall and beautiful against the brightening sky. The creek ran a bit less rapidly since the rain ended, but Melissa still slogged carefully through its higher than normal waters. Her old hiking boots were used to the wet by now.

Melissa set her raincoat on the ground and plopped down on top of it to lean against Grandpop. The saturated ground molded to her body as she shifted into a settled spot beneath his high limbs.

"I was beginning to wonder when you'd get here," he said. "The light of the sun should be your awakener on such a day."

"Well, as a matter of fact, it was," she replied with a grin. "But then I had a little bit more rest after that."

"Walkers," he said. "The sun rises and sets for a reason, you know. Follow the flow of it and you creatures might actually amount to something."

It was a familiar exchange they had shared for years. He chided her each weekend when she slept late, and then she coaxed him out of his crabbiness. The light-hearted conversation let her fears over the future recede in her mind so that she could enjoy the day.

The sunlight on her face was almost tactile as she basked in its rays just as the trees did, drinking in its gentle warmth after the days of chilling rain. The air was still blanketed with moisture, a kind of mist rising from the forest floor.

Melissa looked over at a Grandpop's closest neighboring tree, Billy's cousin Buddy Black Gum, most of whose orange and garnet leaves lay plundered on the ground after the hard downpour. In the lowest of his limbs, she saw a garden spider, the brown ones so prevalent in the autumn months, restoring its web no doubt damaged by the lengthy rains. Drops of moisture still glistened on the edges of the web, but the spider deftly and diligently moved around them spinning her spiraling threads.

"I used to be afraid of spiders, you know," she said to Grandpop.

"Yes, how well I recall. You reacted as if you were the insect that Spider was after," he said. "But Spider is much more afraid of you than you of she."

"I guess it was just my programming. My mother is so scared of them, and my father isn't much better. Kevin would as soon kill spiders as look at them.

"But I started to change my mind about them when I read *Charlotte's Web* in second grade. You remember me telling you about that?" Thoughts of that beloved book flooded her mind as she transmitted the memory to Grandfather Poplar.

"And then you helped me understand them better, which made me a lot less afraid. Now I can look at this one and admire her for the beauty of her web and even for her own gracefulness."

"Then you have learned something," he said.

"But, Grandpop, I had a strange dream last night that kind of scared me. Not that most of my dreams aren't abnormal anyway," she added. "I'd almost forgotten about it after all that sleep, but it was what woke me up early this morning. Seeing the spider made me think of it.

"I dreamed I was surrounded by very large spiders, but I wasn't afraid of them exactly, because I was becoming one of them. I actually saw myself in the dream shaping into this huge spider. Ugh! That really gave me the willies."

Grandfather Poplar was silent for a moment, and then said, "Little sapling, trees don't dream as you do. We simply *are*. But I can tell you something of your dream, I think.

"When walkers see Spider, they think only of death and their fear of her. And it isn't wrong to think of death with Spider, because it is the blood of the insects that sustains her life while ending theirs.... Not so different from humans eating animals, I think, but perhaps you know more about that....

"When I see Spider I am reminded of the flow of creation and the cycle of existence. She spins her great wheel of life and death with the silk of her own body and creates a masterpiece each time."

Melissa watched the garden spider, appreciating each intricate stroke of the silk as she flawlessly built the beautiful web. "So what does my dream mean?" she asked. "It's a nice thought and all, but you kind of left that part out, Grandpop," she said with a smile.

"Did I," he said. "I think I said it quite well. But I suppose you walkers need to be 'beaten over the head with a stick' as you sometimes say," he added with a chuckle.

"Your dream means, I think, that you're becoming a creator and learning about the flow and cycles of life. That may well frighten you at times even if it is a natural thing."

"I guess that's something I'll have to think about for a while," Melissa said. She wasn't quite sure what he meant or even if he was right about the dream, but something about his words held the ring of truth, which Melissa could usually recognize.

The two of them remained silent for a while just enjoying the sunshine and the energy and love that flowed between them. The majestic Red-tail hawk took off from its perch high atop Grandpop's limbs. Melissa heard the flapping of his massive pinions as he gained altitude and then watched him soar as he caught the updraft of wind that lifted his long, broad wings in flight. She longed to be up there with him having a raptor's eye view of the world, flying above the worries and the thoughts of what was to come.

"So what's stopping you," said Grandpop, admonishing her gently.

"Hmm...Let's see. Could it be that I don't have wings?"

"That doesn't mean you don't know how to fly," he replied.

"True enough," she said. "Thanks for the reminder."

Long ago the regal red-tail had called her to come fly with him. The first time must have been when she was nine or 10. She had heard his screech above the treetops and felt his mind touch hers, an invitation to sail among the clouds, to caress the sky.

Melissa closed her eyes and let herself sink into a now familiar state of stillness. She inhaled deeply the misty morning air, breathing slow, even breaths that filled her lungs and quieted her mind. Her heart expanded with immense love for the hawk, complete recognition of his beauty, power and magic.

And then she set her mind adrift upon the breeze and let her consciousness rise, as she had done before, to the heights of the hawk in flight, sending out a silent inquiry.

As always, just as Adahy and Grandfather Poplar had taught her, she asked permission with all her being, to merge with the pure consciousness of Hawk. His spirit responded a soundless assent, and so she climbed to his altitude. She sensed the air currents almost pressing against the underside of flight feathers, the sunlight warming from above, the feeling of gliding from one pocket of air to the next, just as one ended being lifted upon another. Gravity was for the earthbound. The skies were filled with streams of air on which to dance.

Lost in flight high above the trees, Melissa hardly heard the cracking of twigs underfoot as her biology teacher approached. His voice brought her back to the ground with a thud. She opened her eyes to see him standing just a few feet away slightly down the embankment.

"Melissa, good morning," Mr. Brown called. "What great maps you draw," he added. "Led me right to the spot. But it took some doing to get rid of the developer and head out on my own."

Mr. Brown closed the gap between them with long strides up the hill. As he approached, Melissa got to her feet and picked up the damp raincoat beneath her.

"Thanks for coming, Mr. Brown," she said.

"By the looks of it, your tree was worth the trek," he said, brushing his fingertips along the expanse of Grandfather Poplar's trunk.

"And away from class you can call me Tom. We're not in school now," he said smiling. He leaned a hand against the tall tree to steady himself as he put down the knapsack he was carrying.

Melissa took a shallow breath in and held it. If he could hear Grandpop's voice, now would be the time. Grandfather Poplar had agreed that as soon as Mr. Brown touched him, the giant tree would use all his powers of communication to reach the mind of her teacher. "Please let it happen," she prayed within her mind and heart. "Let him be the one who can hear the trees."

Having balanced himself, Mr. Brown stepped away from the yellow poplar a few feet. "This really is a remarkable specimen of Liriodendron tulipifera," he said. "They're known for their straight trunks, and this one is quite twisted.

"And you're right about it being an old tree, Melissa. You don't see many poplars in the area this large," he said excitedly. "It's going to be difficult to get an accurate measure of its circumference because of the trunk deformity, but I'd guess it could be close to 20 feet, and I'm going to say the height must be almost 120 feet."

As her beloved biology teacher spoke, Melissa's heart sank. He was too busy thinking and talking to listen. How many times had Grandpop said that about humans—their brains are too full of their own voices to hear the quiet murmurings of the trees. She fought the tears that threatened to appear in her eyes.

"Melissa, would you hold the other end for me?" Mr. Brown had pulled a tape measure from his bag and with her help began to scale the breath of Grandpop's trunk at his very base.

"I was close," he said, having returned to where she held the other end of the tape measure. "Eighteen feet, four and a half inches as best I can measure." He made a notation in his binder and then took a small camera from the bag.

"Melissa, I'm going to get a wide angle for the first shot; so I'll need you to step away a few yards if you would," he said, walking down the embankment.

She longed to touch Grandpop's trunk, to secretly share the thoughts in her mind and hear and feel his, but she did as she was asked. Moving back to a distance, she could see his crown rising above the other trees as if reaching for the heavens, his last remaining golden leaves shining like the brightest topaz as they bathed in the sunlight. "I love you, Grandpop," she called out with every cell of her body, every molecule, every atom that composed her being.

"I love you too," his voice returned, vibrating through the soles of her feet from his roots stretching deep beneath the ground. "Try not to judge him, little sapling. He's just a walker, after all."

She turned toward her biology teacher, who was taking photographs from several angles.

"Now let's get a few with you, Melissa," he said. "Add a little human interest to the story."

Despite her dislike of being photographed, she swiftly complied and posed in front of Grandpop. Leaning on him, she sat with her head back against his misshapen trunk.

"That should do it," Mr. Brown said.

He replaced the camera and pulled a small instrument out of the bag. "This is a clinometer," he said. "Just a fancy name for a handy little device to measure tree height," he added smiling.

Melissa helped him measure the distance from Grandfather Poplar as he walked away along the ridge carrying his clinometer and his notebook.

"Perfect. I can see the treetop fine from here." After a few calculations, he returned and said, "Well, this is really great. Your poplar friend here is right at 122 feet tall as close as I can figure. I'm no pro at this, after all.

"But I think that should make for a newspaper story at least and maybe, just maybe, a public appeal that will save this rather imperfect beauty," he added, once again running his hand along Grandfather Poplar's oddly shaped trunk.

He scanned the tree line and then looked along the embankment below at the creek flowing gently through the forest.

"You know, I wouldn't mind having a home here for real," he said. "But we teachers don't get paid enough for me to think about that at this point," he said with a grin.

His dark eyes looked sympathetically into hers. "You really do care about these trees, don't you, Melissa?"

She had hardly spoken during his visit to her favorite hillside and felt the words escape her lips with a raw intensity.

"Yes, you were right calling him, this tree, I mean, my friend. The forest has been my companion all my life. That hawk up there and his mate, the squirrels you can hear chattering in the distance, the birds, the rocks and the water, and most of all, the trees. I love this place, and these are my friends."

Right now she didn't care if that sounded crazy. It had to be said.

"I see what you mean," he said, surveying the landscape again with his gaze. "It's peaceful and picturesque indeed—a wonderful place to hike and have fun or just be by yourself, eh?"

Of course, he had no idea what she really meant. That was clear now. But he loved nature and was willing to help, and for that she felt grateful.

"Thanks so much for meeting me here today," she said. "Please let me know what else I can do to save the trees," she added.

"Well, I'll be seeing my newspaper friend this weekend to give her these photos and figures. She sounds pretty interested; so we'll get the ball rolling. She likes to do stories like this whenever she can but has to keep her own views out of the news if you know what I mean. I think we can come up with a suitable pitch to her editor for this one though.

"So I'll be seeing you in class on Monday and will let you know then how things are progressing. As for your participation, if we can get a group together for the county commissioner meeting next week, you're welcome to join us—with your parents' permission, of course," he added in his teacher voice.

"I'd better get back to my car now," he said. "Don't want our developer friend coming to look for me, do we?"

"Thanks again, Mr. Brown. I mean Tom. I can't tell you how much your help means to me."

"I can see that," he said. "Besides, we share a common interest in saving the environment, and every tree counts. I'm happy to help, Melissa.

"See you on Monday," he said, patting her shoulder with his hand. "Chin up. We may just save this one yet."

With that he picked up his canvas bag and headed back in the direction he had come. Melissa embraced Grandpop's trunk, pressing her face against his craggy bark.

"Hope isn't lost, little one," he said, his voice a gentle fluid echo flowing through her veins and into her mind. "We believe in you. We know you'll do your best."

She gazed out across the forest at the treetops of the many companions whose names she knew so well, whose souls had touched her own with laughter and a wealth of wisdom and joy. Home. As surely as the birds, squirrels and other creatures of the woodland made their nests and homes within this forest, so did her own heart.

"The heart of a tree," said Grandpop. "The walker with the heart of a tree."

"Thank you," the words and feelings floated along the channel of thought and sinew back to him. "That's the highest compliment you could ever give me," she said quietly.

Time grew short before Arthur's arrival, and she knew she had to leave this *home* and head for her more human dwelling. Grabbing her raincoat, she whispered farewells and hurried to the house.

There was barely time to wolf down a quick bite of lunch before Arthur was due to arrive. Her emotions waffled from anguish and anxiety to expectation and excitement. This would be a day to remember.

Chapter 16:
The Wisdom of Grandmother Fox

Arthur was as courteous and charming when meeting Melissa's parents as anyone she had ever seen. His usual playfulness and air of mystery seemed to be replaced by a serious and oh-so-wholesome demeanor. Yet, it didn't appear to be an act—just a side of him she had not seen until now. His sister Hannah, who resembled him with long flowing black hair and dark brown eyes, came across as sweet, open and responsible as well.

Melissa's mother still seemed slightly reluctant beneath her pretty smile and charming voice, but she told them to have a wonderful time and added, "Drive safely," to Hannah as they went out the door.

In the car Hannah was warm but somewhat quiet as she sat in the driver's seat next to Melissa. Arthur, who had opted for the back seat, said he enjoyed meeting Melissa's parents.

"Well, you certainly won them over," she remarked. "I could tell my mother actually liked you." No small feat, she thought.

"Your parents aren't so bad, you know," he said. "Your mother's just a worrier; that's all. And your dad, he's an interesting one, isn't he? A lot like you. I think maybe that's where you get your Cherokee blood, huh?"

"How did you know?" she asked. He smiled and turned to look out the window. "Never mind," she said. "I'm getting used to your knowing everything. Looking at the side of his face, she could still detect his grin broadening.

Hannah turned on the radio and began to sing along as the three rode in relative quiet most of the way along the winding back roads of the foothills. Trees lined these roads as far as the eye could travel, and Melissa felt the magic of their presence as they embraced the roadsides in lush colors of autumn interspersed with the deep verdant hues of the evergreens.

After more than half an hour on the road, they turned onto a gravel side road that wound through a thick wooded area, dipping slightly and then rising. The tires rumbled as they drove across a wooden bridge that carried them over a small stream filled with rocks. They passed another wooded area and then came to a pasture, where a few cows and chickens roamed loose. A hen house on the right was followed by an old barn with peeling white paint and a rusty tin roof. Just a bit farther ahead the driveway ended in front of a cabin with another small barn or outbuilding beside it. An elderly woman sat on the front porch rocking.

She put down her sewing basket and stood slowly as they got out of the car. "Come here, you young rascals," she said, hurrying to meet them.

"Ulisi," Arthur said.

"Hi, Mamaw," added Hannah.

"How are my beautiful grandchildren?" the old woman asked. "Up to your usual tricks, my fine grandson?"

Arthur beamed and his cheeks colored with warmth. "Not too many tricks," he said.

Hannah gave her grandmother a hug and told them she wouldn't be staying. "I have a date," she said, smiling shyly.

"Not with that son of a hound dog Sam Pigeon," the old woman bemoaned. "Apples don't fall far, you know."

Hannah rolled her eyes. "He's not a good-for-nothing like his father. He's a nice guy and has a job too. He'll be graduating this year and plans to go to Appalachian State next fall."

"Well, I'll give him the benefit of the doubt for you then, sweet child." Her grandmother hugged her good-bye and Hannah stepped back into the car, turned it around and headed down the sloping drive.

"Now, at last we meet," she said, walking toward Melissa and looking her over.

"It's nice to meet you," Melissa said shyly.

Arthur's grandmother was a tall woman with weathered brown skin deeply furrowing at the corner of her eyes and around her mouth. Her long silver mane still held a few strands of shiny black in places. She looked familiar to Melissa somehow, but clearly they had never met.

She placed her palm gently on Melissa's cheek for a moment and then led her up onto the porch, where she motioned for the two of them to join her in weathered wooden chairs.

"You're as pale as if you'd been locked in a cellar," she said. "But your nose and cheekbones tell a different story. How much Cherokee are you?"

"An eighth. But a proud eighth," Melissa said with a smile. "My name's Melissa, by the way."

"Yes, my grandson told me your name. But that's of little importance in the scheme of things. It's spirit that matters," she said.

With that, the elder closed her eyes still facing toward Melissa, who had the strange sense the old woman was staring at her from behind closed eyelids. For a long time, Arthur's grandmother was silent.

Melissa looked over at Arthur, who held a finger to his lips indicating the need for silence. He closed his eyes as well. Melissa decided to join them since there was nothing else to do. Quickly she became more aware of her other senses. She heard the clucking of the chickens in the distance, the soft sound of water washing over rocks in the stream, the slight wind moving through the trees and felt it wafting over her bare hands and face. The light of day filtered orange, gold and green through her eyelids. She sensed the breathing of Arthur and his grandmother and imagined she was breathing in unison with them, inhaling and exhaling at exactly the same pace.

Following her breath always quieted her mind. The repetitive flow of air in and out brought a stillness to everything. The sounds of nature retreated into silence, the smooth darkness of her inner core bringing her into its peaceful hush. In that inner sanctuary of silence, she found Adahy. He stood beside her, his hand on her shoulder. But he looked much, much older than her usual vision of him. His hair was streaked with silver like moonlight on a dark pool of deep water. His face was older too but as unmistakable as his presence itself.

"Listen to Awenasa," he said within her mind. "She can help you remember *home*. It is the meaning of her very name."

Melissa felt his strong hand on her shoulder and a great sense of belonging filled her heart. "I will guide you," he said, and his voice trailed off in her mind like the end of an echo.

Melissa opened her eyes. She had no idea how long they had been closed, but she found that both Arthur and his grandmother were looking at her.

"I'm sorry," she said. "I was lost in thought."

"Not lost at all, I think," said Arthur.

"Hush, boy.... What have you to say to me, child," she said, looking pointedly at Melissa.

She wasn't at all sure what she was supposed to say. But somehow what came out was, "Your name means 'home,' and you're supposed to help me remember *home*." Melissa could feel her cheeks flush with redness. How could she have said such a strange thing out loud?

"Good," said the old woman. "We don't have time for pretense or games. I'm glad you know how to listen."

Arthur was grinning so widely he looked like he would soon burst into laughter.

"Grandson, I told you today was serious," she said to Arthur, but a twinkle in her eye gave away her lack of temper, and, when he started to laugh, the old woman joined him.

"All right. All right. You were correct. She's the real thing.

"I'm sorry, my dear," she added, looking once again at Melissa. "I know you feel as if you've been left out on the punchline of a joke that may well have been at your expense.

"It's just that my grandson came to me so excited after meeting you earlier this week. He was certain he was reading you right, and it seems he was. He is a fairly gifted child when it comes to connecting with people's spirits, and he was sure you held a soul of great kinship with us. Indeed it appears you do.

"But I want to know more. The first thing you need to do is tell me about your dreams—you know the ones I mean—you've had them all your life."

Melissa had never spoken about these things to anyone, never shared the dream landscapes and events that had made her sleeping life more vivid than her waking hours, except for those spent in harmony with her cherished friends, the trees. But she felt safe here, accepted, just as she was among the world of nature. So the stories within her spilled out on that front porch, memory after memory of her dream life and her companion, Adahy, whose name she was careful not to share, because she held it sacred between them alone She felt as if he stood beside her, acting as her unseen editor, revealing exactly which stories to tell, which details to communicate among the countless adventures within her world of dreams.

After what must have been more than an hour in which she did most of the talking, Melissa fell silent, her throat feeling parched but her mind at ease as if a great burden—carried for so long it seemed a part of her—at last was set down.

"Come inside," said Arthur's grandmother. "Let's get some water for you."

The warmth of the kitchen felt good after sitting on the cool, shady porch for so long, and the water soothed Melissa's throat. She drank the full glass in one long gulp. Arthur reached to refill it smiling knowingly at her.

His grandmother turned on the stove to heat a tea kettle and then went to the open cupboards and pulled down several Mason jars. Melissa noticed that shelves containing numerous containers filled with dried herbs lined much of the room.

"A little blackberry bark and goldenrod, a hint of angelica and some chamomile. This should do wonders for your throat in no time," the old woman said, placing the items inside a thin gauzy cloth and into a mug. As soon as the water boiled, she poured it over the cloth into the cup and handed it to Melissa.

"We'll let that steep for a short time and then you'll be able to drink it."

The odor from the mixture wasn't altogether enticing. But the minty smell of the chamomile coupled with the familiar scent of blackberry encouraged her that it wouldn't be too bad. While the concoction steeped, Arthur's grandmother pointed out the many herbs in her kitchen, briefly explaining the use for some of them.

"I don't expect you to remember all of these things now," she said. "But someday soon we'll have to begin a real teaching."

"Mrs. Fox, you have so many herbs. How do you keep track of them all?"

The old woman smiled. "I prefer Grandmother, but Mrs. Fox will do. As for my herbs," she continued, "this is nothing, child. You should see my cellar. And perhaps you will but not today.

"It's time to drink your tea."

Melissa removed the delicate cloth of herbs and started to sip. The taste was unusual and familiar at the same time. Almost instantly her sore throat felt soothed. She was curious about so much and wanted to ask Grandmother Fox a flood of questions. But sensing the need to allow things to unfold in their own time, she remained silent.

"The tea helps, yes?" Arthur's grandmother said.

"Yes, it helps a lot," Melissa replied. "Thank you," she added, remembering her manners amidst her curiosity.

"Good. You've talked enough for a while. Come sit by the fire and I'll talk to you."

The three of them moved to the adjoining living room where a woodstove kept the cabin warm. Arthur opened its black cast iron door and added another log, stirring the embers to bring back the flame. Then he sat in a faded blue wingback chair nearby that looked like a familiar perch for him, like somehow he belonged in just that very spot.

"You feel a kinship with my grandson, don't you?" the old lady said pointedly.

Melissa blushed deeply. "I...uh...I guess you could say I felt when we met like I already knew him," she managed to reply.

"It's all right, child, he feels the same way about you," she said, winking at Arthur, who fidgeted slightly in his seat. For the first time in the days since they had met, he appeared slightly uncomfortable and ill at ease.

"Oh, he doesn't like me saying so," she smiled. "But it's no less true.

"I suspect we're all very distantly related way, way back like so many of the folk in these parts. But that isn't the whole of your kinship, is it now? The two of you share a certain path, common gifts, after all."

She looked intently from Melissa to Arthur and back again. As her gaze landed on Melissa, she felt as if the eyes of an eagle held her transfixed. "Mrs. Fox," she said, "I'm not sure what you mean."

"Of course you are, my dear. You can't sit there and tell me about your dream life and then pretend that you're like everyone else.

"I've trained Arthur since he was a lad.... It would have been better if I'd had him full time, but they lived up around Snowbird and didn't want to travel the hour or so to see me as often as they should...."

It sounded like a sore subject, Melissa thought.

"But I had this one for the summers since he was two, and he's progressed fairly."

"Just okay, ulisi?" Arthur interjected.

She grinned at him, and Melissa could see where Arthur had inherited his distinctive smile. Then she closed her eyes briefly as if in communion with some deep inner part of herself.

Opening her eyes, the old woman continued, "Thankfully, Melissa, you have had your own teachers among those in spirit and among the Standing Trees."

Melissa hadn't spoken of the trees. She had told them much about visiting the forest with her dream companion during sleep, and, of course, Arthur knew about her trying to save the trees in waking life and how deeply she cared for them. But she was sure she hadn't mentioned her communication with trees.

"Your guide who stands beside you shows me you are deeply regarded among the trees," continued Mrs. Fox. "The Tree Spirits hold great wisdom and ancient knowledge from the Earth, but it is a rare thing indeed for them to allow a human into their world. If for no other reason, that would be enough for me to embrace you and call you kin, child."

The old woman gazed lovingly at Melissa as if waiting for an answer.

"My guide?" Melissa said.

"Your spirit guide. Your counsel. Your friend and ancestor. Adahy, *who lives in the woods*, I believe is his name."

Searching her mind, Melissa *knew* she hadn't given his name.

"Of course, you didn't say his name," Arthur said, reading her thoughts again. "*He* did."

"Grandson, didn't I ask you to be silent?"

Arthur looked at the floor and became still. Melissa felt as if she were inside one of her dreams. She almost pinched herself to be sure she was awake. Feeling the familiar touch on her shoulder, she turned and caught a glimpse of Adahy out of the corner of her eye.

"Yes," said Mrs. Fox. "He's there as always." She smiled. "You haven't just seen him in dreams either," she added.

"What I want to teach you is to see and hear him whenever you need to as easily as you do in your dream world."

Melissa was quiet for a long while. Finally, she looked up at the old woman. "Grandmother Fox," she whispered tentatively. "So I'm not crazy?"

Arthur let out a small laugh in spite of himself, and his grandmother shot a stern look in his direction. "All right. I'll let my grandson answer this question since he's so given to making noise."

"I used to think the same thing as a small boy," Arthur said. "But ulisi taught me pretty early that I was just different and not nuts," he said grinning. "Unless, of course, she is too."

"Young whelp," his grandmother said. "His only real flaw is not taking things seriously enough. But be assured that you and my grandson are quite sane—more sound than most of those in this world to be sure."

"And you both see and hear things too?" Melissa asked.

"See and hear. Feel and sense and know. Someday, it will all be as natural as breathing to you, child."

"It's easy to swim with the fishes and soar with the eagle, to feel the power of the puma or experience the cunning of the Fox," Arthur said, winking at the last phrase.

"But you've already learned some of these things on your own," said Arthur's grandmother. "You just need to become a little more aware and adept in your gifts. It will make your path a lot easier. You still have much to learn.

"The most important thing for you to know now is that you're not alone. Your helpers in the spirit world have guided you to helpers in this world. Some things require a human touch and tangible teachings."

"When can we begin?" Melissa asked.

"We already have," said Grandmother Fox.

Chapter 17:
Embarking on a Path

After the soothing tea and conversation, Melissa went with Arthur and his ulisi for a long walk around the land. Along the way, Mrs. Fox, who leaned heavily on a gnarled walking stick, pointed to a variety of plants to see if Melissa knew what they were. The many hikes with her father in childhood, the quizzes that were like a game to them, proved to be of great benefit now. One after another, Melissa could tell Arthur's grandmother the names of the plants, fungi and trees. But the knowledge of their uses remained a mystery to her.

A cluster of sassafras trees held onto the last of their golden orange and red leaves at the edge of the wooded area. Melissa recognized their familiar three-pronged foliage and cinnamon-brown bark at first glance.

"Ganasdatsi," said Grandmother Fox, "can make a good wash for irritated eyes and a strong poultice for sores. You do know what a poultice is, don't you, child?"

"I think so. Is it sort of a medicated ointment?"

"Something like that. It's kind of an herbal paste. Of course, with sassafras, like all plants, you have to know how to use it and must honor its wisdom."

She pointed to another small tree with reddish foliage and said, "Devil's Walking Stick. Also good for sores and boils."

Melissa listened intently to every word Arthur's grandmother said. The elder often tested Arthur about the uses of the plants along the way. Melissa noticed he seemed quiet and more serious than usual. But he answered each of his grandmother's questions with confidence.

"I've been teaching him since he was knee high to a grasshopper, but the lore of herbal remedies is the learning of a lifetime and not to be taken lightly.

"Child, what do think of all this," she said, looking intently at Melissa.

"I thought I knew plants before I came today. Now I realize I didn't know much," Melissa said honestly. "It seems like I'd need more than a lifetime to learn about plants' medicine."

The old woman smiled broadly. "Good! You've got some sense in you, I see. This is a road not taken carelessly. Be sure you want to embark on it if that is your choice."

After walking for quite a while through the wooded area, they came back out into the sunlight by the small stream. The old woman sat down on a large stone that overlooked the sparkling water. Arthur took a seat on the ground to her right, and Melissa followed suit to the left facing her.

"Now it's time for a different sort of lesson," said Arthur's grandmother. She bent to pick up a small stone from the ground and handed it to Melissa.

"Hold this one in your hand. Feel it, sense it and know it. Tell me what you can about the stone." She placed the stone in

Melissa's left hand and asked her to cover it with her right hand, holding it gently.

Melissa had done this before, she thought, perhaps in a dream. Instinctively, she understood that sensing the stone was exactly the same as soaring with the hawk as she had done earlier in the day and also much like merging and melting her consciousness into the trees or the Earth herself. So she let go.

Doing her best to quiet her mind and calm the nervous need to perform, she began taking slow, deep breaths. Just feeling the flow of air in and out, focusing only on the motion of her breath, the rest of the world seemed to fall away little by little. The ground was cool beneath her, but she felt an inner warmth flowing up from the earth through the center of her being, merging with her breath. With each breath, her mind became more at peace.

In her soul, she knew the rock, like all things in nature, contained its own beautiful magic. She felt a great love for this stone and for all the rocks and minerals of the earth. The more she experienced this love, the warmer the stone within her hand began to feel. Basking in that heat, Melissa allowed her consciousness to drift just as she had with the red-tail hawk. But instead of soaring up toward the clouds, it floated down into the stone she held lovingly in her hand, seeking permission to merge with the life and spirit of this gem and then feeling the portal open between them.

In her mind's eye, she saw a beautiful radiant golden light, glowing, pulsing, shifting. The light flickered and danced like a candle flame in a gentle breeze but shone much more brilliantly. An inner voice said softly, "I am the spirit of the stone, the golden light. I am the rays of the sun embodied in rock. In harmony with me, your own light shines brighter, your inner glow knows peace."

The voice within her continued for a time until only silence and warmth flowed between Melissa and the stone. With a deep inhale, Melissa drew herself back into her body gently. She was not a stone nor a light as vibrant as the sun but just Melissa once again.

Not certain how long she had been aware only of the stone, Melissa gradually opened her eyes. She saw Arthur smiling quietly. He wore a look of peacefulness rather than his usual playfulness. His grandmother appeared serene, showing no emotion, her face like a motionless, undisturbed pool of water. No ripples. Only stillness and a sense of patient waiting flowed from her.

When she could find her voice, Melissa spoke. "The stone was washed here by the stream many years ago after breaking off from a much larger rock. Her surface changed and smoothed as she tumbled through the stream, bathed by time and flowing water. The banks of the stream were wider then, and, as they receded, the stone left her journey and landed here, where she has remained beneath the sun and the moon, in rain and snow, in heat and cold, for countless seasons.

"She's golden and bright like the sun, and I feel her glow inside my stomach, so warm and comforting," Melissa added. "I feel alive and strong and, well, bright myself," she said, knowing this sounded a little strange.

"And she says—the stone, I mean, says—that she can help me remember to shine and wants to come with me when I leave here today."

Melissa looked at Arthur's grandmother, who had closed her eyes while listening to the account of what the stone had shared.

"Yes," said the elderly woman. "Your education hasn't suffered in regard to listening and knowing the silent ones of Earth.

"You may take the stone but only if you leave something in return, a gift in exchange."

Melissa searched her pants and jacket pockets with no luck.

"But I don't think I have anything to give," she replied.

The old woman smiled. "You have more to give than you know," she said. "But for now give your spit."

"What?" Melissa said confused by such an odd suggestion.

"Your saliva is a gift of moisture to the ground. It comes from your own body; so you can offer it freely. Feed the earth your spit."

Melissa felt more than a little strange doing so, but she sensed there was something right about this. So she spat on the ground where the stone had passed its days.

Arthur laughed. "You'll get used to it," he said. "Of course, there are other gifts you can bring to exchange, but spit's the easiest," he said. "Don't worry. I do it all the time." Then he blew out a large patch of spit beside where he sat. "A gift for Grandmother Earth," he said.

"Now place the stone in your pocket," said Mrs. Fox. "Its spirit will stay with you as long as you need it, and then one day you'll feel it's time to give this companion back to the Earth," said the old woman.

"Mind that you do so when you're asked, or else she'll have to get up and walk away on her own," the elder added.

Melissa giggled at the thought of the stone walking.

"You may laugh," said Arthur, "But it happens. I hung onto mineral friends after they told me it was time to move on twice, and they just disappeared from where I kept them."

"See that it doesn't take *twice* for you to learn this, Melissa," added Arthur's grandmother. "And give your new friend a bath each week in the waters of a stream. Also see that she gets the morning sun whenever you can to restore her power. It's kind of like recharging batteries. Being among humans, especially you young ones with the whirlwind of your emotions, can be a drain and a trial for our friends of the mineral kingdom."

Melissa assured her wise new teacher that she would do as instructed. Feeling somehow exhausted and energized at the same time, a sigh escaped her lips.

"You're tired, child," said the elderly woman. "And these bones are a bit weary too," she added, rising slowly with the aid of her walking stick and Arthur's hand beneath her elbow. "I've still got more energy than most my age though," she reminded her grandson with a gentle grin.

"Let's get back inside and warm ourselves. Your sister will be back soon to take you two home."

Arthur and his grandmother walked ahead of Melissa, who ran the fingers of her left hand over the smooth citrine in her pocket, wondering at the connection she felt with its light, its spirit.

Arthur's grandmother nudged him affectionately. "Go on with you now. I don't need your help. Walk with your friend. I know how much you want to."

Arthur hung back a bit and fell in step with Melissa. He seemed almost shy compared with the openness of his grandmother. Melissa felt so drawn to him. The stone within her pocket became warm as she held it, and she felt as if its inner light shone from her solar plexus. A sense of comfort and belonging filled her heart.

"Life force," Arthur said, and she knew just what he meant. "It flows through everything, and the stones have the power to amplify it. But ulisi will explain it better than I can. I feel Spirit in everything just as you do," he said.

Arthur's hand brushed lightly against her own as their strides matched side by side. She felt a glow in her chest being near him. The stone within her pocket seemed to pulsate in tune with her heart beat, which raced a bit faster as his hand touched hers.

As if the old woman had eyes in the back of her head, she shouted back to them, "Go ahead and hold her hand, young pup. I doubt that anyone or anything on earth or in the heavens could object to that." His grandmother's soft chuckle floated back to them on the chill and quiet air.

Arthur's left hand gently and tentatively reached out for her right and clasped it. He didn't look at her but just walked beside her silently. But Melissa didn't have to gaze into his eyes to know he shared something still and precious with her in that moment. She'd known this sensation in the realm of dreams when Adahy took her hand and felt it in each communion with the loving spirits of the trees. *Home.* This too was home.

After they returned to the cabin, Mrs. Fox took out a tattered leather journal from the cabinet of an old sideboard. Melissa could see several others similarly worn inside the cupboard. The elderly woman handled the item with the care one might show an infant. She rubbed its leather binding gently and blew off the dust that covered it.

"If you decide to learn about plants, this will be your study book. It was written in my own hand many decades ago, and I've added to it over time just as everyone who came before did as they learned new wisdom from our plant friends.

"Each generation of my family has recorded and passed on the wisdom of our forebears, the plant medicine we've held safe. Each of us has to make our own copy—both because the act of doing so helps us learn and because none of us is willing to part with the copy we have," she added with a slight grin.

"You'll only be allowed to study this when you come here to visit me," Arthur's grandmother continued. "I may tease about not wanting to part with this volume, but truth is I hold its pages sacred and have never lent it—even to Arthur or to his father, who was not much interested in any case." Her face held a look of silent dismay, but she continued.

"Take a look at these pages now until Hannah gets back. See what chord is struck as you do and if you actually want to study more. As I said," she added firmly, "This is a lifelong path of learning. You have to choose deep in your heart if you wish to follow it.

"If you decide beyond a doubt that you do, next time you can bring a proper journal to begin writing your own copy."

"I'd really like to do that," Melissa said, anxious to get her hands on the book.

"Don't say so now and then change your mind as you young people are so fond of doing. Wait. Listen to your inner wisdom. Consult your friends, the tree spirits, and your ancestor guide who walks with you," she said, nodding to Melissa's right at what appeared to be empty air although Melissa knew better.

"I understand," she said. "I'll let you know another time after a lot of consideration," Melissa promised.

The old woman carefully handed the volume to Melissa, who held it delicately like the rare and prized treasure that it was.

"I've got to start some supper for myself if I want to eat before nightfall," Mrs. Fox said. "Just call me if you have any questions my grandson can't answer."

As Melissa began to turn the pages of the book, the musty smell of aged paper mixed with the faint scent of a multitude of herbs, whose oils no doubt had transferred from the wise woman's hands as she thumbed through its pages over the years. Melissa's eyes watered slightly and a sneeze threatened to erupt from her nose, but she was able to keep these at bay as she nimbly touched the pages of this revered text.

Arthur's grandmother had drawn pictures of the plants to correspond with each entry. There were notes about leaf size, colors of blossoms and time of flowering, along with instructions for the plants' use in tinctures, poultices, teas and more, and a notation about direction—East, West, North, South—that Melissa thought might mean where they grew, although this didn't feel quite right. Melissa imbibed every word as if it were a tonic for her soul.

Arthur, who sat down beside her on the small sofa, spoke softly about his own learning of each of the herbs. "Of course, it looks like your education is going to be really different from mine. She had me learn all about the ancestors and the stories of creation, the four directions and the paths of wisdom, the sacred numbers, and a whole lot of other stuff before she even let me *near* this book."

He looked a little annoyed, and Melissa was afraid she was causing some rift between them. She was concerned that he might be mad at her as well.

"Don't worry," Arthur said. "It's okay. Things are just different with you. You know this is the first time she's ever even thought about teaching anybody who wasn't in the family. What's more, she's always said that the teachings had to be started at an early age. She got really mad at Hannah for not wanting to learn when she was little."

"I can hear you, you know," said Grandmother Fox from the kitchen. The smell of pork frying with onions made its way to their noses.

"I never thought you couldn't," Arthur said with a chuckle. Edging a little closer to Melissa, he pointed across her lap to the page opposite him with the record of an herb called Adam and

Eve root, its Cherokee name, *tsigeyui*, written next to it. Melissa could sense her face flush as she read the description of its use: *For ceremonial joining of a man and a woman in marriage.*

Arthur laughed at her uneasiness. "It'll be a long while before we have to worry about that, eh?" he said. "But it's a powerful way of seeing if a marriage will last," he added, pointing to the continuation of the description. "Maybe if everybody used it, people wouldn't get divorced so much."

The sound of a car pulling up outside drew Melissa and Arthur's attention away from the pages of the herb book. A car door slammed and moments later Hannah walked through the door.

"Hi, Mamaw. I'm back. You two ready to go?" Hannah said matter-of-factly.

The old woman came out of the kitchen. "You can stay for dinner if you will," she said.

"Sorry, Mamaw. I've got plans. And I guess we better get Arthur's friend back to her folks, huh?" she said gazing at Melissa.

"Yeah. I did say I'd be back by dinner."

Melissa stood and carefully handed the book back toward Arthur's grandmother.

"Leave it on the sideboard, child. My hands are oily from the kitchen.... Now before you go we need to get a few things straight between us. The two of you go ahead and scoot out to the car while I talk to Melissa."

After Arthur and Hannah left the house, she continued. "What my grandson said is true. I've never taught anyone outside the family our ways and the knowledge that was passed down to me. And I've never taught anyone who wasn't a full-blood Cherokee. But my guides and yours have agreed on this.

"Sit down and close your eyes a moment, child. Go into the silence just as you did when joining with the stone."

Melissa complied. Her breath slowed as she went into that quiet place within, focusing on breathing, allowing her mind to become still, the nurturing energy of the Earth flowing effortlessly through her.

"Good," said Arthur's grandmother softly. "Now look within and see who stands beside me."

As Melissa drifted quietly into that state of heightened awareness, she saw a plump, brown-skinned old woman smiling at her from just over the left shoulder of Grandmother Fox. Melissa gasped a sudden, sharp in-breath and opened her eyes.

"I know her," she said. "I've seen her before."

"Yes," acknowledged Arthur's grandmother. "My ancestor and life-long companion as your spirit friend is yours. She tells me you know her sacred name." The old woman smiled broadly.

Melissa's face offered recognition of this.

"It's my name too," said Grandmother Fox. "It means 'my home' in English. Of course, I was always called by a nickname growing up, and I was Mary Fox in English to the rest of the world. We don't go around sharing our true name, after all," she said looking intently at Melissa.

"Don't worry. I won't tell anyone," Melissa assured her.

"I knew that already, young one. These days I expect you're rather a rare thing—a teenaged girl who can be trusted to keep a secret." She smiled.

Melissa remembered what Adahy said earlier in the afternoon. "She will help you remember *home*." Melissa felt so at peace here in the company of someone she had met only this very day.

As if the elderly woman had read her mind, she said, "Our clans have been friends for centuries, and a strong trust exists between us at the deepest level of our knowing. My ancestor was a medicine woman from one village and yours a medicine man from another. The two sat in council together.

"So you see, I am bound to be your teacher. Your people long ago let that wisdom passed on from your ancestors die in their minds, but it lives on in your blood, in your heart and spirit. And you are the one to bring it back to life in this world.

"You're in need of much proper schooling, and, while I prefer a more circular path of teaching, wisdom unfolding in layers over time, I'll have to speed your training because you come to it so late.

"But I can't stress this enough. *You* have got to be certain. Our ancestors can only lead us if we are willing to be guided. This is a sacred path of great knowledge and spirit. Only those who are ready progress very far on it." With that, she became silent, staring into Melissa's eyes.

"I understand," Melissa said. "I'll be very sure."

Arthur's grandmother took an envelope out of her pocket. "This is a note to your parents explaining that I will be glad to take care of you and teach you the lore of your ancestors if they're willing. It's not for you to read. Just present it to them. With their permission, I'll see you again next Saturday."

Melissa stuffed the note into the pocket of her jacket, which she slid back into for the ride home. Promising to visit Mrs. Fox again as soon as she could, Melissa offered her profound thanks for the afternoon.

"You have no idea how much this means to me," she said.

"I think I do," answered the old woman. "But I can sense impatience in my granddaughter and it's getting late; so be off now. And remember to honor what you've learned today and hold it in silence."

"I will," vowed Melissa, walking out to the car. Hannah leaned against the driver's side door looking like she was more than ready to leave. Arthur sat on the front fender; sliding off as she approached, he opened the front door for her.

"Quite a day, huh?" he said.

"That's about the biggest understatement of the year," said Melissa grinning at him as she climbed into the front seat.

Closing the door behind her, Arthur hopped into the back, whistling a tune that was both foreign and familiar, a song she'd heard in dreams perhaps. His whistling was soft yet strong and almost flute-like. On the drive back, he continued for quite some time as the three remained otherwise silent. The sun began to sink behind the mountains, its orange glow back-lighting the trees along the roadside. The sky was ablaze with golden, peach and violet streaked clouds blending into the deepening azure horizon.

Leaning back on the headrest, Melissa felt a great sense of peace. She palmed the small yellow stone inside her pocket and perceived the familiar inner radiating of light and spirit. "Spirit is forever," a voice whispered softly within her. And her mind felt washed in a temperate sea of serenity.

Chapter 18:
Time with Family

Melissa was even quieter than normal that night. Her parents took them out regularly on Saturday evenings. Usually dinner out was a treat, but Melissa felt spent from these last few days. Although wondrous and filled with magic, this day seemed to span a lot longer than the hours contained in it.

The crowded restaurant was alive with conversation and wait staff scurrying to keep up with orders. Emotions inundated Melissa's being from every direction. She imagined a shield of purple light around her on all sides filtering out some of the feelings that flooded her senses. She tried to tune in to her inner sanctuary of peace, but there was too much commotion. So she just endured the assault unknowingly sent out by such a crowd.

Kevin took up the slack talking about sports and other things that didn't interest Melissa much. Eventually, though, her lack of participation in the conversation became noticeable.

"You've been awfully quiet," said Melissa's mother. "Don't you want to tell us how your day went?"

"It was great," Melissa answered, aware she wasn't sounding as enthusiastic as she actually felt. "As weird as it sounds, I guess I'm kind of tired from, well, from getting too much sleep last night," she added.

"That doesn't sound weird to me," her father responded. "I sleep late to catch up on the weekend and end up feeling more exhausted than I did when I was sleep deprived all week."

"Well, if you weren't a chronic insomniac, or better yet, if you'd do something about that snoring, you might not be so sleep deprived during the week," said her mother, grinning at him. "Kids, I just hope you take after me in the snoring department," she teased.

This was an old wisecrack between their parents. Her mother often complained that she wouldn't have bags under her eyes if her husband didn't keep her awake with his snoring.

"Don't let her fool you, Melissa and Kevin," their Dad added. "She snores too—just doesn't realize it." He gazed at his wife with a look of affectionate amusement.

"Only when I have a cold," their Mom interjected. "I think we'd better change the subject before I get peeved, Robert," she added, raising her eyebrow but still smiling.

"Okay, Melissa, so let's hear all about your afternoon with your friend and his grandmother," said her father. "He seems like a nice young man, by the way."

"Oh, he is," said Melissa trying not to let her tone give away how much Arthur had come to mean to her in just a few days.

"Ooh, does Melissa have a boyfriend?" Kevin chimed in.

Melissa ignored him. "And Arthur's grandmother is incredible. She knows so much stuff. She comes from a long line of medicine women and was taught by her own grandmother to use herbs as remedies for everything from headaches to arthritis.

You should see her garden, and the land; it's just beautiful." Melissa allowed the excitement she felt to ease her tired mind and body as she shared some of the day with her parents while keeping secret any part that might divulge the elder's teaching.

"That sounds wonderful," her father said. "You know I feel kind of sad that I didn't learn more about the Cherokee side of my heritage. My mother was completely closed mouth about her upbringing, and I didn't get to spend much time with my grandparents. But I heard them say once that we were descended from medicine folk. Don't know if it's true though."

Melissa held her tongue. How she would have loved to confirm that truth, tell her father all about Adahy, who was indeed their ancestor as she now knew. But her father wouldn't understand, she thought, so she remained quiet and managed to keep the conversation light.

"You know," Melissa said, "I'd really like to learn more about the Cherokee part of my roots. And Arthur's grandmother even said she'd share some stories and history with me. She gave me this to give to you."

It seemed like a natural opening, and there might not be a better time; so Melissa pulled the note out of her jacket, which hung on the back of her chair, and handed it to her father, who would probably be the most receptive recipient.

He and her mother scanned the note together.

"Hmmm," said Melissa's mother. "She says she'd be willing to take you in one day a week to learn the ways of the Cherokee— whatever that means. I think we'll need to meet her and find out more about what she has in mind," her mother continued.

Melissa was afraid of that. Although Mrs. Fox was an amazing person, Melissa wasn't altogether sure how the old woman would come across to her parents.

"But you know what, if it keeps you out of the woods for a day a week, it might not be such a bad thing," her mother said.

"Still we will want to meet her," said Melissa's father. "And we want to be sure you'll be properly chaperoned all the time you're with Arthur. He may be perfectly nice, but I remember what it was like to be a boy that age. All those raging hormones."

"Please, Dad," Melissa said. "I can assure you there's nothing like that going on."

"Yeah, come on, Dad, why would he like a metal mouth like Lissa," Kevin interrupted. "Holy halitosis!"

"Kevin, how many times have I told you not to make fun of your sister's braces?" their mother admonished. "You're lucky enough not to have to wear them. But that doesn't mean your sister needs you to give her a hard time."

"Aw, c'mon, you know I was just kidding," Kevin said sheepishly.

"Well, let's not kid like that anymore, Kev," said their dad.

"Your sister's a lovely young woman," their mother added. "And I think it's good if she has a boyfriend even if she is a little young. It's still going to be a year or two before you get to date, Missy, but for now we're just as happy to see you have a little interest in something besides *nature*."

"You're too young for a boyfriend in my book," added her father. "But it's okay to have a friend who's a boy. Right, Gwen?"

Melissa's mother winked at her without her father or Kevin seeing. "That's right. It's fine to have a friend who's a boy." A small smile passed her lips, and Melissa felt for the first time in a long while that her mother actually approved of her.

By the end of dinner, it was agreed that Melissa's mom would contact Mrs. Fox this week and set up a time to meet her before or on the following Saturday. Even in the midst of this encouraging decision, Melissa felt the weight of anxiety. She'd managed to escape it for a while with Arthur and his grandmother, but concern over the fate of the trees never left her mind for long.

She realized that the commitment to study with Mrs. Fox meant time away from the trees and knew she had to work fast and furiously to save them now. As she lay in bed pondering this later that night, she sensed the silent touch of her spirit guide.

"All will be as it is meant to be," Adahy murmured through the corridors of her mind. "Sleep now and be at peace." The comfort of his presence stilled her thoughts. Tired from the day of adventure, Melissa let her consciousness recede into the respite of slumber.

Chapter 19:
Her Woodland Cathedral

After church services that morning, Melissa sat as patiently as possible through lunch with her family. But the day was bright, clear and warmer than usual for this time of year, and the trees called to her as surely as if their voices shouted out loud. She felt more perfectly the presence of Spirit, the purest and deepest love, in her woodland cathedral than anywhere else in the world. The forest sang the hymns of her heart in tune with her soul.

Melissa gathered her English books and told her parents she planned to work on her assignment for this week outside, since that was where she drew her greatest inspiration. As long as she was studying, they felt compelled to send her on her way.

"Just be sure to wear a jacket. I know it's warm today, but it's still damp out there," reminded her mother.

"Got it," Melissa said, hurrying out the door with her bundle.

She hiked through the forest to settle in the lap of her friend Slippery Sally, the magnificent elm she dearly loved. Sally's leaves covered the forest floor beneath her, still damp from the moisture held in the ground.

Melissa spread out an old, faded quilt and dropped her books and notebook on it as she plopped down, crossing her legs under her. As her back nestled in its familiar spot at the base of Sally's trunk, Melissa felt the instant connection between them that had grown from years of contact.

"Bright glories of the day," said Sally lovingly, her smooth tone filtering through Melissa's veins to her heart and mind.

"It is a beautiful day, isn't it?" Melissa agreed.

"Yes, life is precious in every moment, but on days like this it's just a little easier to cherish what we have in this world," said Sally, her inner voice imparting a hint of sadness. "If only it would last," she added.

Realizing for the first time how completely open she was today, Melissa worried that Sally might have picked up the secret she held inside. As quickly as possible she tried to secure her thoughts and camouflage her inner turmoil and anxiety.

"It's all right, my young friend," Sally said softly. "I already know. It's been the talk of the forest since the elder trees decided to spread word of what's coming. Don't worry yourself about keeping secrets."

Over the years, Melissa had experienced the world through Sally's senses countless times. She'd felt the silken flow of life that was unique to this gracious tree; she'd savored her laughter and known her wisdom and shared the alchemy of tree magic, turning sunlight and water into liquid life that flowed through her leaves and nourished her body. Embraced by Sally's trunk, she'd seen the Earth Mother through the loving essence of one who called Her home. The thought of losing this bright life evoked a deep despair in Melissa, and tears began to etch her cheeks.

"Don't feel so sad," said Sally, her smooth even tones seeming for all the world like a lullaby from a mother to her beloved child. "We're aware that the world changes. We don't want to leave this place or end this life, but we're ready for whatever comes."

"How can you be ready," Melissa snuffled, the tears still coming. "I'm not," she said. "I'll never be ready to lose you."

"I don't want that either," said Sally. "Your friend, the grandfather of poplars, says you're fighting to save us. At least that's what I hear. Is it true?"

Melissa quieted her sobs. "I'm working on it. I just don't know how successful I'll be. But I am trying."

"I have faith in you," said Sally. "I don't know about these things or what walkers do, but I know *you*. If anyone can save us, you can. You've got the noblest spirit a walker could have. Even the oldest inhabitant of the woods agrees with that," she said referring to Grandfather Poplar. "He's been unusually kind of late," added Sally. "I think perhaps you helped him find his tree heart."

"He already had plenty of that," Melissa said. "He just doesn't always like to show it. But he's got a great big heart.

"As for saving you and my other friends, your faith in me means more than I can say, and I'll do whatever I can."

Melissa felt tiny in comparison to the spirits of her tree friends and smaller still when facing the daunting task at hand. But she sensed she had the bravery of her forebears flowing through her veins, and the spirits of both Cherokee and Scots-Irish standing behind her, a great line of ancestors extending back through time as far as her inner sight could see. She imagined a throng of souls guarding her back—all the Celts and the Cherokee whose bloodlines passed down through centuries to create the life that coursed through her now. This image filled her with a sense of security and assurance. She might not be much on her own, but she had the heart's blood of her lineage to lend her strength and courage.

"I sense your vision," said Sally. "And I understand. It's the same for us trees. We feel the kinship with our parents and grandparents and all the trees of our kind that ever stood upon the Earth. Their energy flows through us as our limbs spread out to embrace the sky; their bodies, fallen ages past in the forest, nourish us now as part of the soil that gives us energy. We stand upon the lives of all who came before." As she spoke, Sally's voice pounded through Melissa's mind like the march of many footsteps—quite different from the lilting stream that was the Slippery Elm's normal tone.

Sally rarely sounded so reflective or measured in her communication. Her disposition usually light-hearted and uplifting, she was one of the trees Melissa generally counted on to raise her spirits. But today she was understandably more pensive.

"You know, Sally, you're starting to sound a little like Grandpop," Melissa said.

"Oh well, maybe he's wiser than I've given him credit for," Sally replied in a lighter timbre. "I never thought too much about such things until recently. I just lived in and of the moment as trees do. But now in looking to the future, I feel the need to take solace from the past."

Melissa did her best to brighten Sally's spirits, repaying the favor the beautiful elm had so often given her. They talked for some time until Melissa's longing to visit Grandfather Poplar urged her to leave this comfortable spot.

"Give the grizzled old hardwood my regards," Sally said, as Melissa hugged her trunk lovingly in farewell.

Packing up her blanket and books, Melissa realized she hadn't gotten anything done on her English assignment yet. The visit with her favorite tree would have to include a mix of homework and conversation. No doubt the communication would come first, she thought.

Making her way through the woods, song birds greeted her from their perches overhead, a mockingbird darting down to ward off intrusion as she walked by too close to his nest, which was far out of reach high up in the crook of Percival Pin Oak's branches. Despite the mockingbird's protests, Melissa patted a greeting to Percival, a most even-tempered and noble tree whom she had dubbed after the heroic knight in King Arthur's court. She'd read the story to him a few years past, and he delighted in being named for this seeker of the Holy Grail.

"Tree lives are a great adventure too," he had said. "Our quest is for life, and Mother Earth is our Grail."

No time to stop today, Melissa thought, continuing past many tree friends, crossing the edge of her family's land and making her way over the creek to the most familiar and comforting place she had ever known.

"How are you, Grandpop," she said after securing her quilt on the still soggy ground.

"As well as can be expected. Isn't that what you like to say? Seems appropriate enough under the circumstances," he replied.

"Well, I'm hoping things will get better this week. I'm sorry I had to leave in such a rush yesterday. Mr. Brown took so long I was afraid I'd be late."

"And how was your adventure with your young friend and his grandmother—not that I need to ask. By those images pouring from your mind and that feeling in your blood, I already can tell much more than your words could say. You seem a bit like those capering jay birds at the rush of spring."

There was no need to explain what he meant. The channels of communication forged from years of connecting with

Grandfather Poplar made it impossible to keep anything from him. She also knew that since yesterday any reference to Arthur was likely to make her heart beat just a little faster.

"I don't know how to describe yesterday," she said.

"Then just think of it and let your memory flow," replied Grandfather Poplar.

Focusing her mind, Melissa allowed the experiences of the previous day to envelop her. Although she still preferred to express herself in terms of human language, Grandpop had taught her the easiest communication was wordless—the tide of thought and feeling conveyed in pictures, sensory impressions and emotions. She quickly downloaded all of yesterday to Grandpop in this way.

After digesting her human impressions, the yellow poplar finally said, "You've stumbled upon the path of your soul, it seems."

Melissa remained silent for a time knowing that Grandpop still sensed the current of feelings that whirled within her. At last she said, "I think you're right."

"Do you only *think* it?" he asked. "Surely the soul path requires more certainty than that."

"Let me rephrase that then," she said emphatically. "I know you're right." She smiled inwardly and outwardly. "Where would I be if you didn't call me on things all the time?"

It hit her again in that moment. That question, said jokingly, renewed her fear of losing him.

"I know, little sapling," said Grandpop. "Fear is a strange thing. You walkers carry it around like a bag full of boulders that you seldom set down for long. But while we trees don't want to end our days under the sun, we don't feel this curious emotion. We wonder at the cruelty of such an act as annihilating a forest, but we have no fear. Everything my spirit knows from this long life and the memories of my ancestors tells me there is no use to such a thing. From what I can see, fear changes nothing except to destroy the joy of each moment spent in its grasp. It consumes like fire everything in its path. What purpose does it have for you, little one? Why do you allow it?"

"I don't know, Grandpop." She pondered the question for a long while before she answered. "The only good thing that comes from it, I guess, is that sometimes it causes a person to act in ways to stop the bad stuff from happening."

"Hmmm. But wouldn't it serve that purpose as well if you felt it for just an instant instead of dwelling on it during all your waking moments?"

"You have a point there, Grandpop. I'll have to think about that one. Maybe making the choice to act is enough to help the fears go away. I only know that when I actually *do* something about what I'm scared of, it always helps me be less afraid."

"Well, you've already started doing something about saving us, haven't you? And you're continuing to make other efforts. So why do you still have the fear?"

"If I knew that one, I guess I'd be able to solve anything."

"That sounds like a good plan," he said, inwardly sending her the feeling of a smile. "But I don't think walkers really need fear at all. Seems to me action should grow out of the flow toward life. I feed on sunlight; so I stretch my limbs upward. I need water; so my roots extend through the layers of ground beneath me."

"Grandpop, humans are just different. I don't know how to explain it."

"Something tells me *you* could get beyond it and be more like us if you had a mind to," he added with an air of assurance. "I don't know about the rest of the lot, but you could change and, perhaps in doing so, others would too."

"Right now overcoming my fears isn't my biggest goal," Melissa answered. "But I'll work on not inundating you with them."

"If I should have to leave you, young sapling, I want you to remember something."

"Don't say that, Grandpop. I'm not going to let that happen."

"Even so, I want you to remember this. It might just help you with that thing you call fear. Join with me deeply. Know the oneness."

At his invitation, Melissa closed her eyes, slowed and deepened her breathing. Leaning firmly against Grandpop's trunk, she shifted her back to a snug position and felt his awareness begin to blanket hers as she merged into his giant spirit. She sensed first his physical being, the flesh of his bark, the flow of sap moving slowly through his body, the sensation of sunlight on his leaves, the water being drunk by his roots. Then she went deeper, allowing herself to be swept into the vastness of his consciousness, knowing the connection between him and all the other trees past and present. At last she traveled further than she'd ever gone before in her connections with the trees. Not only her mind but her spirit blended into his. And she felt *Life*. Energy danced through everything and all that existed was enlivened by it. Ebb and flow. A silent waltz. No, not silent. There was a chord of Life that echoed through everything, the soul song of the Universe. Lost in soundless music, she became one with every particle of soil, every drop of water, every molecule of air, every creature great or small.

I am the ceaselessness of Spirit. I am life unending. I AM. These truths came from no inner voice; no words; just awareness. *I AM. Life IS.*

After timeless moments, Melissa felt herself rising back upward, disengaging her body, mind and spirit enough to perceive herself again. Even more than when she had merged her mind with Mother Earth, she realized with absolute certainty that this union had changed her forever. As she came into full awareness of her own body, she felt as if each one of her cells were vibrating very fast—almost as if she might levitate at any moment. Her hands trembled.

Needing to feel some sense of solidity, she touched the ground. Firm, strong, real.

At last Grandfather Poplar spoke softly, more gently than at any time she could recall. "You see, sapling, what it means to have no fear.

"We experience what you might call sadness when our brothers and sisters fall. Even though we realize they live on, their life force unending, we simply miss the unique spark of spirit that each one shared with us. And like all creatures, we feel the longing for our lives, our uniqueness, to continue and thrive. It drives all life forms in Earth Mother's garden. But there is no fear. Only life. Forever."

Tears rolled silently down Melissa's cheeks. "I wish I could be like you, Grandpop, feel everything, feel life, like you do. I wish... If only we humans could all have the gift you just gave me."

"Perhaps someday you will, little sapling. But for now I only ask that you hold that gift in your own spirit and remember what it feels like to be a tree."

Melissa realized her fears had been banished at least for now, and she wanted to hold onto that as long as she could. "You can count on it, Grandpop," she said. "I won't forget that feeling for as long as I live."

Melissa remained in silent communion with Grandfather Poplar for a long time, sharing the joy of the warm afternoon sun that beat down on her skin, his bark. Finally coming back to the realities of mundane existence, she gazed down at her English text and notebook. She wasn't sure how much time had passed but knew that she would need to rush through her assignment.

"I'll help if I can," said Grandfather Poplar. "That is if tree lore can offer any insight. What are you studying?"

"In English class we've been learning about mythology for the last two weeks. First, we had to define it and then we studied common themes in various mythologies, and we've spent a good bit of time on the Greek and Roman pantheon."

Realizing this didn't mean much to Grandfather Poplar, she channeled many of the memories from class to him and also sent some of the pictures she'd formed while reading the myths.

"Now Mrs. Wentworth wants us to write an original myth. Students who are better at art can draw theirs, creating pictures of their gods and goddesses, and a few people got to work in groups if they decided to play out scenes of their myth. But I chose to write, of course. Just don't know where to start, and I have to have the first three pages to turn in tomorrow so Mrs. Wentworth can check on our progress."

"It seems these myths are just stories of how to live, how people see the world and what they believe. Is that right?" asked Grandpop.

"Yeah, that's pretty much it."

"Then I think you ought to know just where to begin," he said. "How do you see the world? What's in your heart?"

"But I can't tell them that. *Can* I?"

"It's just a *myth* after all, isn't it?" he added. "Your realm is the truth of Earth Mother, the wisdom of her children, the lore of lifetimes of tree spirits and nature beings, the knowledge of the unseen worlds. Can't that be your mythology?"

"You mean I should tell them about everything I see and feel and sense and know?"

"Not everything. How long is this story supposed to be?" He sent the gentle whisper of a smile. "Just make a beginning, a little insight into the vast wealth of wonder we've shared with you. Bring our world to life in your words. Perhaps it will mean something to someone one day. If nothing else, you will have something to offer your teacher."

Melissa's mind whirled with the possibilities. Where to start? What aspect of her world to include?

"Begin with Mother Earth and Father Sky, sister Moon and Grandfather Sun. Be still and the rest will come."

She closed her eyes again and wound her way down into that place of inner twilight. There Adahy greeted her. He knelt beside her and placed a hand on her shoulder. "I will guide you in the telling," he murmured within her mind. "Just be open and write."

Chapter 20:
Arthur's Foreboding Dream

Arthur woke early Monday morning, long before he needed to get up. It was still dark outside his window. Sunrise this time of year came late, after 7:15, and most days began in the pitch black stillness of pre-dawn. Arthur adjusted his eyes to the darkness and tried to shake off the dream that had awakened him.

In sleep he was walking through a wooded area where the trees had been felled, the nubs of their trunks all that remained of a once great forest. Far away he heard someone sobbing and recognized the energy of the person. Melissa. He felt her calling to him in the distance out of eye shot. He ran toward the sound and the sense of her as fast as he could, but the cries never got any closer. He stopped and listened. Putting his head to the ground, he tried to hear her footsteps or sense her presence. But the barren forest spoke no wisdom, and the earth was still and voiceless. Then even the sobs trailed off. He couldn't find her. He continued to race toward where he thought she was, a sense of urgency growing in him. That was when he awoke, feeling out of breath.

Arthur knew the dream hadn't ended. He came to wakefulness because he didn't know what else to do. But he understood he had to go back now—this time choosing consciously instead of following the path of the dreamscape. So he closed his eyes, set his intention and drifted back into sleep.

Once more in the dead forest of his dream, Arthur found his way to a clear stream he knew would be there. The water was virtually still, and he could see his reflection in its surface. He looked at the mirror image of himself and merged with it just as his ulisi had taught him long ago. He slithered into his dream skin in an instant, leaving behind his view as observer and becoming the dream self. Now instead of watching from the outside as before, he looked out of his own eyes.

Facing East, he called out Melissa's name. No echo. No sound. Turning to the South, he shouted again. Still no response, and the West offered the same result. Crying out toward the North, he heard her answer. He began to stride Northward, toward the cold. The landscape grew more barren, a blue sheen covering the ground. Along the path the bodies of small animals lay still as stone.

He called again, and her voice in response seemed closer. So he ran toward it. There in the distance he saw Melissa. Coming to her side, he knelt next to her. She sat atop the remains of a huge tree trunk. Tears covered her cheeks. She looked small and cold and pale.

"He's gone. They're all gone," she said as he embraced her, her voice muffled against his shoulder.

In the midst of this death, he felt alive holding her. He stroked her long hair and whispered into the still void of this place, "I'm here. I'm here. You're not alone."

Her body quivered against him as her sobs continued. "We will rebuild the world," he said. "There will be no end."

Arthur woke again with a start and sat up in bed. It was late now, and he needed to hurry to get ready for school. As he pulled off the T-shirt he slept in and donned his day clothes, he knew he had to see Melissa as soon as possible. Not all of his dreams came true, but many of them did, and this one had that raw quality of a warning. He and his friends had work to do and time was drawing short.

Arthur visited the guidance counselor first thing after arriving at school to see about switching two classes. He had to come up with a logical reason besides just needing to take English and chorus at the same time as Melissa. He explained that he got too drowsy after lunch to devote his full attention to English and that singing made him feel livelier.

"That sounds reasonable," said Mr. Raeburn, the 9th grade guidance counselor. "Since Mrs. Wentworth teaches 9th grade English both periods, changing to a different class is feasible. Ordinarily, it would be too late in the year to switch your classes, but, since you just moved here, I think we can allow for the change."

Mr. Raeburn altered Arthur's schedule and wrote a note for his homeroom teacher. Arthur felt a little more at ease as he headed to class. But he would still have to wait until fourth period to see Melissa. At least having two courses together might allow them more time to discuss what they would need to do.

The morning passed slowly as Arthur's classes presented him with little real knowledge. As a child he used to pass the time by catching the stray feelings that his classmates or teachers so openly blared out to the world. But his grandmother had been quite firm in her teachings regarding such things, and he now knew better than to intrude upon the inner worlds of others.

Still, there were times when he felt an invitation to read others a little, when thoughts and feelings danced before him in a person's energy so clear and easy to perceive. He knew, for example, that Mr. Hendricks, his history teacher, wasn't really interested in the lesson and would rather be fly-fishing with his son. He could see that his classmate Lisa Collins was angry at her friend Heather, who sat next to her. Lisa's energy fluctuated and bubbled in deep murky reds around Heather. The only way to avoid sensing these things was to close his eyes and go completely inward. He'd been caught doing just that on more than one occasion, and teachers always assumed he was sleeping. So he diminished his insight as much as he could and focused on listening to the lesson.

When fourth period arrived at last, Arthur entered Mrs. Wentworth's classroom and handed her the altered schedule sheet. She was somewhat surprised but directed him to a seat near the back. He smiled at Melissa, who looked puzzled but pleased, as he walked by her desk.

"Class, we have a new student: Arthur Fox. Let's all make him feel welcome," Mrs. Wentworth said. "Did everyone complete the first three pages of their assignment to turn in?"

Arthur pulled out the opening pages of his myth. He'd started writing one of the stories his grandmother had taught him in childhood. He opened with the tale of the Boys, Anitsutsa, who left their lives behind and became the star cluster known as the Pleiades. The story had been passed down for ages, but the words used in the telling were his own. Arthur passed his paper forward and wished for time to speed by more quickly so the chance to talk with Melissa would come sooner.

When class finally broke for lunch, Arthur took the opportunity to escort Melissa to the cafeteria. Walking by Mr. Walters' room on the way, they met Cheryl as she came into the hallway.

"You two look so serious," she said.

"We were talking about the trees," said Arthur.

"What's the latest," Cheryl inquired as they took their place at the end of the cafeteria line.

Arthur sensed Cheryl wasn't as interested in the trees as he and Melissa, but he could easily discern how much she cared for her long-time friend.

"I had a dream warning that we'd better do something soon," Arthur said. "Let's just say it was a bad omen."

"A dream, huh? You two are a perfect pair," she said, nodding toward Melissa. "A daydreamer and a night dreamer," Cheryl added with a grin.

Arthur smiled and so did Melissa, who stared at her shoes looking embarrassed. But he could sense it was just shyness on her part.

Arthur decided not to go into details about his dream. He would tell them only the meaning. "In the dream I was called to the North, the place of troubles," he said. "It could be worse though. At least it wasn't the West."

"What's worse than troubles," said Melissa.

"West is the direction of death," he replied. "But this dream was just a warning, I think, showing me what we have to prevent." Again, he chose not to elaborate. Melissa didn't need to hear the vision of her beloved trees laid waste. This would only worry her, and Arthur could perceive already how deeply concerned she was. Anxiety would only sap the energy she needed now to fight for her friends.

"Well, we definitely need to act fast then. I trust your dreams, Arthur," Melissa said looking into his eyes. And he felt that trust, something solid between them. Strong.

After getting their food, the three found an empty spot and continued their conversation.

"I talked to Mr. Brown after class this morning. He signed us up with his ecology group, WENOCA, to speak at the County Commissioners' meeting tomorrow. He says they only allow half an hour for public comments, so you have to get on their list if you want even a potential chance to talk.

"Anyway, can you both get permission from your parents to go? I think I can persuade my dad to take me. Mr. Brown says the more of us who go, the more they'll pay attention to what we have to say."

Arthur would find a way to the meeting even if he had to walk.

"I'll definitely be there," Cheryl said.

Melissa told them about her father's idea to contact the television station and about Mr. Brown's friend who wanted to write a feature story for the newspaper.

"Sounds like our biology teacher is quite a guy. I haven't had much chance to get to know him yet," Arthur said.

"Yeah, he's cool," Cheryl said. Turning to Melissa she added, "What was it like seeing him outside class?" Cheryl's tone revealed a mix of curiosity and mischief.

Arthur felt a twinge of discomfort coming from Melissa at the question. Without intruding on her thoughts, his gut told him that she had a crush on this Mr. Brown. But Arthur didn't seriously view the man as a rival. Deep within he knew that someday Melissa would stand by his side. He understood it from the moment they met—even before that. He recognized her spirit.

"Kind of weird, really," Melissa replied, shrugging. "He was pretty much all business, measuring height and width, taking photos. I guess he has a very objective approach about things, but maybe that's good. He can discuss the trees from a scientific perspective and an environmental one. All I can do is tell people about them from my own point of view."

"That's the most important thing," said Arthur. "When you talk about the trees, they come to life for people. That's way better than science," he assured her.

"Well, I'm not so certain about that. But thanks anyway," Melissa said smiling. Her blue eyes shone as she looked at him, and he could feel a shift in her mood whenever he held her gaze.

"I'll tell you what, Melissa, Arthur's right," Cheryl said. "Your love for those trees is downright infectious. I guess you could say you're a carrier for environmental flu," she added, giggling at herself. "You've even got me fighting for your cause, and I'm not exactly what you'd call a nature girl."

Cheryl's comments brought a little lightness to the conversation, but the three still felt the urgency of the task—Cheryl picking up on it from Melissa and Arthur.

"If we can reach just one person on that board," Arthur said. "I think it will make a difference. So if any of us has a chance to speak, and it ought to be you, Melissa, tune in to which one that is and focus your eyes on them."

"But how am I supposed to know which commissioner will listen?"

Arthur smiled and peered into her eyes. "Oh, you'll know," he said with a steady tone. "I have faith you'll pick the right one."

Chapter 21:
The Classroom of Life

Excitement churned just beneath the surface as Melissa considered the possibilities before her. Between working with Mr. Brown and brainstorming with Arthur and Cheryl, ideas to save her friends were beginning to take shape. She'd never encountered so much support outside the world of trees.

Inside her jeans pocket, she tumbled the warm smooth citrine between her fingers. The rock's energy, its life, seemed to pulsate against Melissa's fingertips. When she held the golden-white stone in her left palm, she sensed the nature spirit's consciousness providing her with the courage to act.

"Thanks, my friend," she whispered inwardly, as a feeling of warmth coursed through her hand and up her arm, traveling to the pit of her stomach. A sense of calm passed over her.

Arthur mentioned at lunch that he would be in her chorus class next period; so the two of them walked there together. Melissa's citrine companion vibrated in her hand while she was close to Arthur, or maybe it was just her imagination. But she had learned through the years of communicating with the trees that what most people attributed to fantasy was often just a truth they were unable to recognize.

"I'm glad you're keeping the stone with you," said Arthur as they walked into the music room.

She almost asked how he knew, but she was starting to get used to his level of awareness, which seemed even greater than her own in a lot of ways.

Arthur presented the transfer sheet to their chorus teacher, Miss Fairchild, who was one of Melissa's favorite instructors. She was young with blond hair and a sweet smile, and she genuinely loved music.

Since Melissa was an alto, she sat between the sopranos and the tenors. As it turned out, Arthur was a tenor; so Miss Fairchild seated him on the same row just two seats away from Melissa. He grinned at her as he strolled to his chair.

Both sections of chorus were preparing for the autumn performance given to raise money. School funds had been slashed, and concerts and special events brought in just enough to keep the music and art programs going every year.

Melissa loved to sing although she wasn't particularly good at it. Her range was limited, but she could stay on key at least. Today they rehearsed an old Celtic song that was an annual favorite with the countless people in the area who celebrated their Irish and Scottish ancestries.

Arthur's voice sounded clear and strong—just as Melissa would have expected. She timidly sang along, doing her best to blend into those around her. But by the third chorus, she felt herself letting go as the melody began to take hold, to flow through her blood much like the voices of the trees. A flash of her Scottish ancestors played in her mind, and she knew this song had been sung by them for generations. She envisioned them dancing and reeling, stomping their feet in time with the music—fiddles, harps and pipes playing. It was as if a distant chorus sang to her, their music resonating in her soul.

Without realizing it, her voice grew louder as if bolstered by this inner vision. She closed her eyes and felt her ancestors singing with her. As the chords of the last chorus ebbed, she looked up to see her teacher and the entire choral group staring at her.

"It seems you found your voice today, Melissa," said Miss Fairchild. "You sounded great. But you were singing the melody rather than the harmony. I had no idea you were a soprano disguising herself as an alto," her teacher said, smiling. "Would you like to join the sopranos from now on?"

A little in shock, Melissa looked around at her classmates. Arthur gave her his usual broad grin.

"I, uh, I don't know. I mean, I think I'll just stay where I am."

"All right. It's up to you. We can always use you as an alto. But it's good to know you can double as a soprano if we need you."

As the class returned to rehearsal, Melissa tried to understand what had happened. She really wasn't a soprano, or at least she didn't think so. She'd just been so lost in the tune. An inner voice whispered, "Blame it on the ancestors," and the thought almost made her laugh midway through verse two. She still felt a little shaken and took pains to remain her usual alto self, her harmony blending subtly with the rest.

Melissa was gratified that the remainder of chorus passed without incident. Yet, she continued to wonder about her unconscious soprano *debut* into her next class.

She gazed out the window at a bluebird who landed on a bush outside. Of all the song birds, these were her favorites. They nested in the caverns left by woodpeckers or weather damage or in hollow trees that had passed long ago. Melissa often delighted in their soft, melodic warble and at the glimpse of bright electric blue feathers in flight. At the moment, here in the dull monotony of civics, she marveled at the cheerful sight and sound of the female bluebird. This small chirper lacked all self-consciousness. She sang fully with her whole heart.

In dreams Adahy had told Melissa often that no creature crosses our path without a message for us. There was nothing hidden about the meaning of the bluebird's appearance so soon after the incident last period. She had to stop hiding in the shadows and sing the music of her soul. She didn't plan on doing any solos in chorus class, but she would find other ways to express her heart song.

The true revelation of her spirit came always when she connected with the trees. After the school day and long bus ride home, she followed the frequent, well-worn trail through the forest as usual. Red-tail greeted her affectionately from his perch high atop Grandpop's crown. The wind and rain had stripped bare the giant poplar's bright golden foliage. His tall light gray limbs stretched naked toward the wispy clouds overhead. Melissa sat on the bed of leaves, still slightly moist even after two days of sun, and let her consciousness be enfolded in his, Grandpop's familiar and fluid communication filling her once more with the sense of home.

"Little sapling, it's good to see you again so soon," he said. His tone through the years had often been as rough as his aged bark, but of late the timbre of his voice flowed more softly through her body and mind.

"Grandpop, you know I always miss you when we're apart. You're about the brightest spot in my day," she replied.

"You know flattery is as useless to me as the droning of a tree frog," he said, the pretense of brusqueness in his words betrayed by the inward smile she recognized quite well.

"Oh, Grandpop, the truth is you like compliments as much as Randy Red Maple, and you know it. I'd say it's more like fertilizer for your ego, if you had one, that is," she teased.

"Egos, hmmmph. From what you've told me of this state of being, I can hardly fathom it. You know we don't have such nonsensical things. We live in harmony. I daresay those with egos, limited to you walkers from what I can see, don't do the same."

"Ah, Grandpop, there's nothing quite like a little verbal, or non-verbal, jousting with you. It makes my day," Melissa said with a laugh. "Of course, you're right about egos. They can make us confident or crazy, depending on our mental health. At least that's what my history teacher said last year. She gave us some pretty prime examples of shadow egos run wild."

Melissa thought back to her American history class. So many stories of darkness and death among the ones of liberty and sacrifice. Although she liked history for the most part, she could envision it so easily and feel it all too much. Waves of pain had spread through her when she read the account of the Sand Creek Massacre, the murder—that was the only word that fit—of a village of over 200 Cheyenne men, women and children in 1864. A chill ran down her spine remembering the history.

"When walkers destroy each other so easily," said Grandpop, "it should be no wonder that your kind spreads death to so many other forms of life." His voice hummed low and somber through her veins.

Melissa realized instantly that the pictures in her mind evoked by the memory of what she learned in history class had transmitted to Grandfather Poplar without her intention. "I'm sorry," she said. "I didn't mean to paint such a terrible scene for you, Grandpop."

"I know, little one. But it's not as if we trees had no knowledge of such things. The past passes through us from generations long gone and from far across the expanse of land on all sides. Our ancestors told the stories to those who came after them and on through to those who stand today.

"We've watched in silence through the ages. But we've never come to understand. For myself, though, I can only say the walker I know most deeply shares the soul of a tree. And you, dear sapling child, sing with the life of the Mother, strong and deep, wondrous and light, sure and steady."

Tears welled in Melissa's eyes. "I hope that's true," she said. "I hope I take after you, Grandpop, as if you were my own grandfather for real."

"Count on it," he replied, gently conveying his love along the channels to her mind and heart.

"But you know, I'm human too, Grandpop. Can't do much about that."

"Yes, I guess you'll just have to accept it," he added, trying to lighten her mood. "Not everyone can be as perfect as a tree. And not every tree can be as insightful as I." A slight chuckle from Grandfather Poplar rattled through her being.

"Seriously, though, Grandpop, I'd like to think we're not all full of so much venom. But I get really angry sometimes. There are moments—and not so few and far between—when I just want to haul off and hit somebody, usually my irritating brother. And sometimes I feel like I *hate* people for the horrible things they do. I may not be like the people who killed those Cheyenne, but I have to deal with my own ugly feelings. Of that you can be sure."

Grandfather Poplar was quiet for a while. At last he said, "Do you think I don't know who you are after so many seasons together, sapling child? I've seen the workings of your mind and felt your human emotions. But I see beyond all that to who you are, Melissa.

"You know sometimes when you relax your eyes and look across the water to the trees in the distance you get a glimpse of the light that emanates from them?"

"Sure. It's one of my favorite pastimes on those lazy days when I have nothing to do."

"Well, I see, or rather sense, your light too, and it's not so different really. Even your brother has that light, if you can believe it, and your teacher and every walker who has passed by this hillside in my time. So I recognize something that you walkers usually seem to forget or ignore: We're made of the same stuff. I don't often admit it but it's true. The radiance that shimmers around and through us also shines in you. You have *potential*. You could live as we do in oneness with all.

"Search your heart," he added. "You know it's true."

Melissa gazed out toward the small stream and across to the trees on the other side of its banks. She allowed her eyes to lose focus just a little, the way she learned to do when looking at hidden pictures in those "magic eye" books. Surveying the tops of the trees against the azure blue sky, she could easily detect the gentle white glow around them. She stretched her hands out toward the trees in the distance, fixing her relaxed gaze on them against the background of the sky. Easily she perceived the same radiance around her own hands. As she concentrated on it, this luminescence seemed to expand outward, and after a few moments she could discern colors, blue and green edged in golden white. Watching this display with curious joy, she began to feel more at peace. A flash of white light flowed into her field of color, and she suddenly sensed Adahy's presence.

Closing her eyes, she let her mind still as she was learning to do more easily now. Breathing in and out slowly and consciously, she went into the centered place within her heart.

Adahy's voice within her mind said, "I was here all the time but only now made my presence known. Continue to hold the peace and love in your heart and open your eyes."

Doing as she was instructed, Melissa gazed up at her guide who stood beside her just where she had seen the white light appear. She could view around him now the same colors as she had seen when she looked at her hands.

"Yes, we're much alike, dear daughter. We carry many of the same gifts; so it's natural that our energies would appear very similar.

"Listening to your communication, I want to share something with you.... Don't despise your humanness, Amadahy. For every shadow within the human mind, you'll find the balance of light within the heart, and you can always decide to follow your heart and your spirit.

"You have the capacity to choose conscience instead of guilt, wisdom instead of fear, love rather than hate. For every iota of shadow, you hold an infinite amount of love."

"I feel nothing but love when you're around," Melissa said peacefully.

Adahy smiled. "That's not quite true, is it? I'm with you in every moment. I've never left your side. I was there when you wished your little brother would fall off the side of the earth. I stood by you when you imagined your fifth grade teacher would meet her doom and never come back to school and when you envisioned the bully in your third grade class turning into a toad."

Melissa didn't want to look at Adahy and realize this truth. She closed her eyes, but he was still there in front of her.

"It's all right, Amadahy. You were just learning to be human, learning how to live in this realm. You're on your path of spirit becoming one with humanness, and humanness becoming one with spirit, and it's all part of this reality.

"So when you see what you think of as ugliness in others, remember they're doing exactly the same thing: learning to be human. Every experience serves a purpose—even those you do not understand."

She opened her eyes again, but Adahy's aspect faded into the background. "Grandpop," she said. "Between Arthur's grandmother, Adahy and you, I feel like I'm getting lessons every day lately. I might as well be in school," she added with a half grin.

"Seems to me you've been in school your whole life, little sapling. I think that's what your friend is trying to tell you. It's not just some building you go to five days a week. It's a planet and every vibration of existence on it."

"You've got a point there, Grandpop. All I want to know is what happened to recess?"

The two of them shared a quiet laugh reverberating through their inner cores.

"No rest for the weary today though. I've gotta run and get back to the house before my parents come home. But before I go, I wanted to fill you in on the latest news. In a flurry of picture thoughts, she shared the day with him and promised to return tomorrow if time allowed before she went to the County Commissioners' meeting.

"You're welcome, day or night, upon this hillside, sweet sapling," he said, as she hugged him wholeheartedly and said farewell for the day. Embracing Grandfather Poplar, she could almost feel arms wrap themselves around her. But his limbs remained still in the autumn afternoon.

Chapter 22:
The Age of Wishes

At the dinner table that evening, Melissa asked her father if he would take her to the County Commissioners' meeting.

"I hate to disappoint you, sweetheart, but I have to work late all this week. We're under the gun to get the Donaldson campaign done by Friday."

Melissa felt let down. She had been sure he would agree.

"You said your friend Cheryl is going. Couldn't one of her parents give you a ride?"

"Robert, you know I don't care for that girl. She's wild and has always done her best to get Melissa into mischief."

"Oh, come on, Mom," Melissa said. "Cheryl's not any wilder than anybody else. She's just herself instead of being what everybody thinks she should be, and I think that's pretty special."

"Well, if you're intent on going, I'd rather take you myself. I'm not that crazy about Cheryl's mother either. What time do you have to be there?"

Melissa hadn't expected her mother to volunteer.

"It starts at 4:30, but they won't take public comments until 5:30 or 5:45, maybe later."

"I'm not sure how you expected either of us to get home and go that early," her mother said. "So I don't see how we can get you there."

"Well, there is one other option. My biology teacher, Mr. Brown, said I could go with him and his friends from WENOCA. I could stay at school, I guess, until he gets off and go from there."

"Isn't he the one just out of college," her father asked with a slight frown.

"Yeah. But he's a really great teacher and he cares a lot about the environment."

"I met him at parent-teacher night last month, Robert. He seems fine, and it would solve the problem. Melissa, I know we won't hear the end of it if you don't get there," her mother said glancing at her father with a look of approval. "So I'll come by there after work and pick you up. I don't think we need to ask Mr. Brown to drive you home as well."

As soon as the plans were arranged, Melissa proceeded to press her father about calling the television station.

"You don't skip a beat, do you," he said with a smile. "I haven't forgotten. I'll see about doing that during lunch tomorrow if I get a chance. Don't worry."

But she did worry. She needed everyone to follow through, because the trees had to be saved.

Later that night as Melissa began to drift into slumber, she heard the unmistakable and reassuring voice of Adahy whisper, "Trust."

"I'm trying," she replied as she felt her conscious thought ebbing into the edge of sleep. "I am trying."

She awoke in the wee hours. The clock read 3:33. Struggling out of the warm covers, she rose and went to the window as if guided by an unseen hand. The night sky was clear, a blanket of stars shimmering against the backdrop of midnight blue black. The forest called to her, a deep longing filling her senses. Opening the window, she felt the wave of chilly air rush over her body. In that moment a star burst from the sky cascading across the horizon. Then another and another arced a downward path in the distance. The Orionid Meteor Shower—she'd heard about it on the news. Although the moon was over half full tonight, it had set just after midnight; so its light wouldn't mask the glory of this spectacle for those who made the effort to fight sleep for the wonder of the skies.

Her old autumn and winter companion, the constellation Orion, the great hunter, had risen high in the sky, the red supergiant Betelgeuse glowing at his shoulder, and Rigel, the blue-white supergiant, shining brightly at his left leg.

"Wonder if this means I get three wishes," she mouthed, her breath wafting into the cold air like a whisper of smoke.

A warm comfort spread across her shoulders as Adahy's spirit hand touched her. Wondering if this were a dream, she turned to see his figure gleaming beside her in the darkened room, the same colorful energy emanating from him as she had seen earlier in the day.

"Wishes are for children," his voice rang softly within her mind. "The age of wishes is ending. The time for creating is at hand."

"Does that mean I can't wish anymore?"

"Only that wishes carry no power. In truth they say to the Universe, 'I am powerless. I am a babe who must be fed.' You move beyond that now."

"How do you figure," Melissa thought.

She felt Adahy's laughter ripple through her mind much like that of the trees.

"Accept your truth. Honor your path. The light flows through you. Use it to envision, to create, to build," he said. "Much better than wishing," he added.

"If only I knew how," Melissa said quietly.

Adahy looked deeply into her eyes. Seldom had she seen her guide in waking hours, and rarely did he speak without some level of reserve, his wisdom so often imparted in riddles or in ways she found difficult to fully comprehend.

"Hear me, Amadahy," he insisted. "Do not ask how when your heart already knows. If you want three wishes, instead build three dreams. Birth three truths. You have the power. In oneness with Spirit, we all have.

"Sleep now and consider your three visions to bring to life."

With that he became invisible again although she knew his presence remained. She simply didn't need to see him anymore. Leaving the window cracked, she crawled back into bed and watched the clock tick by until 4:44. That was the last she remembered until morning.

Chapter 23:
Letter from the Heart

"Class, I have an announcement to make," said Mr. Brown. "One of your classmates brought something to my attention a few days ago," he said, nodding in Melissa's direction. "There's a development being built off High Ridge Road, and it looks like they plan to destroy most of the trees in the process.

"I and some of my friends from the regional chapter of Sierra Club, as well as a few of your class members, will be pleading the cause of the environment at this afternoon's meeting of the County Commissioners. So today I thought we might include a little civics and English in with biology and work on composing a letter from the class that I can share at the meeting later today. How does that sound?"

Realizing her mouth hung open, Melissa regained her composure. She could hardly believe this turn of events. Mr. Brown stood smiling at her, obviously aware of both her surprise and elation.

"Melissa, would you like to say a few words?"

Without thinking, she began to rapidly shake her head, a look of panic no doubt distorting her features. Speaking in front of class had never been easy or pleasant. Stutters, stammers, the wave of embarrassment flooding her neck and cheeks. Ugh.

"Come on," he entreated gently. "You know those woods better than anyone. And it will be good practice for later today."

Cheryl eyed her with enthusiasm, her head motioning Melissa to the front of the room.

Closing her eyes for an instant, Melissa took three long, deep breaths, the last exhale almost a sigh. She could sense Adahy's presence blanketing her like a protective cloak. She felt the flow of Earth Mother's energy rising through her feet and took a moment to imagine herself barefoot against the cool ground, rooted in the Earth.

Slowly rising from her seat, Melissa stared at Mr. Brown, his warm brown eyes signaling an invitation to stand beside him. She walked to the front of the room.

In the wee hours, she had rehearsed what she might say to the commissioners, but the words from the night before fled her mind as she stood before her biology classmates. Melissa felt her throat tighten as Tracy Beaman leered at her with the usual display of loathing. But she had to do this. So, fixing her focus on Cheryl, the friendliest face she knew, she began to speak.

"Most of you know that I'm not a person who talks a lot. But I can say that I love the forest around where I live. It's a great place to escape to, to have adventures, to just *be*. The trees there are so beautiful—poplars, oaks, elms, maples, beech and birch, dogwoods and redbuds, cedars and pines—and the woods are home to lots of animals too—rabbits, squirrels, groundhogs, deer and pretty much every kind of bird you've ever seen.

My favorite tree, a giant yellow-poplar, has a hawk nest in the top. There's a stream nearby where the animals drink. It runs slowly when we have a drought but washes over the rocks when there's a lot of rain.

"I haven't been to a lot of places—just to the beach on vacation once in a while, to Tennessee and Virginia and once to Atlanta. But of the places I have been, this one is the best, the most beautiful, the one where I belong," she said, her voice beginning to break.

She looked down at the floor on the way back to her seat, her face warm and flushed with heat. *Why did he make me do that? I sounded like an idiot*, she thought.

"Thank you, Melissa," Mr. Brown said. "That was a perfect and clearly heartfelt description.

"Now I'm going to pass around a few photos of the tree that Melissa mentioned as well as some of the landscape around the area."

After distributing the photographs to the first person in each row, her beloved teacher held a large picture of Grandfather Poplar for the class to see.

"I made an enlargement of this one to give you some idea of the size. Photos don't really do it justice. This specimen of Liriodendron tulipifera, yellow poplar or tulip tree to most of you, is at least 120 feet tall. If you want to wrap your mind around that, think of a 12-story building."

A couple of seats away from Melissa, Jared Moloney said, "Wow. That sucker's huge." Mr. Brown ignored the comment.

"In the pictures circulating, you'll see examples of other trees in this forest as well." He showed them photos of several, offering scientific names and data for each.

"Here's an example of *Acer saccharum*, or sugar maple, and this one's *Acer rubrum*, that is, red maple. As you can see, these two look similar in autumn, but closer inspection reveals their bark varies slightly in color and in texture as does the leaf shape."

Mr. Brown continued to go into detail about the properties of *Betula* or birch, *Quercus rubra*, better known as red oak, *Quercus palustris*, or pin oak, *Liquidambar stryaciflua* or sweetgum, *Nyssa sylvatica*, whom Melissa knew as black gum, although her father had taught her its other names were black tupelo or sourgum.

Melissa felt her attention drifting. The science of trees wasn't nearly as interesting as their character. When she looked at the photo of Buddy Black Gum, Melissa could think only of her friend, who was Grandpop's neighbor, how the birds and opossums loved to feast on his small indigo-colored fruit each autumn, how the bees gathered nectar from his tiny greenish-white flowers, their buzzing accompanying many a daydream on lazy summer afternoons.

"So these are your inspiration," Mr. Brown concluded, his eyes sparkling with enthusiasm. "You can think about the trees you love, the animals as well, about camping trips or hikes, whatever. Put some feeling into it. Let them know that saving over 200 acres of trees means something to you.

"Take the next 15 minutes or so to write a letter to the County Commissioners. After that anyone who wants to share their letter aloud can do so. If we have a masterpiece, I'll pass it around for everyone who is willing to sign. I'll take all of them with us today to the meeting and present them along with those written in my other biology classes.

"We'll make this an extra credit assignment. If you don't want to write a letter, you can review Chapter 9 in your book. But if you do decide to write, make it good. No jokes or fluff."

Almost everyone started taking out paper and pens. There were a couple of people whose parents worked in logging who chose the other option, one being Tracy, whose father owned a local sawmill. But given a choice between plodding through a review of their textbook and writing a letter to save the trees, most of her classmates found the latter more appealing.

For Melissa, this was perhaps the simplest assignment she'd ever been given, but it also held the deepest significance, which lessened the ease with which she wrote.

> *Dear County Commissioners:*
>
> *I've lived all my life, 14+ years, on the land that Cherry Hill Development Company just bought. Over 110 acres belonged to Mrs. Cora Reynolds, who was our neighbor and my friend until she died a few months ago. The rest was my family's property—96 acres of proud, beautiful trees.*
>
> *On that land I've sat beneath the oaks, elms and poplars on summer days in the coolness of their shade. When I was little, I climbed tall trees and pretended they were my jungle gym, and my father and I hiked every inch of the land, exploring each trail as he taught me about all the plants and animals of the forest. In first grade, I gathered fallen leaves in a scrapbook for Show and Tell. The teacher was impressed that I knew all their names by heart.*
>
> *Playing alone, many times I was the only human witness to the forest wonders: flying squirrels leaping from limb to limb, opossums carrying their babies on their bellies, young wrens taking their first flights, deer pausing to drink at the stream in early morning,*

the water flowing slowly as it glinted with sunlight amid the reflections of the trees. I've seen rainbows kiss the treetops and sunsets blazing through the forest in fiery hues. I've looked on as countless butterflies danced together in the summer. I've watched falling leaves in autumn glowing brightly beneath the waning sun as they spiraled to the forest floor, sprouting blossoms in the spring and summer that scented the air with sweetness, tendrils of sunlit spider webs fluttering in the wind, robins pecking the ground for juicy grub worms, hawks gliding high in search of prey. I've seen what seemed like a thousand starlings descend upon the trees and then suddenly ascend at once murmuring against a cloudless sky. Once when I was younger, a red fox walking upwind from me came within five feet before he caught my scent and stood stunned and motionless for just a second before high-tailing it in the other direction.

I remember the time before Christmas when I was eight. My Daddy took us out in the woods to cut down a small cedar. But he finally changed his mind because I cried and pleaded the whole way, begging him relentlessly not to kill one of my tree friends. That's how I feel about them, you see. They are my friends—every tree, every animal, every rock, every insect and arachnid (except maybe mosquitoes and ticks), every fern, mushroom or weed in those woods. Just like I've witnessed the quiet miracles of nature there, they've looked on as I grew and became the person I am now. They've stood beside me while I argued with my brother, while I cried about something someone said or did to me, while I complained about school or chores. They've inspired me, supported me, listened to me, shaded me in the heat and sheltered me in the rain.

My favorite tree of all is one I call Grandfather Poplar because this yellow-poplar is the biggest one I've ever seen anywhere. Every tree in the woods is unique, but this one is the most unusual of all with a trunk that winds its way toward the light. This tall tulip tree is my resting place, my haven, my heart.

My brother has a tree house he calls his own, but I feel like every tree is my home. And that's what I'm asking you to save. Maybe you can't stop the development; I don't know. But you could keep them from clearing almost every tree the way they did in Cherry Point. You could save the trees that are my home.

I understand the land will belong to others now, but the kids whose parents build houses there deserve to know what it's like to live among the tall trees just as I have. They deserve to hear the bluebirds warble and watch the fledglings fly, to chance upon a chipmunk stuffing his cheeks with acorns fallen from the massive oaks and to play in the leaves gathered up each fall. And my friends, the trees, deserve to live, to make a home for the animals and insects of the forest and a sanctuary for kids like me who long to be where the wild things are.

So with my whole heart, I ask you to do all you can to help the forest live on, to rescue as many trees as

> *possible, and to save most especially my favorite tree of all. Please help.*
>
> *Most sincerely,*
>
> *Melissa Kincaid*

Melissa was glad she had used a pencil since she had to erase so often. But this was it. Exactly what she wanted to say and just in time. As she added her signature, Mr. Brown began asking for volunteers to read their letters. When no one immediately raised a hand, he began calling on people. Feeling raw after writing such a heartfelt plea, Melissa sent out with all her might the message that she didn't want to read aloud. Whether from coincidence or telepathy, Mr. Brown didn't point to her.

A few of the letters sounded really good. Melissa was surprised that some of her classmates shared deep feelings and special memories about times in the woodlands. Cheryl's letter, especially touching, talked about the times she'd played in the forest with Melissa when they were younger. Melissa smiled at her friend after hearing it.

"I told you your nature flu was catching," Cheryl whispered with a grin.

"We're about out of time," said Mr. Brown. "So go ahead and pass your papers forward. I appreciate what a great job you all did and will gladly give these to the commissioners tonight."

After passing her letter to the person in front of her, Melissa gathered her books. The bell rang not long thereafter. As her classmates filed out of the room, she walked up to her teacher.

"Thank you so much, Mr. Brown," she said. "I seem to be saying that a lot lately," she added. "Looks like I'll be going with you after school today after all."

"Did your parents say that would be okay," he asked.

"Yeah, my mom even wrote notes, one for the front office and one for you. Here's yours," Melissa said pulling the folded paper from her biology book. "She's going to pick me up near the end of the meeting if you'll just give me a ride there."

"Absolutely. Your friend Arthur will be going with us as well. He told me yesterday afternoon that he wasn't able to get another ride. He's supposed to bring a permission slip with him today too."

Arthur hadn't mentioned riding with Mr. Brown, but Melissa was glad he would be coming. As much as she liked her biology teacher, being alone with him outside the classroom had proved to be a little awkward with her fumbling for words and unclear about how to behave. Still, she wasn't certain things would be any more comfortable with both of them—her first crush and her second one—in the car.

"My friend Hilary is meeting us here so we can carpool. She's the newspaper reporter in our group. You'll like her. She cares as much about trees as you do."

His brown eyes sparkled with a hint of humor. "Hil likes to anthropomorphize them too," he added. "She's not much of a scientist, but her heart's as big as Nebraska."

"Well, I'd better get going. I'll be back here after last period. Okay?"

"See you then," Mr. Brown said as Melissa turned toward the door and made her way to her algebra class.

At lunch that day Arthur announced that he would be riding with Mr. Brown to the meeting.

"I know," said Melissa. "I'll be sharing the ride too."

Arthur smiled.

"Won't that be cozy?" Cheryl said, one of her wicked Cheshire cat-like grins spreading across her face. She nudged Melissa with her left elbow. Melissa didn't have to read her friend's mind to know that Cheryl was thinking about the fact that she would be in the same car with both Arthur and Mr. Brown.

Intentionally ignoring the comment, Melissa added, "Did you know the newspaper reporter was coming with us?"

"Yeah, he mentioned something like that. Cool, huh?" Arthur said. "She could do a whole story on how much the forest means to you."

Melissa sensed Arthur's sincerity, which shone from his features like the radiant gentle glow around a full October moon. Realizing for the first time the common trait shared by her two friends, Melissa couldn't help thinking how pleasant it was to be with people who were exactly what they seemed. Nothing hidden, no agenda. Just being themselves for all the world to see.

"Sounds like a double date," Cheryl said with a slight giggle. "I'd call my mom to see if I could go with you guys, but I wouldn't want to be a fifth wheel."

"Oh, you're just too much," Melissa replied.

"Yeah, isn't it great? What would you do without me to tease you?"

The three of them laughed. But Melissa noticed that Arthur's eyes never left her. Fidgeting ever so slightly under his constant gaze, she continued to discuss their plans, eating only a few morsels of creamed corn and barbecued chicken during the focused conversation. Even amidst her concern for the trees, she became enveloped in the warmth of sitting beside this boy, whose life was beginning to mesh into her own so seamlessly she felt as if she'd known him forever.

Chapter 24:
Plea to Those in Power

Arthur was glad when school ended that day. Filled with anticipation and quiet elation, he strode toward Mr. Brown's classroom. Melissa arrived coming from the other direction at almost the same time. He watched her walking toward him down the hall. There was nothing girlish about the way she moved. Always with a purpose, this one. She reminded him of one of the forest dwellers she loved so much; yet, he realized she had no sense of her own inner strength.

Sensing her mild discomfort at his gaze, he looked down at his books for a moment but then resumed his somewhat blatant stare. *She'll have to learn to deal with looking me in the eye*, he thought. Arthur usually avoided direct eye contact with people outside his family or those he didn't know well. It was the way of his people. But Melissa was no stranger to his heart. It was as if he had known her always, and he felt the call of her sparkling eyes and answered it with his truest self.

"Someday you're going to get over being shy," he said.

Melissa sighed. "How is it you *always* know what I'm thinking. Am I that open a book?"

Arthur grinned. "Pretty much, yeah. I don't have to read your energy when you show everything on your face."

Rolling her eyes, Melissa added, "Well, I guess I should get better at hiding my feelings if I'm going to hang around with someone who reads people so well." She smiled.

They stood outside the door of the biology classroom in silence for a moment. Her blue eyes held tiny glints of yellow and reminded him of cornflowers dusted with specks of sunlight.

A chair screeched slightly as it moved across the bare floor, and Arthur turned toward the sound. Mr. Brown rose from his seat and came toward them.

"Come on in, you two. It's still 40 minutes before I can leave; so get comfortable. You can do your homework while I work on my lesson plans."

The two of them sat next to each other at the front of the classroom. Arthur took out his biology book to work on the assignment Mr. Brown had given them. Since they wrote letters in class, they had to read Chapter 10 and prepare for questions the next day. Clearly, Melissa had the same idea since she pulled out her biology book as well.

"You can look on with me," Arthur said, starting to scoot his desk closer to hers.

"Probably not a wise idea," she said smiling. "I'll be able to concentrate better on my own."

"No problem." He knew she was right, but the truth was he wouldn't be focusing much anyway. He felt the closeness of her warm and vibrant spirit. In the time of their ancient ancestors, he would have asked her to be his usdayvhvsgi, his wife, at just a couple of years older than he was now. But that was far off in today's world.

Arthur watched the minutes tick by on the clock above the chalkboard behind Mr. Brown's desk. In his peripheral vision, he could see Melissa do the same thing, checking the time about every two minutes.

At five minutes before 4:00, the time teachers got to leave for the day, a young woman strolled into the room. Mr. Brown looked up with a wide smile and turned toward her as she came to the desk. Embracing her lightly, he said, "Hi, Hil."

Her long sandy hair fell just beneath her shoulders and curled around her lovely oval face, and her body looked toned and fit like a runner's. Arthur could see Mr. Brown's attraction and felt it coming off both of them like a wave of warmth. At the same time, he sensed the slightest flinch of surprise from Melissa, who sat next to him looking intently toward the stranger.

"Hilary Braithwaite, meet a couple of my favorite students, Arthur Fox and Melissa Kincaid."

She beamed an infectious smile in their direction. Arthur liked her already—good energy.

After a few pleasantries, it was time for them to leave for the commissioners' meeting. Sitting in the back seat of the small Honda with Melissa, Arthur had little room to stretch his long legs, but the nearness of his friend made the discomfort worthwhile. She sat in silence as they rode downtown. Little effort on his part was required to sense the turmoil and expectation within her. She exuded nervousness. As they wound along the sometimes steep and curving roads toward town, he could almost see the pools of anxiety expand in the energy around her.

He reached out silently and took her left hand in his. An almost soundless gasp escaped her lips, but she continued to look out the window. Closing his eyes, Arthur focused on allowing the life force of Nature to flow through him as his ulisi had taught him. He felt energy rising up from the Earth through his feet and pouring into his head from the cosmos. It flowed into his hand and then into Melissa. He was careful not to give her his own energy, which required a lot of focus since he was concerned about her agitation, but he knew the strength of the Universe was a better bolster for her than his own.

As the warm, quiet flow of energy passed through him, his mind was quieted, his breathing slowed, and he could easily reach out to her with his thoughts.

"It's going to be okay," he said inwardly. "You will do great and say just what is needed."

Arthur sensed Melissa begin to relax a little. Her breathing slowed to match his own. As she leaned her head back against the neck rest, he could see her close her eyes. Her hand tightened in his for a moment as if to say "thank you." Then her shoulders sank against the back of the car seat and her arms fell to her side. She began to breathe consciously—slow, even, deep breaths.

"How are you two doing back there," said Mr. Brown, looking back at them in the rearview mirror. "You're awfully quiet. Hil and I have been talking so much, but we haven't heard a peep from you."

"We're fine," Arthur answered. "Just getting in the right frame of mind."

"I was hoping you might tell me some stories about the woods by your home, Melissa," said Hilary.

"She's been a little nervous about all this," said Arthur, sensing Melissa's need to be quiet. "I think maybe we just need to focus on what the meeting will be like."

"Well, I can fill you in on that," said Hilary. I've covered a bunch of these for the paper. They're mostly a bit of a snooze fest to be honest. The most interesting part is always the public opinion portion of the meeting.

"Anyway, they begin with calling the meeting to order followed by the Pledge of Allegiance. After that it's pretty similar each time with approval of last month's minutes, old business updates, various resolutions, reports and ordinances, budget info—you know, really riveting stuff—until it's time for public comments."

"Sounds like something our Civics Teacher Mr. Aldridge would find just fascinating," Arthur interjected.

Melissa laughed lightly. He was glad her mood had brightened. After the brief interlude, both Arthur and Melissa turned inward again into the place of silence. Arthur could feel their guides with them and knew the support and wise counsel they offered were greatly needed. As they pulled to a stop in the parking lot across from the county courthouse, he released Melissa's hand. Her bright blue eyes opened, and she gazed briefly at him in unspoken recognition of the bond between them.

Hilary was right about the commissioners' meeting. The level of excitement was much less than that of watching a snail plod along a garden path. So instead of paying attention, Arthur passed the time by surveying the energy of the people present, particularly the commissioners themselves.

He'd looked them up on the internet and shared his findings with Melissa at lunch. One was a former school teacher and principal, two were lawyers, one a businessman and developer who grew up on a farm and the other was a retired veterinarian, who might make the best candidate for directing her plea for help. But in person his earlier determination changed. The former vet's energy was closed. Arthur didn't need to invade his thoughts to sense the man had had a bad day and was angry about something—not in the mood to listen. The female attorney was likewise shut off from the proceedings, and the man who practiced law had an air of arrogance coupled with an inability to really hear what people were saying. Arthur couldn't imagine him being very successful if he couldn't listen.

So pickings were slim. Arthur bent to tell Melissa his sense of the situation, but Mr. Brown glared at him before he got more out than "The vet isn't the best one." So he remained silent and trusted that Melissa would *know* just as he had told her she would.

At last the time came for them to offer their comments about saving the forest. The contingent from WENOCA was rather large and all went up to the microphone en masse with Mr. Brown at the front. Since they only had a short time allotted to present their case, Mr. Brown spoke concisely. After only a minute or two, he introduced Melissa, who timidly walked forward.

Arthur felt his own pulse racing, surely matching her own. He sensed her reluctance and anxiousness being overcome by a most profound courage. Clearing her throat, she began, tentatively at first, like a small child suddenly thrust in front of a mob of strangers, but then Arthur felt a quiet confidence rise in her. He could sense, almost see, her guide and ancestor standing beside her, his spirit hand upon the small of her back. Arthur let his senses expand and realized there was a throng of spirit beings gathered around her, their light buoying her. The nature spirits, the guardians of the standing trees, the crystal spirits, the elementals, and the ancestors spread a wave of light around his friend. Letting his attention return to Melissa as she spoke, he watched her gaze fix on one commissioner, the developer who once was a farmer, and he knew this was the perfect choice.

"Think back to your childhoods," Melissa continued. "Do you recall the first time you went hiking through the woods? Maybe with your father or grandfather, your older brother or your best friend, maybe alone. Do you remember the quiet magic of the trees, the rocks or leaves you collected as your treasures or the songs of the birds? Do you remember the way you felt—like a pioneer, like Daniel Boone when he explored these foothills and mountains? He might have walked the same footpaths you hiked, your ancestors and mine, making their homes here in the world of nature, living in a place where they could feel most alive....

"When you go into the forest, the world disappears, the chaos of your life, all your troubles, get left behind. There's nothing like that feeling. I came here to remind you of that and to ask you to save that gift, not just for me but for yourselves and your children and their children.

"The woods by my home are the best place in the world to me, and I love those trees; every one of them is a miracle; every one of them reminds me of the ways this world can be perfect. In the woods when it's quiet, I remember who I am. I feel like a part of everything. I'm asking you to save that feeling," she said, her voice breaking slightly.

"I could appeal to you to save the trees in the forest and all the animals and all the beauty just for the sake of Nature, but I'm asking for something more: Save them for that feeling you get in the stillness of the woods that doesn't come from anywhere else in the world. For all the kids growing up who will treasure that feeling as I have and as I know you have."

With that she returned to her place beside Arthur. He squeezed her arm gently. "You did great," he whispered, his pride in her emanating from the core of his chest.

Mr. Brown came forward again and asked if he could present the commissioners with the letters of appeal from the students in his biology classes. Removing a thick handful of papers from his satchel, he walked to the commissioners' table and gave the stack to the presiding board member, the former principal.

"Thank you for your comments and for the considerable efforts of your students," said the commissioner. "We understand that expeditiousness is needed and will take your appeal under advisement."

As they turned to leave, Arthur saw Melissa's mother standing near the doorway. He doubted Melissa had seen her come in. Mrs. Kincaid dabbed her eyes with a tissue, her face streaked where the tears had washed through her makeup.

Melissa's mother tentatively hugged her daughter. "I'm sorry, honey," she said. "I never heard you speak so eloquently." Her eyes welled again with tears. "I wish now we hadn't sold it," she added. "I never wanted to break your heart."

Melissa's face was wet with tears as well. Arthur wanted to reach out and embrace her but realized this moment was for her and her mother.

"I know, Mom," she said. "I know."

Chapter 25:
Omen of the Owl

On the way home, Melissa and her mother spoke very little. There was an implicit understanding between them now. The look in her mother's eyes at the commissioners' meeting had said it all—guilt and regret written so clearly there. It was obvious that she now understood how deep a betrayal it was to sell the woods. The stubborn confidence that it was the right decision had fallen away from her mother's demeanor like the last leaf dropping from a slender elm as winter's harsh reality set in.

"Melissa, I wish we could go back and undo things," her mother said softly. "But we can't. So I'm going to call tomorrow and see if I can get an appointment with the development company. I'll implore them to leave as many trees as possible on the property. Of course, now that they own the land, they don't have much reason to listen to me. But who knows. Maybe I'll make a dent."

"If you do meet with them, can I go with you?"

"As long as it's after school, I don't see why not. I'll make it as late in the day as possible both for your sake and mine. I'd rather not have to take off from work anyway."

Melissa never imagined she would have her mother's support in this. Her father loved the forest, but her mom seldom sojourned beyond the boundaries of their yard and wasn't exactly outdoorsy. Funny how things can change so swiftly, Melissa thought.

The next day her mother followed through on the plan and actually went a step further.

At dinner Wednesday evening, she said, "I spoke with one of the owners of Cherry Hill Development Company this afternoon. Melissa, I don't know if I mentioned that it's owned by two brothers. At any rate one of them is coming to dinner tomorrow night." Her mother's face shone as she shared the news.

"You're kidding," Melissa said. Not sure how she felt about sitting down to eat with someone who had the nasty habit of clear-cutting trees for his subdivisions, she flinched at the thought. But Adahy and the trees had taught her the wisdom of seeking peace.

"Melissa, if you can help me out by setting the table and making the salad and rolls, I might just manage to get a decent meal on the table by 6:00 when he arrives."

"Sure."

"Kevin, I'll need you to pick up the family room and make sure your video games and toys are all put away." Before he could protest, their mother added sternly, "And I don't want to hear any complaints. You'll both need to help."

Kevin glared at his older sister, and she felt his contempt pelting her like a hard sleet, bombarding her skin and sinking into her pores. Instantly she placed a shield around herself, an impenetrable wall of energy, that she had learned to build as a protection against emotional onslaughts.

"Dad, did you call the TV station today?" Melissa inquired.

"Oh, honey, it's been such a crazy week. I just didn't have a free minute. But I'll do my best to find the time tomorrow."

"That's what you said yesterday," she replied, extreme disappointment easily discernible in her tone.

"Melissa, give your father time. I know he'll get to it," her mother said. "Robert," she continued, turning toward him, "This really is important to our daughter. If you'd heard her speak to the commissioners, you'd know that this is something we both need to help with."

Her mother clasped a hand on her father's forearm. "We made this decision without the input of the children, and now we've got to fix things as much as we can."

"Okay, okay. I get it. You went on about it all last night, Gwen. I'll call tomorrow," he said, looking at Melissa. "That's a promise."

Satisfied, Melissa let the subject drop, but the plight of her tree friends continued to gnaw at the edges of her consciousness like termites silently and relentlessly devouring wood. Anxious thoughts seldom left her mind for long except in the company of the trees.

After dinner and homework, Melissa went to bed. She desperately needed sleep. The night before she had replayed again and again her speech before the commissioners, wishing she had said this or omitted that. She had a habit of reviewing and analyzing the day, imagining that it went differently. It was a tendency she was trying to overcome since it had caused her many sleep-deprived nights.

Tonight, however, the welcome respite of sleep found her soon after her head touched the pillow and with it the time of dreams. It had been several nights since Adahy had come to her in slumber—perhaps because she was seeing and sensing him more in waking hours—but tonight she walked the familiar dream path through the shimmering wall within the woods.

Adahy's hand in hers, she was guided to a council meeting once more. All those she had seen in the dream rain dance were there around the fire. As the plump older woman, whom Melissa now knew as Awenasa, Mrs. Fox's ancestral guide, gave her a welcoming smile, Melissa basked in warmth and comfort. Taking her seat with the others, she and Adahy looked at each other across the firelight—acknowledgment and kinship wordlessly spoken in their gaze.

Looking directly at Melissa, Adahy spoke solemnly, "Tonight in council we kindle the green twigs of the sacred cedar, known to us as atsina, whose smoke is powerful medicine.

"Long ago when the world was created, the animals and plants were asked to stand in wakefulness for seven days and nights. All tried to remain vigilant; yet, as the long nights passed, one after another fell into slumber. Only a few sustained until the end. Those animals who hunt by night with keen sight were given this gift as a reward. Among the trees, only those who are ever green—cedar and her companions spruce, pine, laurel and holly—lasted until the end. All others must become bald each winter, but these few remind us that there always shall be spring.

"Amadahy," he said, "look now at the outer edges of our circle and see what before you have failed to notice."

She scanned the forest around the entire circle. How could she have missed this: In every direction—East, South, West and North— cedar trees stood tall, vigilant protectors surrounding their circle. As she tuned into their essence, she could almost smell their distinctive fragrance, even in dream state, so deeply ingrained was the memory of this scent. As the firelight glimmered upon their towering frames, she imagined them standing like silent watchers through the time of Creation.

Adahy continued: "We do not burn the cedar to warm ourselves, for its strength and power are meant for something more. All things upon this Earth have a purpose that we must honor.

"When our brothers, the Standing Trees, sacrifice themselves to provide the warmth of fire and lodging, they render the gift of their bodies. So it is when our animal and plant brethren make the sacred offering for nourishment. In the time of your ancestors, we knew this, Amadahy. We asked permission before taking the life of our fellow children of Earth, and, when this was granted, we honored their gift with thanks and blessings for their spirits.

"There is no honor in what men do now, my daughter. The way of balance has been lost. For every tree cut another must be planted. For every death must be a birth. This has been forgotten.

"In this land where you live, you bring the keys of remembrance. And we are pleased at your efforts to save those among the Standing Trees who are not ready to make that sacrifice.

"But we ask you to remember that not all will be saved. Some have already made their peace within the heart of Earth. The willingness to transform and be of use to others has become their truth. Do you understand this?"

Melissa felt as if tears were flowing down her cheeks even here in the realm of dreams. "I know I can't save them all," she said, a sense of surrender beginning to wash away her resoluteness. "But I will rescue as many as I can."

"We ask no less and no more of you than this....

"Soon comes the time of the harvest moon. Do what you can before that time, for the earth begins to move again as the rains have dried, and the days remaining to preserve the forest inhabitants grow short in number.

"And, daughter," he said, brushing her cheek gently to wipe the tears. "Always hold the gift of cedar in your heart. He placed a small twig of cedar into her hand and then pressed it to her chest. Remember that the spring always comes."

Melissa heard the creak of a tree branch, and moments later a small owl silently swept across the encampment, its golden eyes shining in the firelight like a cat's. Perching upon the low branches of a nearby tree, the owl peered down at the circle of humans. With its reddish-brown feathers and tufts that looked like ears, this little one was clearly a screech owl. As if in reply to her recognition, the owl's low and tremulous whinny-like whistle pierced the still air.

"To many Tsalagi, we whom you now call Cherokee, Owl is a symbol of death. Yet, like the cedar, Owl remained wakeful through the seven days and nights of Creation. You must be like our friend ugugu," Adahy said. "Learn to see in the dark."

The owl swooped again from its perch, flying just over her head, and dream time ended.

Back in her bed, Melissa awakened with a start, almost as if she could feel the rush of wings above her. The scent of cedar seemed to fill the space. Shaking her head, she glanced over at the clock: 4:04 a.m. The room was pitch black except for the dim red radiance of the digital readout. Melissa adjusted her eyes until even in the darkness she could discern shapes.

Rising from her bed, she strode softly to the barely cracked window, allowing the cool air to coax her into wakefulness. She perceived a strange sound in the distance and raised the window slightly to hear better. As she did, the unmistakable low cry of the male Eastern screech owl greeted her, its utterance reaching out from the edge of the forest.

"See with your spirit eyes," said a voice within her.

Closing her lids to shift to inner sight, she breathed slowly, deeply. Although the frigid air stung her lungs a little, she continued until the full breath sharpened her focus. Reaching out with her internal vision, she saw into the border of the woodland. There on the branch of a Sycamore the small tufted owl sat. With open eyes now, she gazed in the direction of the screech owl. Suddenly she felt as if her senses were telescoping outward and she could *see* the owl. With only starlight to illuminate her view across the expanse between them, her mind said this was impossible, and just as swiftly her sight returned to normal. Her usual 20-20 vision and nothing more.

Sighing, she returned her thoughts to more pressing matters and considered Adahy's warning. The moon had set hours ago; so, again closing her eyes, she summoned forth the picture of how it had looked earlier in the night. She remembered: a waxing gibbous moon, perhaps three or four days away from being full. This realization struck her like a blow to the chest. Adahy said her work had to be completed by the harvest moon. She turned on the adjustable reading lamp next to her bed and focused it on the calendar that hung on her bulletin board. Sunday. The full moon was only four days away.

After more than an hour of restless worry, Melissa fell into a fitful sleep until the alarm woke her not long thereafter. She rose slowly, ragged from the dream journey and the anxiety that weighed heavier than the day before. Still so much to do and so little time.

Chapter 26:
The Texture of Dreams

Because dinner plans on Thursday would prevent a visit with the trees, Melissa had set her clock to get up early. She dressed hurriedly and bundled up for the frosty morning. One of those times when it was hard to shake sleep, her mind felt thick with an inner haze. As if to match her mood, there were pockets of mist hugging the ground outside. Between the darkness and the fog, she took care to tread softly as she entered the woods.

Melissa decided to stop and see Sydney Sycamore tree, on whose branch she thought she'd seen the owl. The tall sycamore was easy to detect by touch since his older gray bark was split and scaly, peeling off to reveal smooth new bark beneath. Even if she didn't know her way well enough to navigate in the dark, all she had to do was feel for his rough and crusty trunk.

As she rubbed lightly against his bark, fragments fell off in her hand. She embraced Sydney's trunk tenderly and inwardly sent the message, "Good morning."

"I don't call it morning until the sun comes up," Syd grumbled, sounding a little drowsy himself. "You walkers saying that morning starts at midnight in the darkest time of day is quite loony, you know," he added.

Melissa's laugher merged softly into the mist. In that moment, she heard the unmistakable quivering refrain of a screech owl above her. As he called again, she determined how far up he was and looked in that direction. For an instant she thought she saw a tiny glint of yellow eyes peering down at her.

"I'm no threat," she whispered softly, accompanying the words with waves of love expanding outward from her heart to the small raptor perched above her.

She felt a crispness to the air like tiny pinpricks on her skin, a sense of movement and a tingle up her spine. Closing her eyes, she allowed her inner awareness to open, acknowledging the presence of Adahy. With her internal sensing, she could hear his voice inside her mind.

"The screech owl is your teacher, he said. "Although he is diminutive in comparison to the other owls, he is a fierce protector and hunter, as mighty in spirit as his cousin the Great Horned One. His courage spans far beyond his size. And he sees through the darkness and the mist, discerning what others cannot. That is the wisdom he offers you, Amadahy."

As Adahy spoke her dream name, Melissa sensed stirring above her. In soundless flight the owl wended its way to the open yard, and with the swiftest motion he scooped something tiny, a field mouse perhaps, in his talons and flew back into the forest to eat. A surge of sadness washed through Melissa.

"Bless the spirit of Mouse, tsisdetsi, on his journey. But do not judge Owl for nourishing himself and his kindred. His hunting is part of the cycle of life. If all lived as much in the flow of the

Mother as ugugu and tsisdetsi, your battle would be at an end."

With that, Melissa felt Adahy's presence fade once more into the background of her psyche.

"Your friend is wise," said Sydney. "Would that all walkers could hear the guidance of the unseen ones who stand with them."

A hint of melancholy sounded in the inner voice of the great sycamore tree.

"I suppose you've heard the news," Melissa said.

"Yes, everyone has."

"My father said he kept three acres of trees near the house, Syd, so you'll be safe here near the yard."

"Thank you for trying to set my mind at ease, sweet child," Syd whispered through her veins. "Even so, I pray for my brothers and sisters, for all my kindred. In the truth of my spirit, I already can feel them leaving the bosom of the rich Earth."

"I'm working hard to save them," Melissa reassured him.

"I have heard this too, beautiful tree who walks. But the fear within you cannot be quieted—although I sense you trying to hide it. Like me, you suspect it will not be enough. Many will fall as some already have.

"But don't be afraid," added Sydney. "I know you'll keep as many safe as you can, and no matter what happens, the trees who stand after the great culling will remember you all our days. Our children and theirs for all time will tell the story of She Who Walks with the Spirit of a Tree."

Melissa was struck deeply by his words. She hadn't spent a great deal of time with Sydney through the years although she preferred to wander farther away from the house and from her brother most of the time. But his humor and crustiness had always reminded her a bit of Grandfather Poplar, and she held a warm spot in her heart for him as she did for all the trees of the forest.

Wiping tears from her cheeks, she said, "I love you, Syd. I need to run now, but we'll talk again soon."

Melissa continued taking careful steps as she hurried through the forest. At last she greeted Grandpop as the birds began to chirp. Gently embracing her favorite tree, she knew she had to share her concerns and the ominous message of the dream, which was still vivid in her mind.

After the dream scene filtered from her mind into his, Grandpop said, "Yes, the ground dries and the gnawers will begin to move again soon. I can feel it. They tried to stir their massive machines a day ago but then stopped short in the oozing mud. As the sun beats upon the land, it seems the death march won't be forestalled much longer."

Just as the chill air nipped at the pores on Melissa's face, the truth within his words pierced holes in the armor of her courage. Consciously, she stilled her breath and felt the Earth beneath her feet. With her whole self, she called on Earth Mother for the strength of Her brave heart.

Reinforcing her waning faith with a powerful infusion of Earth energy, she said, "I'll fight them, Grandpop! I'll fight them with every ounce of my being." She imagined herself like a knight from olden times, sword and shield gripped firmly in hand, doing battle with a faceless foe.

Grandpop's light bass chuckle thundered through her mind. Lessening her touch upon his trunk, she laughed too, a much-needed release of pent-up emotion.

"I guess I come up with some pretty silly pictures in my head, eh, Grandpop?"

"Silly indeed," he agreed. "But not so far from the truth,"

he continued. "You are a warrior for our cause. Your weapons are love, wisdom and passion—as well as your words. Not so different from your imagining at all."

"I never really thought of myself as a warrior," she said. "I've always been pretty timid and done whatever I could to *avoid* a fight."

"You just never had the need before, sapling child. You might not be willing to stand up for yourself often, but when someone threatens your loved ones, why, you're as ferocious as old Red-tail up there roosting in my highest branches. He may be quiet now, but he's as mighty as they come when the time is right."

"Seems like being compared to raptors is somehow my lesson for the day," she said. "Adahy said I should be like the screech owl, and now you compare me to the hawk. I'll take both as a compliment."

"You should. I may complain about the pair of them, but I do indeed admire the red-tails' determination and passion for life. If I were a bird myself, that's likely what I'd be."

"Well, Grandpop, on that interesting note, I'm afraid I have to say 'good-bye' for now."

"Will you come again very soon?" he asked, his voice suddenly subdued and introspective.

"I can't come back today because we're having a guest for dinner tonight, and I have to help get it ready. But I'll be back tomorrow and I'm praying I'll have good news to share."

"No matter your news, I will take comfort and joy in your presence, little one. Go with the light of Earth Mother and the love of one gnarled old poplar at your back."

Hugging him tightly, she said her farewells and traveled back through the forest. As she walked into the yard, she took a look back toward the woods. She longed to remain with them in the quiet of the forest. "I love you," she mouthed, reluctantly turning toward the house and the day ahead.

At lunch that afternoon she shared a small portion of her dream with Arthur and Cheryl. She knew she could have told all of it to Arthur but still felt the need to withhold such notions as spirit guides and dream councils from her longtime friend.

A brief opportunity for Arthur and her to be alone, or as private as two people can be in a cafeteria filled with noisy people, came when Cheryl went to buy an ice cream bar. Arthur's intense gaze held Melissa as Cheryl left the table.

"You know they're not just dreams, don't you?" Arthur said as soon as Cheryl was out of earshot.

"I'm not sure what you mean," Melissa answered.

"Of course you are," Arthur said with a grin. "They're journeys, not just dreams. You can tell the difference."

"Well, they do *feel* different from a normal dream, but I'm not sure how to explain it."

"Part of it is—I'm not sure how to put it either—the texture, I guess is a good word. Dream visions and night journeys are somehow more real than real life." His face looked serene, but his eyes revealed an inner passion as he spoke.

Melissa understood completely. How often she'd thought exactly that about her sleep encounters with Adahy.

"I always feel like I belong there too," she said quietly. "I guess you could say it's my other life."

Laughing softly, Arthur said, "You don't know how right you are. Our people believe the dream vision world is as real as this one. My ulisi says that in times past if a person was bitten by a rattler in the dream world, the medicine man or woman treated them for snake bite in waking. Ulisi still believes this, and I can't say she's wrong."

Melissa was instantly reminded of awakening to the downpour after the dream rain dance last week and was about to share this revelation when Cheryl returned to the table.

"Well, I leave you two alone for two minutes and you're deep into something. What's up?"

"Just talking about dreams," Arthur said in a matter-of-fact tone that told Melissa he understood her wish to keep this between them.

"Well, that's a subject I could go on about for ages. I've had some pretty lively dreams myself lately."

Cheryl went on to share three of her most *interesting* dreams from the last two nights. One of them, of course, featured Ricky McManness, whose attention Cheryl was still trying to attract without great success. Another seemed to be just a jumble of details from the previous days thrown into a kind of dream stew. But the third was most telling about Cheryl, and she recounted it without a thought about how much of herself she was giving away.

"Anyway," Cheryl said, "I have these vampire dreams a lot. Guess I watch too many scary films. But the creature in my dream wasn't much like those gorgeous vampires in the movies. It was old and ugly and downright nasty. It chased me for what felt like *forever*, running around my house from room to room. Finally, when I was cornered in the family room, it disappeared, and there I was, just standing there beside the sofa with my mother watching TV with her beer in one hand and the remote in the other. Weird, huh?"

"Yeah, that is strange," Melissa agreed, but neither she nor Arthur offered an interpretation.

Adele Harris had always seemed a little *off* to Melissa. Cheryl, who was outgoing with everyone else in the world, became strangely subdued around her mother. Reflecting on the times she had spent with Cheryl in her home, Melissa remembered sensing a kind of energy drain in her friend whenever Mrs. Harris was present.

Long before she could give a name to them, energy vampires were something Melissa could discern. Instinctively shielding herself around Mrs. Harris, Melissa understood the need to be free from such influences in her life. Thankfully, Cheryl herself was completely different from her mom.

After the dream discussion, the three speculated about what dinner with the co-owner of the development company might be like.

"I just hope he'll listen to reason," she said.

"Just be as persuasive as you were at the commissioners' meeting on Tuesday, and no doubt you'll win him over," said Cheryl. "By the way, have you heard any more about that?" she added.

"No more than you," Melissa said. "I know Mr. Brown says that government can move slowly, but we don't have time for them to do that!"

"We're all doing what we can," said Arthur. "You most of all. No matter what happens, you can be proud of that."

But pride wasn't what mattered, Melissa knew, and she felt certain Arthur did as well. Something concrete had to be done.

"You know I've heard about some groups that actually sit in the trees or chain and lock themselves to trees to save them. Maybe that's something we could do. We'd probably get in a heap of trouble, but I'm up for it," Arthur said.

"You know I'd do it in a heartbeat," Melissa replied. "Let's see how tonight goes. Maybe we won't have to. But if we do, I'll be headed to the hardware store," she added with a grin that disguised her inner turbulence.

Chapter 27:
The Art of Persuasion

A strange calm came over Melissa as she prepared for dinner that evening. Humming as she set the table, she took note of her unexpected composure. There was a sense of anticipation, even a mild uneasiness, just beneath the surface of her demeanor. But it was hardly perceptible amid the deeper serenity that pervaded her consciousness. Considerably out of character, Melissa wondered at her inner state. It was as if the sun radiated within and around her.

Feeling a hand on her shoulder, she turned but saw no one. Melissa smiled to herself. Adahy must be very close, she thought. Her guide no doubt enveloped her with his reassuring energy.

Her mother came home in a frenzy, bustling around the kitchen in a rush to have dinner ready when their guest arrived. Melissa could hardly recall a time when her mother put so much energy and effort into doing something for her sake. Must be a day for rare occurrences, she thought. She felt almost as if she and her mother had a bit of a personality switch, trading nervous anxiety and confidence so that Melissa got the better trait for a change.

Just as her mother was taking the chicken out of the oven, the doorbell rang.

"Oh, no. He's early. Your father isn't even here yet. Melissa, please get the door," her mother said, "while I call Robert's cell and see what's keeping him."

As she headed for the front door, Melissa's inner calm evaporated. What would this man be like? Would he listen to her or her parents? She wished her father were here to welcome him.

Opening the door, Melissa was greeted by a major surprise.

"Good evening," said the man. "It's good to see you again, young lady. When your mother invited my brother to dinner and he was too busy, I decided to come instead."

The tall, somewhat thin man, had on the same light gray suit he'd worn at the commissioners' meeting on Tuesday. His tan brow was etched in feathery lines beneath a receding hairline. He held a black brief case in his left hand. These things registered within Melissa's brain on some level as if she were watching from a distance.

"I can tell you're surprised to see me," the man said. "Are you going to invite me in?" he added.

Finding her voice at last, Melissa said, "I'm sorry. Please come in."

Following her inside, Commissioner Newman, the very man to whom she had directed her focus at the meeting on Tuesday, stood awkwardly in the entry of their home.

"Mr. Newman," her mother said walking into the foyer. "When your brother said he'd be sending his partner, I didn't realize that was you, one of our county commissioners, that is." Recovering quickly, she added, "Please come into the living room and have a seat. My husband should be home in about five minutes. Would you like something to drink while we wait?"

"Some iced tea, if you have it, would be wonderful."

After her mother went to the kitchen, Melissa sat in a wing chair opposite the sofa. She wasn't sure what to say or do. Fortunately, her mother returned quickly.

"There you are," she said, handing him a tall glass. "I must say it's a delightful surprise to have you join us for dinner."

"Yes, most folks don't realize I'm partnered with my brother Don. He handles the business most of the time now. Being so busy in other areas with two companies of my own, I've become more of a silent partner these days. But I'm still co-owner of Cherry Hill Development."

Directing his gaze at Melissa, he continued, "You're an excellent speaker, young lady. You might make a fine commissioner yourself someday."

"Thanks," she said. "I don't much like speaking in front of people. This is just something I had to do."

"Well, you made me think back to my youth and how much I loved tramping about in the forest. So I'd say you're a pretty effective speaker anyway." He smiled.

"You impressed me so much that I read most of the students' letters, yours first, and even made the mistake of sharing some of them with my wife, who immediately took on your cause."

"We really didn't consider how devastated our children would be when we sold your brother the land, Mr. Newman," her mother interjected.

"Well, we can certainly sympathize with you. My wife and I have made some decisions that have riled up our three girls over the years, and, believe me, I never hear the end of it when those three get stirred up."

Commissioner Newman grinned pleasantly between sips of iced tea. The three of them sat silently for a while, an awkward stillness densely pervading the air around them. At last Kevin sauntered into the room. With his usual careless, slacker attitude, he plopped down on the rug in the midst of them.

"This is my son, Kevin," their mother said. "Honey, why not sit in a chair, or there's plenty of room for you on the sofa?"

Melissa allowed herself a tiny, almost imperceptible, grin. Although her mother's tone remained extremely controlled, she could detect the touch of ire bubbling just beneath the surface of her words. She didn't need to be a mind reader to know that her mother wanted to tell Kevin to act like he had some sense.

After a few minutes of polite conversation, Melissa's father walked through the door.

"I'm sorry to be late," he said, coming in and shaking Commissioner Newman's hand sturdily.

"Think nothing of it. I've just been enjoying the hospitality of your charming family," said their guest.

"Robert, why don't you show Mr. Newman into the dining room, and I'll have dinner on the table in just a jiffy. That is, unless you would like to freshen up first, Commissioner?" her mother added politely.

"I'm fine, ma'am. And please call me Lawrence."

Melissa went with her mother to bring out the food.

"You'll forgive us if we're pretty informal around here," her mother said, setting the plate of hot biscuits on the table. "Most of the time we just help ourselves." She offered the plate of baked chicken to Mr. Newman so that he could select the most choice piece.

Their dinner conversation was light-hearted and polite, and the subject uppermost in Melissa's mind hadn't come up again since the commissioner's comments just after arriving. She ached to speak to the issue at hand, but the right moment never seemed to present itself.

Mustering her courage, at last Melissa simply broke into the conversation.

"Commissioner Newman, will you please do all you can to save the trees?"

An awkward moment to be sure, but she felt a weight lift from her chest as the words were spoken.

"That's why I'm here," he replied.

"Why don't we let the commissioner enjoy his meal, Melissa?" her mother interjected, politeness always her primary concern. "We can discuss it *after* dinner."

"I must say I'm enjoying this delicious home cooking. My wife's from up North, and just between us I do miss the kind of good Southern cooking I grew up with."

"Gwen's a *fine* cook when she gets around to it," Melissa's father said with a smile and a wink at her mother.

"Oh, Robert," her mother said. "You see, commissioner, or rather Lawrence, I usually work too late to prepare dinner on weeknights. But I still like to keep my hand in every now and then."

Impatience swelled in Melissa as if a bee had stung the inside of her stomach. She could hardly eat, so she spent the remainder of dinner quietly picking at her meal.

Afterward, she and her mother cleared the plates. Kevin, conscripted to assist them, grumbled under his breath.

"Melissa, you and Kevin go ahead and load the dishwasher. I'm going back in with your father and the commissioner."

"But I wanted to be there to talk about the trees and see what he's going to do," she pleaded urgently.

"I know. Believe me, I understand. But I think it's best if your father and I talk to him ourselves."

Melissa knew frustration showed on her face.

"Melissa, listen to me," her mother said quietly. "You made your case on Tuesday, and I can see it eating at this man's conscience. It's written all over him. So you've done your part. Let us grownups see what we can do to persuade him. All right?"

"Okay," she said, resigning herself to the obvious. Once her mother's mind was made up, there was little she could say to change it.

Her mother turned to leave the room but then came back as if she'd left something behind. With a tentative gesture, she reached out to Melissa's hand.

"Honey, I really will do my very best," she said looking intently into Melissa's eyes. Her face wore its mask of resolute composure, a look Melissa had come to trust.

"Thanks, Mom."

"When you and your brother finish, you can wait in here or go upstairs. Just don't interrupt."

As she did the cleanup—with little assistance from Kevin—Melissa strained to hear through the sturdy walls of their old house, but she could only make out a word here or there and intermittent bouts of laughter. In her mind, there was little about the situation that would evoke even the slightest chuckle. But adults had their own strange way of looking at things.

After more than half an hour, Melissa heard them walk into the foyer to say their good nights. This seemed to be the perfect opportunity to ascertain their mood and let the commissioner see her face one more time—a little reminder of what was at stake.

"I was just leaving, young lady. I'm glad I had the opportunity to bid you 'good evening' before I went."

Melissa tried her best to read what might lie beneath his charming smile and cordial banter with little success. "Thanks for coming," she said.

"It was my pleasure. Thanks again, Mrs. Kincaid, for a wonderful meal and to all of you for a delightful evening." With that he turned and walked out into the night.

As soon as the door closed behind him, Melissa pleaded, "Well, what did he say? Is he going to help?"

A smile spread across her parents' lips almost in unison.

"Yes. He is," her mother said enthusiastically.

"He's a really nice fellow," her father added. "He's going to talk to his brother and see if they can work with their landscape planner to be sure that every plot has at least several of the older trees left on it.

"We appealed to him on several fronts. Treed lots, although more difficult in the planning and implementation, always sell for more than ones without trees. And it's great PR for them to be working with the local environmental chapter on this.

"Mind you, sweetheart," he added. "They'll still be cutting down more than they save. But that's a whole heap better than clear-cutting the entire acreage."

Melissa should have been elated, she thought. Better saving many than having all destroyed. But the sentiments of Sydney Sycamore and Grandfather Poplar kept ringing through her mind. The loss of their kindred. Would those who were spared feel joyful or mournful for the countless brothers and sisters, parents and children who were lost? Tears came unbidden to her eyes.

"Honey, we thought you'd be happy," her mother said, a quiet kindness in her voice.

"Oh, I am. Really. I just wish that all of them could be saved. Like Dad said, more will be cut down than left standing."

Then an important thought came to her.

"What about Gran—I mean, what about the giant poplar tree where the hawks roost? Did you ask about that tree?"

"We wouldn't forget your favorite tree, Melissa," her father reassured. "He said he'd have to take a look at it and see. But he sounded at least cautiously optimistic.

"And before you ask, Melissa... No, I didn't have time again today to call the TV station. But it's still on my agenda...after the presentation tomorrow afternoon. Then I'll be able to get something done besides focusing on this one account."

"Please don't forget this time, Dad," she said meekly, the energy drained out of her after being on pins and needles for so long. "We've got to save him, the hawk tree, most of all."

"Your father will come through," her mother said smiling. "But right now you'd better get upstairs and do your homework."

"Mom, you know I asked about having Arthur over to see the hawk tree before the workmen get too close? Is it all right if he comes home with me from school tomorrow? His sister can pick him up before dinner."

"You mean you want to take him out there by yourself?" her father asked, his face contorted with a frown.

"Yeah, it's not like he's a weirdo or anything. He's a nice guy."

"Just take your brother on this trek with you, and it's fine," he said.

"Oh come on, Kevin is so annoying...."

"You heard me. Take Kevin along or forget about it. That way neither you nor your brother will get into mischief before we get home." Her Dad looked pleased with himself at this solution.

"Okay," she said reluctantly.

"And see if your friend wants to go out for pizza with us. We'd like to get to know him better," her mother added with a smile. "We can give him a ride home afterward."

"That sounds great. Thanks," Melissa said, surprised by her mother once again.

"Now get on that homework. I don't want to see your grades slipping because of all this uproar about selling the land."

That sounded more like the mother she knew. Upstairs in her room, Melissa found herself unable to concentrate on her homework again. She looked out the window into the moonlit yard and the forest beyond. Who would be spared, and who would be taken? The developers held the fates of her friends in their hands in this bizarre and senseless lottery in which the losers are razed from the earth.

An inner voice she had come to recognize well spoke softly within her mind. "Stand apart from the chaos, Amadahy. Allow the quiet balance to still your being. Know that all will be as it is meant to be."

Without finishing her homework, she turned off the light and went to bed. Holding Adahy's words closely in her heart and mind, she lay there with eyes open gazing toward the window. Pale moonlight bathed the floor and furniture, casting shadows upon the far wall. As she closed her eyes, she began to breathe in deeply and slowly, allowing her lungs to fill with the air, and then exhaling gradually and completely. Exhausted from worried days and nighttime visions, she drifted into sleep within a few breaths.

Chapter 28: Introducing Arthur to the Trees

Arthur sat beside her on the bus ride home from school Friday afternoon. Kevin, who took a spot immediately behind them, repeatedly kicked the back of the seat with his feet. There was no rhythm to the jostling her brother's blows brought—simply an intermittent annoyance that came every time she started to relax slightly.

Turning around in his seat, Arthur said, "How ya' doing, bro?" Arthur met Kevin's stare with an amiable grin. "Believe me, I know the joys of irritating your older sister. I've got one too. But do you think you could lay off the seat pelting for a while?"

Without a reply, Kevin straightened up and put his feet on the floor of the bus.

As unobtrusively and quietly as possible, Arthur slipped his hand inside Melissa's. Unless he leaned forward, there was no way Kevin could have seen this gesture, and Melissa could tell that was Arthur's intention. He looked at her and smiled.

Melissa could feel an energy flowing between and around them. Arthur's voice was barely detectable as he bent toward her and whispered into her ear.

"Our energies are blending," he said. He didn't have to explain. Melissa understood that she was normally shielded from the world, aware of the wall she had built around herself. But she just realized that for the first time she had let someone, Arthur, inside that protective barrier. Without so much as a thought, she had invited his energy to intermingle with hers.

He squeezed her hand gently yet firmly. She remained silent but clasped his hand more tightly, wishing she could speak freely without her brother's abrasive presence. Arthur just kept smiling and giving her his most reassuring look.

"Well, here we are," Melissa said as the bus pulled to a stop. The two of them exited with Kevin close behind.

"Kevin, I'm going to put my books up, and then we're heading out to see the Hawk Tree. Dad said you'd need to come with us."

"Yeah, yeah. I know. Tagging along with you and your *boyfriend* is about the last thing I want to do. But who gives a crap what I want?" he said in his surliest tone.

"You can bet I'd rather you went out and did whatever you wanted," Melissa said.

"Well, I'm looking forward to the adventure," Arthur interjected. "So let's make the best of it."

As they trekked through the forest, Arthur engaged Kevin in conversation and gradually warmed his mood. He invited Kevin to show him the tree house and his other favorite spots in the woods and listened with seemingly genuine interest as her brother rattled on about his special haunts. After the tree house, Kevin led them to a woodchuck burrow, which prompted Arthur to share the Cherokee legend of the groundhog dance.

"Once long ago, oganv, what we call the groundhog, was caught by seven hungry wolves. Of course, he didn't want to be eaten; so he told the wolves that catching food was cause for celebration and that the food would be blessed if a dance was done to commemorate the feast. He said if the wolves danced out from the circle, he would sing a song for them standing by seven trees, one for each wolf, and they could eat him after the seventh chorus. The wolves agreed and the woodchuck sang, Ha'wiy̆ĕhï', touching one tree and then another. But oganv was smart. When he sang the last song and the wolves danced out away from him, he made a quick dash for his burrow. Just one step ahead of the wolves, he got safely inside. But the closest wolf caught him by his tail and it broke right off. And that's why the groundhog has no tail."

"That's a pretty stupid story," Kevin replied. "Even if they could all talk, the wolves would have to be pretty dumb to fall for that."

"Yeah, it sounds pretty silly. But there's truth in every story passed down among our people and lessons for us when we're ready to hear them."

"Whatever," Kevin said.

Despite his outer behavior, Melissa could see her brother begin to change around her friend. He even started to walk more like Arthur, picking up an old stick and leaning against it as Arthur had done when they set out into the woods.

Next Kevin guided them to a papery gray hornet's nest several yards up in a maple tree, which inspired stories about episodes with bees and needing remedies for the sting of *usquaduli*.

At last Arthur said, "The sun's getting pretty low in the sky, and I know your sister wants to show me her favorite places too. So why don't we follow you for a while, Melissa."

"I'm gonna head back to my tree house," Kevin said sounding disappointed. "I already know all *her* favorite places."

Finally, Melissa thought. It was an answer to her prayers.

"Catch you on the way back to the house then," Arthur added.

After Kevin was out of earshot, Melissa felt herself relax; she began to take joy in the presence of Arthur here among her friends. As they walked toward Grandfather Poplar, she passed by many of her long-time companions and introduced Arthur to them briefly.

"I wish we had time for you to get to know them all," she said.

"So do I. But I feel their energy, their strength, and that's a great gift," he answered making his way beside her through the thick underbrush.

"We're almost there," she said as they came out into the slight clearing by the stream.

The sun's orange light sparkled across the water beneath Grandfather Poplar's hillside. Arthur gasped slightly.

"What a mighty tree," he said. "I knew your friend was big, but this..."

"Yeah, he's beautiful, isn't he? Even without most of his leaves."

Without reply, Arthur hopped across the stones in the glistening brook and started up the slope.

"Come on," he yelled to her, an exuberant tone in his voice. "I'm anxious to meet this tree."

Melissa joined him on the other side, and they trudged together up the steep hill.

When they arrived, Arthur stood solemnly in front of Grandfather Poplar. He closed his eyes and gently placed a hand upon the giant poplar. His face became serene and Melissa could discern that his breathing slowed.

"May I have the honor of hearing your wisdom, Grandfather?" he asked quietly.

Melissa stood beside Arthur, placing her right hand in his and touching her left hand to Grandpop's trunk. She sent the introduction within her mind and heart, "Grandpop, this is my friend Arthur."

His voice boomed through her sinew in reply. "You don't have to tell me that, little sapling. He's already made a fine introduction. And I'm pleased to meet this walking one who is so much like you."

Looking somewhat startled, Arthur jerked back his hand for a moment.

"Whoa, I've communicated with lots of trees but never heard their voices so clearly before," he said. "This is different. It's always been like hearing my own voice inside my head, or like just having a feeling or a kind of knowing of what the tree said. But this...It's like his thoughts travel through my blood and ring out in my mind."

Melissa laughed. "That's exactly what it's like," she said. "Wonder why it's different this time though. Maybe it's just that Grandpop is so special."

"You never fail to amuse me, child," Grandfather Poplar said. "It's different because he's with you. He already has a gift, but the two of you together, holding hands as you are, well, you blend your gifts, I guess you'd say. It's like two streams coming together to make a mighty river.

"It's a wonder to me that you haven't noticed something of this already yourselves," he added.

Thinking back, Melissa realized that her ability to tune in to people's energy did seem to be amplified when Arthur was around, and she'd certainly noticed that he could read her better than anyone she'd ever met.

"Makes perfect sense," said Arthur, who had easily followed the communication. "I've got to say this is such a weird feeling though. It's like an itch inside my head when you talk, Grandfather."

Grandpop's roaring laugh rumbled through them so intensely that they fell to the ground aching with giggles. Arthur kept his hand in Melissa's and, once they calmed a bit, the two leaned against the massive misshapen trunk.

"I like your young friend, little sapling. I can sense he walks in harmony with Earth Mother. You've got a good soul, young one," he added, speaking to Arthur. "My sapling kin here who walks on two feet needs people like you in her life. I'm glad you found each other."

"So am I," said Arthur.

Melissa allowed the news she had to share to flow through her in picture thoughts to Grandfather Poplar.

"You're making a difference," he said when she finished. "The help you are giving us speaks to the depth of your love and the beauty of your spirit, sapling child."

"She's fighting for your cause with the fire of a warrior," Arthur said. "I think if she could save every tree in Grandmother Earth's garden, she would."

Melissa felt almost proud as she listened to the two of them speak about her quest. But she knew in her heart that there was too much at stake to get side-tracked by pride. If only she knew a way to save them all.

Hearing her thoughts as usual, Grandfather Poplar said, "If only it could be so, dear child. But you know as well as I that even with your best efforts and those of your loved ones more of us will fall.

"When that happens, don't blame yourself. Don't give energy to guilt and self-reproach. Stand strong and pliant as a tree. Grief and loss may bend your frame, but remain rooted in the joy of the present and the love of those who are still here."

"Don't talk like that, Grandpop," she said. "You sound so resigned to things."

"No, child. Just realistic. I promised I wouldn't give up until the chainsaw was nipping at my trunk, didn't I? And I won't. I'm grateful to have such a fighter, two of them it seems, working to keep us standing.

"But let's speak of pleasanter things." Directing his inquiry to Arthur, he added, "Young walker, tell me about yourself."

"I'm of the Tsalagi people. My kin go back a long time here in these mountains. My grandmother is a medicine woman from a long line of medicine folk, and she's been teaching me since I was a kid about the healing power of the Earth and how to live in harmony with our fellow creatures."

"I knew I liked this young man," Grandpop said. "Thought I recognized a resonance there too. Seems to me your kindred have walked these paths and washed in this stream and hunted in these woods for centuries. I still can see the trails of light they left behind."

Melissa recalled the times she had seen the visions out of time as she sat with Grandfather Poplar. Villagers from centuries past whose imprint remained there by the water's edge. She gazed down the hillside but saw nothing.

"I can see it in your mind," Arthur said to her. "I wasn't even trying and I saw exactly what you saw. That doesn't happen often," he added.

"We three are looking together," said the giant poplar. "Still your mind and look again with your inner eyes."

The two of them closed their eyes in that moment and breathed in unison, deep long breaths in and out, as energy from the earth beneath them flowed up into their bodies. Melissa could sense their energies merging again, completely open to one another and to their surroundings. No barriers. No safety blankets. Just Grandfather Poplar, the Earth and the two of them in the stillness.

Simultaneously they opened their eyes and stared into the distance toward the stream and the forest beyond. Two scenes seemed to overlay one another—each a vision of moments in time when their ancestors stood by the water's edge. Melissa could see Adahy and Arthur's ancestor Awenasa, each of them standing with their kinfolk. They looked up toward Arthur and Melissa and smiled, and then once again the image shimmered into nothingness. Only the quiet stream in the approaching stillness of dusk remaining.

Both Arthur and Melissa said nothing for the next few minutes. The experience needed no words. Their hands held fast to one another as they reclined against Grandpop's sturdy trunk. Although the chill in the air grew as the sun began to fall behind the trees, there was a warmth between them that diminished the cold.

"Wado. Thank you," Arthur whispered to Grandfather Poplar, to Melissa, to his ancestors, to everything around them. And Melissa could feel his gratitude flowing like a sure and steady spring of clear water.

"Grandfather," Arthur said, "when my people communicate with a tree we leave behind an offering of our thanks. Tobacco or corn meal or even the spit of our mouths. What would you like from me in return for your wisdom today? I always carry some tobacco just in case."

"No, young man. I don't need any of these things. But I do have one thing to ask of you. If a time comes when she needs you, be there for my sapling child. Hold her safe. Bring her joy."

Arthur peered into her heart with his deep brown eyes. She thought she detected a glint of tears in them. His voice was soft and intense when he spoke aloud.

"That I can promise," he said. "That I'll always do."

The energy flowing between them now was palpable.

"I believe you," Grandpop said. "This young walker has been my dearest friend in this world," he added. "I've stood with her and she with me. But she deserves someone who can *walk* beside her with a spirit as fertile and, may I say, flawless as that of a tree." A subdued, almost hollow chuckle flowed from him and into their minds.

"Just so long as I get to have both of you as my friends," Melissa said feeling less light-hearted than she tried to sound. "Don't get me wrong, Arthur, I'm really grateful that I've found a friend like you. But Grandpop and I have something special and we go way back; so I'd just as soon keep my friends who can't walk along with my ones who can."

"With friends like this one, I can definitely understand," Arthur said. "I hope I get to be your friend too, Grandfather."

"Well, I don't take to having walkers as friends much, but I suppose you're a special case. Yes, I'd say you'll do. As long as you treat this one with the care and kindness she merits, that is."

"I'll do my best," Arthur said with a grin.

"It's getting late, Grandpop," Melissa said. "I think we'd better get back since my parents should be home soon.

"I'm going to visit Arthur's grandmother again tomorrow; so I'm not sure if I can come to see you. But I'll be back on Sunday for sure, Grandpop."

Standing to go, she hugged her tree friend fervently, pouring love into his bark with every pore of her body. As was his custom, Arthur spat on the ground in thanks even though Grandfather Poplar had said it was unnecessary. They trod back down the hill and through the forest. The sunset glow trickled through the limbs of her many friends along the way. The sun from the west kissed their tree trunks and bare branches with a brilliant golden-orange luminescence, the color of firelight. In awe, she inhaled a cool breath of air and drank in the vista. Walking beside her, Arthur remained quiet as both of them bathed in the beauty of their surroundings.

The moon wouldn't rise until a couple of hours past sunset, but the fading daylight illumined the path to her brother's tree house. Kevin had already called it a day and gone inside; so Melissa hurried the rest of the way.

When they reached the yard she saw her mother's car in the driveway. Melissa felt as if the serene bubble in which the two of them had resided since Kevin's departure evaporated as they approached the house. The usual prickly sensation of the real world intruded upon their inner sanctum.

"Oh, boy. We'd better get inside in a flash. Mom's going to have a fit that Kevin didn't stay with us."

"Maybe she won't be too upset. Just take it easy."

"Arthur, you sure are an optimist. All I can say is it's just a good thing we made it back here before my father got home."

Melissa hurried into the house with Arthur close behind. He reached out and shook her mother's hand just after they entered the kitchen.

"Mrs. Kincaid, it's great to see you again." Arthur seemed completely calm and self-assured. He flashed a bright smile at her mother.

"It's good to see you again too. I hope you'll be able to go out for pizza with us. Did Melissa ask you in time?"

"Yeah, I had a chance to talk to my sis, and she was just as happy not to have to pick me up. So I'm glad to join you for dinner. Thanks so much for inviting me."

"We're always interested in getting to know Melissa's friends."

Her mother oozed charm. Melissa was more than a little surprised that she hadn't even mentioned the fact that Kevin wasn't with them in the woods.

As if in answer to her thought, her mother said, "Kevin's getting cleaned up before we go out. He seemed to have a great time tromping about with you two. I think he really likes you, Arthur.

"His father doesn't have as much time to spend with him as he'd like, and it's nice for him to have another boy around. I hope we'll get to see you more often."

"I'd like that too," Arthur said. "And since you and your husband okayed Melissa's studying with my grandmother, it looks like we'll be spending more time together."

"Yes, I had a lovely conversation with your grandmother on Wednesday. What an interesting woman. I can't say I understand a lot about Cherokee teachings, but I know my daughter will be in good hands with her, and that's all that really matters to me."

Kevin came in wearing cleaner jeans than the ones he had on earlier. He sat at the kitchen table beside Arthur.

Pulling a feather from his shirt pocket, he said, "See what I found on my way back." He looked pleased with himself.

"This is a special gift when a bird leaves a feather behind for you," Arthur said solemnly. "Do you know the blue feathers have a magical quality? Look how it appears blue with the light shining down on it. But see what happens when the light is behind it," he said, holding the feather up so they could view it from the underside beneath the overhead light. "Now it's not blue at all but brown. Pretty cool, huh?"

"Yeah," Kevin said taking back the feather and turning it in the light.

"And the blue jay is an interesting fellow," Arthur continued. "Fearless and clever. Dlayigo reminds us to use our power wisely and act with integrity."

"Well, that's certainly something we try to instill in these two," said their mother.

Ignoring the comment, Kevin said, "Do you know any stories about blue jays, you know, like the one you told me about the groundhog?"

Melissa was somewhat surprised by her younger brother's interest.

"Sure, when you get to know me, you'll find out I have a story for almost everything. Stories are the way my grandmother teaches me, so I'm full of them.

"This is one of the stories of how dlayigo came to look blue.... Like the mocking bird, another powerful and mystical bird, Blue Jay was always a great mimic and liked to confuse other birds by pretending to sing their songs. Sometimes he could trick them right out of their nests. If he wanted to scatter the other birds, all Blue Jay had to do was imitate the high-pitched shriek of the red-tail hawk, and he was really good at it.

"One day dlayigo made a big mistake. He didn't realize there was a young hawk nearby who heard his call. The hawk mistook dlayigo for his kin and flew to greet him. Blue Jay saw the giant raptor headed right for him and left his perch to escape. But the hawk's keen eyes followed close behind as he soared effortlessly on the wind.

"Blue Jay's drab brown feathers were easy to spot against the blue sky, and Hawk was closing fast upon him from above. Many a time dlayigo and his kin had banded together to fight hawk and keep their nests safe. But now he was alone. Fearless by nature, still he had no wish to be dinner for the hawk. So he cried out to Spirit.

"Help me, Creator," he said. "I have nestlings to feed. Do not end my life so soon."

Spirit heard his plea and answered. "Let the Sky kiss your feathers as the sun shines upon you," said Creator. "The hawk in her heights will lose the sight of blue against the azure sky. But from below, the other song birds will see you dressed in brown so that you cannot come upon them by surprise."

"Dlayigo gladly accepted this gift. In an instant, his feathers blended into the color of the sky long enough to escape the hawk. Without the sunlight reflecting on them, they're just a plain brown as they were before the blessing of the Sky. But in the light, we get to see their perfect sky blue."

"That's a cool story," Kevin said, getting up from the table and starting out of the room.

"Where are you going," their mother asked.

"I'm going to put my feather in my room," he said on his way out the door.

"You're an excellent storyteller, Arthur," Melissa's mother offered. "You and Melissa have that in common. My daughter has quite a way with words herself."

"So I'm learning," Arthur said. "She was amazing at the commissioners' meeting."

For the first time that afternoon, Melissa felt self-conscious. She'd never been blessed with the ability to graciously accept a compliment.

"You should read some of her writing. She's been writing little poems and stories since she was in second grade. She must get it from her father's side of the family. I'm certainly not that creative.

"Melissa, why don't you get out one of your poetry notebooks and show it to Arthur?"

She wanted to crawl under the table. "I'm sure he doesn't really want to hear my poetry," she said.

"Sure I do," Arthur said.

"Come on, Melissa. You're always so shy about these things. I'll get one of them out to show you, Arthur."

Melissa was about to protest when she heard her father's car in the driveway.

"Sounds like Dad's home," she said, thankful for the interruption.

Her father came inside a minute later. Looking tired and preoccupied, he excused himself and went into their bedroom.

"I'll be back with you all in a jiffy," he said sounding friendly though exhausted.

Soon thereafter the four of them piled into her mother's car and headed to Rudolfo's, their favorite pizza joint. The aroma of fresh-baked pizza wafted on the breeze in the parking lot, and, as soon as she smelled it, Melissa realized how hungry she was. She often forgot about such mundane things while spending time in the forest. But the physical need for food came on swiftly after prolonged experiences with her friends. It was as if the level of communication she shared with the trees required a lot of energy. Perhaps even calories, she thought with a smile.

"I feel like I could eat a bear," Arthur said, grinning at Kevin.

"Me too," Kevin agreed.

"Well, I think that's one of the few toppings Rudolfo's doesn't serve," their father said with a laugh. "But they've got about everything else."

During dinner Melissa was relatively quiet—not uncommon when they went out. She spent the time watching Arthur interact with her parents and Kevin. She marveled at the way he seemed to know just what to say to engage them and win their approval. But she understood that it wasn't some game or act to him. It was just Arthur being Arthur. He was naturally charming, funny and a wonderful listener, genuinely interested in people and their stories. In no time, he had her father relating family history and telling tales from his childhood.

Remembering what Grandpop had said about their talents being enhanced by each other's presence, Melissa decided to see if she could discern the energy around them. She had read that it was called an aura. No one seemed to notice as she slowed her breathing and stilled her mind, closing her eyes for a moment to get a fix on their energies.

When she gazed again across the table, she allowed her eyes to relax and see what she could detect. As her father spoke enthusiastically about one of his youthful adventures, his energy got brighter and more expansive around him. Melissa almost gasped at the sight. She observed Arthur's energy glowing warm and bright as well. All of them radiated this luminescence. A quiet glee filled Melissa at the sight.

"Arthur, I've been doing all the talking. I'm anxious to hear more about you and your family. What prompted you to move here?"

"My father got a job here. He'd been looking for one in this area for a while so we could be closer to my grandmother. She's old and lives alone. Besides, I like to visit her a lot, and she wanted me to be able to train with her every week instead of just during the summers."

"Your grandmother told me a little something about what she's teaching you. But it would be nice to hear your perspective," Melissa's mother said.

"A lot of it I can't go into because it's sacred knowledge to our people. We can share stories and we can help people with the remedies handed down, but the essential parts of it are kept within the family. Except for Melissa, that is. My ulisi took one look at her and figured she *is* family."

"Well, I'm glad you have the chance to learn about that part of my ancestry," her father said. "This grandmother of yours," he added, looking at Arthur, "sounds like a formidable woman. I hope to get to meet her soon."

"I'm sure she'd be happy to meet you. She always says the apple doesn't fall far, so no doubt she'll like you too."

Since her father's mood had elevated throughout dinner, Melissa took the opportunity to ask him about his promise to her.

"I'm happy to report that I did make the call to the TV station just before I left work today. Unfortunately, the person I needed to talk with was out on assignment, but I left a voice mail message for him with both the home and work numbers. Does that satisfy you, young lady?"

She wanted to say it would have satisfied her if he'd done it on Tuesday as he said he would, but instead she simply nodded.

"It's been quite a week. We gave our presentation today to a large client who was considering another firm. But we won them over, and it's a good thing after all the hours we put in. That's our bread and butter, Melissa, so I'm afraid it had to take precedence even over your beloved trees.

"But I'll come through, sweetheart. You just have to give me time."

"I know, Daddy," she said quietly.

As they left Rudolfo's later, the moon had begun its climb across the ecliptic. *Almost full*, Melissa thought. *Time is the one thing we don't have.*

Arthur held her hand as they sat together in the back seat of the car. Except for Arthur's directions to his house, neither of them spoke aloud. But a dance of feeling and energy played between them all the way to Arthur's home.

"See you tomorrow," he said getting out of the car. "And remember to bring your notebook, or Ulisi will think you're not serious about learning." He smiled but she knew he meant it.

"Thank you for the dinner, Mr. and Mrs. Kincaid. It was a real treat."

"You're welcome, Arthur. Have a good night," her mother said as they started to back out of the driveway.

"I'm pretty impressed with that young man, Melissa," her father said. "Just remember what we've told you about boys that age."

Melissa sighed. "I'm glad you like him. But I can tell you he's not like other boys my age. He's really serious about what his grandmother teaches him."

"Well, that's good. We should always respect our elders. Just be good enough to listen to yours, and everything will work out fine," he added with a chuckle.

The moon was rising toward the mid-heaven as they arrived home. Its subtle luminescence gave an eerie glow to the treetops and the lawn.

Melissa inhaled a deep breath of October air and exhaled a hint of smoky vapor.

"Looks like it might be a hard winter this year," her father said hurrying into the house.

She lingered for a moment beneath the moonlight, radiating love toward the trees in the distance, then went inside to do as much homework as possible before bedtime.

Chapter 29:
Smoke and Broom

Melissa slept later than usual that Saturday morning and awakened to her mother's voice calling her from downstairs.

"Melissa, get up and come downstairs. I've got something to show you."

Pulling on her robe and socks as quickly as she could, she headed down to greet the day. She found her mother in the kitchen bent over the newspaper, a cup of steaming coffee on the table beside her.

"I couldn't wait for you to see this," she said as Melissa entered the room.

There on the front page of the "Features" section of the paper was a large picture of Grandfather Poplar with an article beside and beneath it, the headline reading "Giant Poplar a Local Landmark."

Without a second thought, Melissa grabbed the paper out of her mother's hands and started to read....

> *This misshapen yet majestic yellow poplar,*
> *estimated at over a century and a quarter old and*
> *some 120 feet high, stands among the few trees of its*
> *age remaining from a logging venture in the early*
> *1900s. When the property of the late Cora Reynolds*
> *sold to Cherry Hill Development Company in*
> *August of this year, this tree and others on the 110-*
> *acre estate off High Ridge Road became potential*
> *fodder for the sawmill.*
>
> *Fourteen-year-old Melissa Kincaid, who grew up*
> *on the adjoining 90 plus acres, most of which also*
> *have been purchased by Cherry Hill, is fighting to*
> *keep these trees from being toppled. This young girl*
> *and her friends enlisted the help of WENOCA, the*
> *local chapter of the Sierra Club, and presented their*
> *case before the County Commissioners on Tuesday.*
>
> *She entreated the board 'to remember the quiet*
> *magic of the trees and the songs of the birds,*
> *the rocks or leaves ... collected as ... [childhood]*
> *treasures.'*
>
> *Those attending the commissioners' meeting*
> *were clearly moved by the speech, which was*
> *accompanied by letters of appeal from a large*
> *number of ninth grade biology students at Oakcrest*
> *High School.*

Melissa continued to read, feeling somewhat dumbfounded, as the article went on about the landscape, the trees and animals of the woods. Hilary Braithwaite had asked if she could use quotes from Melissa's talk before the county commissioners, but she had no idea her name would appear so prominently in the article.

Near the end, Mr. Brown's reporter friend had included another quote from her:

> *'When you go into the forest, the world disappears.... All your troubles get left behind. There's nothing like that feeling. I came here to ... ask you to save that gift ... for yourselves and your children and their children.'*
>
> *This magnificent poplar and its fellow trees clearly have a strong advocate. Whether or not such forest inhabitants will be saved remains in the hands of Cherry Hill Development Company, whose owners could not be reached for comment.*
> —Hilary Braithwaite

Melissa was shaking as she fell into a chair beside her mother. Tears filled her eyes as she set down the paper.

"Wow," was all she could manage to say.

"Well, I didn't think I'd be seeing my daughter's name in the paper so early in life," her mother said smiling broadly. "I'm really proud of you. Of course, I wish we hadn't put you in a position to have to take this stand, but seeing as how that's already done...."

"How someone behaves in the face of adversity says more about them than anything, honey, and I have to say we must have done something right in raising you."

"I just hope it makes a difference," Melissa said.

"Oh, it will make a difference. I think it already has. You've changed my view after all, and look what came of that. I really think Commissioner Newman is going to make sure as many trees will be spared as he can. We'll have to wait and see, but I have a good feeling about it."

"I hope you're right."

"Anyway, look at the time. You'd better get ready if you're still planning on spending the day with Arthur's grandmother. And I'd better get your father out of bed so he can take you up there and meet her for himself like he said he wanted. My guess is when it comes down to it he might just have me drive you. You know how he likes to sleep in...."

By the time Melissa got dressed and ready, her father, looking less than bright-eyed, was in the kitchen having his coffee and toast.

"Good morning, sunshine," he said, stretching his long arms up and out to shake off the stiffness of a lengthy slumber. "I see from the morning paper that we have a celebrity in the house." His grin was interrupted by a yawn.

"If this article doesn't save the old hawk tree, I don't know what will. Sure would hate to see that tree get cut down. So I'm with you on this all the way.

"Better grab some breakfast so we can get going," he added.

Melissa felt a little drugged by sleep today too. She often had a fitful night or stayed awake late when the moon was waxing full, but this time she'd slept like the dead and found it difficult to awaken.

Carrying the citrine she had found at Grandmother Fox's in her pocket as usual, she held it in her left hand as she ate her oatmeal with her right. She had been giving her golden mineral friend plenty of time in the light lately, letting it bask in sunshine each time she went out to the forest. At night, it sat on her windowsill beneath the rays of the waxing moon, and the spirit of the stone loved both these means of re-charging and rejuvenating. The citrine's light and life force glowed strongly, and her presence infused Melissa with energy as she held the stone gently and lovingly.

"Looks like breakfast has perked you up," her father said. "Ah, to be young again and able to get energized so easily."

"Oh, Dad." She had no need to tell him about the energizing power of the citrine. Maybe someday. But for now the world of the invisible that remained overlooked right alongside the visible would be something just for her, Arthur and his grandmother.

The sun was bright that morning as they drove to her Cherokee teacher's house. A cloudless sky edged the treetops in pale blue. The citrine in her pocket hummed with energy as they neared the home this stone had known for countless years.

"I wish I knew more about my Cherokee roots," her father said as the car skirted the inside of a steep rocky embankment. "I wonder if your new acquaintance might share a bit of history with me sometime, or if she knows anything about my family. Probably not," he added.

Melissa wondered if she should tell him that their families knew each other for centuries, but she thought better of it. She would leave it to Grandmother Fox to share what she thought was best. Still, a part of Melissa longed to let her father know about her other world. In his dark eyes and high cheekbones, she could see remnants of the ancestry she so cherished. He even bore a slight resemblance to Adahy, although her father was much older than the way she most often saw her spirit guide.

When she failed to answer, her father grew quiet and much of the last part of the ride was spent in silence. Unlike most people she knew, Melissa relished the quiet. It gave her the opportunity to drink in the beauty of the landscape they passed.

Melissa caressed the leather-bound notebook she had found with her mother earlier in the week. Her mom had balked at the price but wanted to lift her daughter's spirits in the face of the current crisis. Certain she had been guided to exactly this journal, Melissa recognized it as hers the moment she saw it, a depiction of a proud oak gracing its front cover. She wished it weren't leather because of her love for cattle, their innocent brown eyes so filled with gentleness. But she recalled that all the bindings she had seen at Mrs. Fox's appeared to be made of hide and went ahead with the purchase despite this reservation.

Acting as navigator on their drive, Melissa read the last part of the directions to her father although she had pretty much memorized the route a week ago on her first trip here. Already there was a feeling of home about Mrs. Fox's land. More than just the perception communicated by the citrine she held, this was a sense of belonging that came from deep within her.

As they turned onto the long winding gravel driveway and drove across the creaky wooden bridge, an air of ease filtered into Melissa's consciousness. The cows in the pasture stood still, unperturbed by their passing, while the rooster greeted them with a hearty crow.

As was the case the week before, Arthur's grandmother sat on the front porch in her favorite rocker. Arthur sat beside her, and both rose in welcome as the car pulled up in front of the house and she and her father got out.

"Mrs. Fox, I'm happy to meet you," her father said, shaking the elder's hand. Arthur's grandmother exchanged cordial words of greeting with her father.

Melissa could hardly wait for the pleasantries to end so that she could proceed with her study with Arthur and his grandmother. Yet, she held her tongue and remained as patient as she could.

"Won't you have a seat with us?" Grandmother Fox asked. "Arthur, fetch some lemonade for your friend's father. Or would you prefer some hot herb tea?"

"No, thank you. I'm fine," her father said. But a moment later he changed his mind and accepted the lemonade.

As they sat on the front porch, Grandmother Fox rocked in silence until Melissa's father spoke.

"My daughter's pretty excited to learn the ways of her Cherokee ancestors, Mrs. Fox. I have to admit I'm a little envious. Wish I'd had someone to teach me these things when I was a lad."

"Yes. Well, not every child has the commitment to learn," she replied. "Do you suppose you would have stuck with it?"

He grinned. "Well, to be honest, no, I rather doubt it. I'm afraid football and girls would have side-tracked me as I got into my teens."

"There you have it," the old woman said. "We'll have to see if this one will bear the responsibility," she added nodding toward Melissa. "But I have a good feeling about her."

Arthur returned with a tall glass of lemonade, which her father sipped politely. Melissa knew that neither lemonade nor herb tea were favorites. Her dad was a cola and coffee man and water if he was really hot and thirsty, but he was clearly trying to be polite and respectful of Arthur's grandmother.

"I wonder if you knew any of my family's people. I don't know much about my Cherokee roots, but I can tell you my grandmother's name if that helps."

Grandmother Fox told Melissa's father briefly about her knowledge of his ancestry, omitting the means by which she had been given some of this information. His face lit up as he listened, and Melissa realized for perhaps the first time that her father's curiosity was deep and genuine. He had seldom spoken about their Tsalagi heritage; yet, his features and his frame bore the qualities of their people on both sides of the family.

"You know I get so caught up in work these days that I forget how much I love breathing in the outdoor air and feeling the call of the land. You've got a really nice place here, Mrs. Fox," he said.

"Seems you needed a reminder of what your daughter knows better than most: We recollect who we are when we're out among the other creatures who share the Earth with us."

"You're right about that.... You know, there have been times when Melissa's mother and I thought she could use a little more human companionship. But she sure does love the woods."

"You've raised a wise child. But I suspect she gets that love of nature from somewhere," Grandmother Fox said, the hint of a smile on her face. "The Earth touches the spirit within our people. We know a kind of truth in her embrace." She gazed intently toward Melissa's father as if trying to size him up.

"Well, maybe one of these weekends you'd be willing to show me around your land," he said.

Melissa could tell from his tone he was getting ready to leave.

"If you can find the time for it, I imagine I can," she said with a smile. "I've been caretaker of these acres for longer than I care to say, and they're my home as surely as that of the squirrels, rabbits, deer and raccoons that roam them. You may be a two-legged critter, but you're welcome here too."

A low and easy laugh rumbled in her chest, and Melissa was struck by how similar Mrs. Fox's words were to those she herself had spoken earlier in the week.

Arthur's grandmother stood and took her father's glass as he prepared to go.

"I understand your granddaughter Hannah will be giving

Melissa a ride home later, but I hope to see you again soon," he said.

Grandmother Fox stood on the porch, her face showing little emotion as she waved farewell.

"Now, young lady," she said sitting back in her rocker, "have you made your decision about learning our ways and teachings?"

"Ulisi doesn't like to beat about the bush," Arthur said with a grin. "Right to the point as usual," he teased.

"Young whippersnapper. You're one to talk since you take right after me.

"So, tell me, child, have you considered well?"

Melissa took in a deep breath. "Yes. I want to study and learn all you're willing to teach me." The words came out in a flurry, and she felt more relaxed as soon as she spoke them.

"Good. I see you've brought your own notebook. Have you blessed it?"

Through her connection to Adahy, Melissa had learned to give thanks for the sacrifice of earthly creatures who gave their lives for the benefit of others, whether for food or shelter, clothing or livelihood.

"I forgot," she admitted. Amid her worries and efforts to save the trees, she had let this practice slip her mind with the journal.

"Then we'll do so now. But know this," Grandmother Fox continued sternly. "The hides on the journals you saw in my cupboard were from animals my people killed. They asked permission first, which is most important. They asked the animals if they would make this sacrifice. And every scrap of that animal's gift was used for food, for clothing and for the covers of our medicine journals.

"You're not a hunter and I don't expect you to do this. But we *will not* forget to say a prayer of thanks and blessing for the spirit of the animal whose skin covers this book, and we'll do the same for the trees whose bodies became its pages."

Grandmother Fox began to chant in a low soft voice. Arthur joined her, and Melissa sat quietly paying reverent homage to the animal and plant spirits. Envisioning their beauty in life, she allowed a swell of love to permeate her chest and flow around her. She felt Adahy beside her as she cherished life in its living and in its passing and prayed for renewal and rebirth.

After a time, Grandmother Fox and Arthur went silent. Melissa opened her eyes. The journal she held in her hand was warm from her touch, but the late morning air around them remained cool and goose bumps covered her arms.

"I'm glad to see you mean it," Arthur's grandmother said. "It's easy to talk the talk. But you carry the love of all life in your heart. That's the only way to truly give a blessing or say a prayer.

"Arthur, grab my shawl, will you? *Gola* comes early this year. We need to go for a walk now to warm the blood."

"Winter," Arthur said looking at Melissa before going into the house. "Gola is winter."

While Arthur was inside, Melissa asked, "Mrs. Fox, may I ask you a question?"

"Yes, you may. Seems you just did," she said with a chuckle. "If you weren't allowed to ask questions, I wouldn't be much of a teacher. Now would I?"

Melissa grinned in assent. The way Arthur's grandmother spoke reminded her of her guide Adahy, who often seemed to answer a question with a question.

"I was just wondering about what you told, or maybe what you didn't tell, my father. You said more about our family history than I would have thought—talking about his great uncles and aunts and all—but less than you could have."

"What would be the sense in telling a man something he didn't need or wasn't ready to hear? Would you have had me say that his ancestor was a medicine man who is now his daughter's guide?"

"No, especially to the last part."

"There's something you should know about your father, child. If I'd gotten him when he was young, he might have proved an apt pupil himself. But he's passed the time of openness to these things."

Melissa was surprised by these words.

Arthur returned with the shawl, which he wrapped gently around his grandmother's shoulders.

"Should I bring my notebook and something to write with?" Melissa asked.

Grandmother Fox smiled. "Not today. It's good you're eager, but you're not ready for that just yet."

The three left the porch and headed out behind the house in a direction Melissa hadn't surveyed on her last visit. They walked along a trail wide enough for three or four people to stroll side by side. Along the way, Grandmother Fox quizzed Melissa once again about some of the trees and weeds that lined the trail.

"You'll soon learn to stop thinking of these plants as weeds," she said. "What others see as a nuisance I see as a teacher and a healer. Each of these plants has its wisdom and its purpose."

After walking for a while, they came upon a clearing with a small hut that looked very old. Grandmother Fox instructed Arthur to wait outside while she and Melissa entered.

Inside the hut smelled with a pungent scent. Contents of the single room shack were minimal. A hollowed rock in the center of the room appeared sooty in its cavity. On a small table nearby Melissa noted a box of matches, a large feather and small bundles of what looked like light greenish straw-like herbs wrapped in four-colors of twine. Grandmother Fox motioned for her to sit on the floor next to the rock.

Picking up the hollowed stone, she placed a small amount of the herbs into its indentation and lit it while chanting softly. Still singing, Grandmother Fox looked toward the left side of the room and toward each of the other three walls, to the floor and the ceiling. She then used the feather to waft the smoke up her body and over her head and shoulders.

Bending to the floor, she sat in front of Melissa, who watched with avid interest. Grandmother Fox then handed the stone and feather to her. Unsure how to proceed, Melissa sat still for a moment until Arthur's grandmother guided her movements. Taking her cue, Melissa in turn fanned the small pile of smoldering herbs with the feather drawing the smoke over her body. There was something familiar in the action that sent a tingle up her spine with a sense of *deja vu.*

When she completed the sweep of smoke over her body, Melissa handed the stone back to Grandmother Fox, who placed it between them on the floor and fanned the remaining embers until the smoke wafted into the air around them.

A tiny straw and wood broom rather like a lint brush leaned against the table beside them. Rising again, Grandmother Fox picked up the small sweeper and, chanting once more, began to brush it lightly over Melissa's back, her arms, her head and all over her. It was a strange almost ticklish sensation and Melissa felt somewhat self-conscious, but she knew there must be a reason behind the ritual albeit one she did not understand.

As the last of the herbs burned to ash, Grandmother Fox spoke.

"Good, now you're ready to begin to listen and to learn. On a warmer day, I would have chosen to take you down to the stream to immerse yourself in the waters, but in this chill I chose the sacred smoke to prepare you. Mind you, I go to the waters every day no matter the weather to purify myself. But you're not quite ready for that, I daresay."

Melissa was just as happy not to be bathing in the cold stream in late October. She could hardly imagine the old woman doing so in the depths of winter.

"What's in that herb bundle? I thought I smelled sage and maybe some cedar."

"You have a good nose. Those and two more besides. But we'll get to that in time. I want to share some of the sacred stories with you now, child."

With trees shading the small building, the daylight filtering in through its two windows offered only dim light to the space. Melissa pulled her coat on tightly. Noting the gesture, Grandmother Fox grabbed a small blanket from beneath the table and handed it to her.

Over the minutes, perhaps hours, that followed, Melissa listened intently as her teacher told her the Tsalagi stories of creation, the four directions and the cords of life, the way of balance and harmony that was sacred to their people. The stories all wound into one another, seemingly without beginning or end. These interwoven and connected tales always came back to the same truths—balance, peace, spirit—yet each with its own unique lesson.

From time to time Grandmother Fox paused, closing her eyes as if envisioning the rest of the story in her mind before continuing. Once or twice Melissa got up her nerve to ask a question only to find that the answer was on its way had she but been a bit more patient.

At last Grandmother Fox said, "Enough for today. I'm pleased that you know how to listen. Another girl your age might have spent the time wondering what Arthur was doing." She grinned shrewdly.

"Well, I guess I'd better confess I did think of him a time or two."

"Ah, yes, I can see a young person's mind at work and detect when it's drifting. I thought as much.

"The fact you were honest about it tells me more about your character than a few daydreams during a long storytelling." She continued to smile.

"Help me up, will you?" Grandmother Fox asked. "These bones don't do as well with sitting cross-legged as when I was your age."

After a thorough stretch, the two of them walked outside. Arthur sat, eyes closed, on the ground beneath an old oak tree. He looked serene as the sun shone from the Southwest onto his features.

Hearing their voices, he opened his eyes and covered his forehead with his left hand, making a visor to shield him from the sunlight. Standing, he looked back toward the tree where he had reclined and spat on the ground beside it.

"Well, I was beginning to think it might be dark before you came out," he said with a grin.

"Sorry to disappoint you," his grandmother said. "A young girl can only hold so much knowledge in one sitting."

As they ambled back down the trail toward the house, Arthur moved closer to Melissa.

"So what did you think?" he asked.

"I think I have a lot to learn," she replied. "But it's the best kind of learning I ever did," she said honestly. "And it all feels really familiar somehow."

"You two go on back to the house," Arthur's grandmother said. "I'm going to pick some herbs, or weeds as you might call them," she added with a chuckle. "Go on with you," she said motioning them down the trail.

"Ulisi is tired," said Arthur when he was certain they were out of earshot. "And she doesn't like to show it in front of me. Plus, I think she likes a little time alone after being with someone else for a long while."

"I didn't mean to tire her out," Melissa said.

"No worries. She'll be fine. She's got more rejuvenating power in her plant medicine than the fountain of youth."

As they walked together, Arthur casually swung his hand next to hers until they touched and then clasped. He whistled as they strode in pace with one another.

"Arthur, I didn't want to interrupt at the time, so I didn't ask.... Can you tell me what that strange smoke ritual was and about the tiny broom-like thing your grandmother used on me?"

"She was cleaning you up," he said. "The smudge is a sacred way of clearing the energy around a person, or a place for that matter. A lot of folks who don't know what they're doing use it now, which irks my ulisi to no end. But those among the First Nations have used it in ceremony to cleanse for centuries.

"Both of the rituals Ulisi used were preparations for your learning. But she'll share all that with you in time no doubt."

"Thanks. It was kind of strange, but it felt right somehow too. One thing she said though was that she'd rather have me going down to the stream like she did every day."

"Yeah, when I stay with her in the summers she always has me go to the stream and face East every morning dipping under the water seven times to be cleansed for the day. 'Course, I don't mind it in the summer, but she does it on the coldest days of winter and doesn't even flinch. Says she's used to it."

"That sounds awful," Melissa said. "Why does she do it instead of using the smoke?"

"Because that's the way she was taught. It's the Tsalagi tradition for purifying. Ulisi honors our traditions and doesn't veer from them unless she's strongly guided."

They walked the rest of the way to the house in silence. The sensation of his hand in hers, his warmth so close, sent waves of heat through her. She wondered if he felt it.

"It's the same for me," Arthur said responding to her silent but obviously easily-read feelings. "Only more so." He laughed somewhat nervously.

She said nothing more until they reached the house.

"I'm getting pretty chilly. There wasn't any heat in the other building."

"Let's go inside and I'll stoke the woodstove.... Don't worry," he added. "I always look for dead trees and fallen limbs, and if I do have to cut one I choose those that are injured or diseased most often and always, always ask permission before taking the wood for warmth."

"Do the trees ever say 'no'?"

"Once in a great while. But mostly Spirit leads me to the ones that are ready to end their time here. And I send a blessing for their rebirth."

Melissa realized how much was taken for granted in all the products that were used from her friends the trees. But the Tsalagi had another way, a better way, she thought.

After tending the fire, Arthur said, "I'm hungry. How about you?"

Since it was well past her usual lunchtime, Melissa definitely felt hunger pangs. Arthur found sausages and some leftover biscuits, which he covered with some honey from a large jar with the waxy comb inside. As famished as she was, Melissa savored this as a feast.

Arthur closed his eyes and gave thanks for the food and said a blessing for the animals. After no more than a bite or two, his grandmother walked in from outdoors.

"Couldn't manage to wait on me, I see, young buck. Well, I can hardly blame you growing youngsters for letting your appetites get the better of your manners." She sounded stern but there was a hint of a smile on her lips.

After their meal, Grandmother Fox sat between Melissa and Arthur on the sofa. She had taken out her prized volume of medicinal herb lore and began to show Melissa the pages relating to the plants they had seen along the trail as well as others in her cupboards. They talked about some of the medicinal qualities of echinacea root, mullein, ginseng, jewelweed and spicewood, about the wisdom in waiting until each plant was ready to be harvested and about only following the tried and true means of utilizing their gifts as cures.

"Mind, you're still a long way from actually using these yourself, child. I've been teaching this one since he was a tot, and still he doesn't use the plant medicines without my approval and guidance.

"I want to be certain you understand this is serious work and not to be taken lightly," she added.

"Yes, ma'am," Melissa said nodding.

"Call me 'Grandmother,'" she said. "It's a term of respect, and I like it a lot better than 'ma'am.'"

"I understand, Grandmother," she replied, the address feeling surprisingly natural. "Speaking of names, I've noticed something. You almost never call me by my name. How come?"

Grandmother Fox was silent for a few moments.

"There's nothing wrong with your name. I believe it means sweet, and certainly there is a sweetness about you," she said, a kindness in her tone. "But the name doesn't speak to your spirit nature. You deserve a name as strong as a tree, *tlugv*, or as powerful as *ama*, water. Maybe someday you'll take another name."

"I've always felt like what my ancestor calls me is my real name, Amadahy."

"Yes. Perhaps we'll have a naming ceremony and give you this spirit name that speaks to who you are," Grandmother Fox said.

"What exactly does that name mean?" Melissa asked.

"I thought you knew. It means the water that flows through the forest."

Chapter 30:
The Child He Chose

After a wondrous afternoon with Grandmother Fox, Melissa rode home with Arthur and his sister Hannah, who wasn't being especially friendly and appeared to resent acting as their chauffeur. Unlike most people, his sister didn't seem to be affected much by Arthur's easy charm, which was able to melt the aloofness or reluctance of others—at least from Melissa's limited experience.

"So how did you enjoy today," Arthur asked.

As if you don't already know, she thought. "It was great. I just keep thinking how much there is to learn though. It feels a little overwhelming when I consider how long I'll have to study just to catch up with you," she replied honestly.

"It's not about catching up. We learn in our own time. Believe me, Ulisi will be more than happy to have me review most everyting I've learned by helping you. No matter how many times I study something or how many tests I pass, there's always more. You'll find that out soon enough," he said with a playful grin.

"Arthur, why did she ask me to bring my notebook when I didn't even use it?"

Hannah laughed. "That's Mamaw for you," she said.

"Truth is, though, you did use it. You blessed it. From my grandmother's perspective, that's *plenty* of reason to bring it. Besides, you've got to know she wanted to see if you were serious," he added.

"Yeah, she made that pretty clear," Melissa said smiling.

"That's the main thing for Mamaw," Hannah said clearing her throat. "If you're not serious enough about learning, that's it."

"My sis here didn't much want to be a medicine woman."

"Hey, I've got a life to live, you know," Hannah said emphatically. "Anyway, it's not like she doesn't have at least one willing student in the family."

Melissa sensed it was a sore subject, so she began to discuss their English class assignment, and conversation remained light the rest of the way home.

When Arthur and Hannah dropped her off at her house, she was sorry to see them go. The day's adventure had ended, and now it was on to an evening with her family.

Unable to share what she had experienced at Grandmother Fox's, she spoke mostly about the land at dinner that night. Her father agreed that it was a beautiful place and noted that he had quickly developed a respect for Arthur's grandmother. He liked people who were matter-of-fact in their dealings and speech.

As Melissa lay in bed that night, she contemplated the events of the day. It felt good to begin her study with Grandmother Fox, and she fell asleep quickly after an exciting day.

After church the next morning, she chose her favorite place—Grandfather Poplar's hillside—to work on the last of her homework. The afternoon was unusually warm, but she carried a sweater with her in case the weather suddenly turned as it could do easily this time of year.

Her blanket placed carefully on the ground beneath the giant poplar, she squatted in the usual spot and reclined against the sturdy trunk of her dearest friend.

"Greetings, Grandpop," she said affectionately. "What a gorgeous day!"

"True enough," he replied. "We seldom see a day like this so late in the season. Yesterday I'd have sworn winter was on the way, but today feels more like spring."

The sunlight felt warm against her skin, and in communion with Grandfather Poplar she knew it was much the same for his bark. High above them both, the red-tail soared in silence as if touching the cloudless sky.

"This is my kind of day," she said, her meaning echoing through her mind to his. "I love you so much, Grandpop, and I have such good news to share with you."

Through their connection Melissa relayed the events of the previous day. First, she transmitted the picture of him in the newspaper and the intent of the article. It would be strange, she thought, if another tree's sacrifice to become paper was the very thing that led to his survival. The irony involved wasn't lost on either of them.

"We shall see what happens," said Grandpop solemnly and softly.

"I thought you'd be more pleased with the news. They can't possibly cut you down after an article like that."

She felt a sigh pass through him into her.

"So much loss already," he said. "They have been working relentlessly, these chewers and sawers, getting closer and closer as they destroy my kin, and the animals flee in distress and alarm."

"They didn't work yesterday, did they?" she asked.

"Yes, I have felt the earth rumble anew with each sunrise since the ground began to dry. I've heard the wailing as the sawing sliced through strong and sturdy trunks. So many, so many. One after another.

"The death is nearby and marches toward this hillside, little sapling. Would that I could spare you this truth, but I thought you needed to know." His voice was so low through her mind it felt like a trickle rather than its usual boom.

"But I thought they wouldn't work on Saturday, and I hoped that the commissioner might actually talk to his brother and *do* something," Melissa said, her emotions running wildly.

Anger, fear and grief whirled within her.

"Let it go," said Grandfather Poplar. "The fear and anger help no one. Remember you're a walker with the heart of a tree."

"It's my human heart that feels so much now, Grandpop," she said, tears staining her cheeks and dripping onto her shirt. "I'm sorry. I just thought I was making a difference."

"You are, little one. You are," he said quietly. "Don't you know what a difference you've made to *me*? You talk about how I'm your closest companion, but *you* have been mine. You help me remember my own tree heart. You make me see the world in a different way...

"My seeds have scattered to the wind in every season, and my children grow beneath the sun, but you are my heart's child, little sapling. You are the child I chose."

She felt as if her heart were breaking. Too full of emotion to think or speak.

"Remember I shared with you how it feels to be a tree?" he said. "Hold onto that feeling now. I haven't given up, sapling child. I *know* your efforts have made a difference. Do you want to hear how?"

She nodded silently.

"I know because you've never failed to touch the hearts of those you meet. If a cantankerous and quarrelsome old poplar like me can be swayed, then no walker would stand a chance once you set your mind to something." She could sense him trying to send her an inner smile.

"I just don't want to lose you," she said quietly. "Grandpop, how close are they?"

"Close enough to make old Red-tail agitated when they were nearby yesterday." He continued more dolefully, "At day's end, I heard the voices of the cedar twins who stood not far from here fade as they fell to the earth. I tried to stop the sound but couldn't. We are all connected, and I've felt the loss of every one."

Melissa got to her feet and turned toward Grandfather Poplar, embracing his trunk with all her might as she wept heavily for her many friends, those rooted and those with four legs or with wings. She mourned for her two favorite cedars, the twin brothers, Cedrick and Cecile, she had called them. Sharing this strong a link with Grandfather Poplar, she could no longer distinguish his feelings from hers. There beneath the loving rays of the sun, they stood together, human and tree, honoring the passing of those they loved.

Through him, she could sense the extent of the loss, the large number of trees who had been razed. Lost in their mutual grief, she wasn't sure how long she stood there holding him. At last, no longer able to stand, she fell again beneath his massive trunk. Leaning heavily against him, she found herself unable to speak.

"Little sapling," he said after a time. "Gather your strength. No matter what happens, my spirit will live on, and I aim to be here in body too if the Fates, or rather the walkers, allow. If not, the light that lives on will always cherish you."

Melissa was too raw to attempt her homework assignment. Her mind focused solely on how she might save her dearest friend.

At last she located her inner voice again amidst the turbulence of her thoughts.

"I've got to go, Grandpop. I want to see just how close they've come, and then I need to head home to let my parents know what's happening. But I don't want to leave you," she said fervently.

"You've never really left me," he said, and his words flowed around her like the gentlest embrace of a loved one. "Just as I've never left you since we first became friends these many seasons past. You leave a part of your energy here on this hillside each time you visit me, and you take a part of mine with you wherever you go.

"That's the way of things. We're bonded for all our days, sapling child. I'm as stuck on you as the hardened sap of a sweetgum tree." He conveyed a slight chuckle along with the last thought, but there was an emptiness to his laughter.

"Grandpop, do you mind if I leave a note on your trunk," she asked.

"What sort of note?"

"A plea to the workers who are grading the land. I want to make sure you're safe while I'm at school tomorrow."

After he agreed, Melissa began to search her backpack for a something to hang the paper in place with no results. Still, she went ahead and penned the note: "Please do not harm this beloved tree. An article in Saturday's paper explains that there are people working hard to save this majestic yellow poplar. Please wait and contact Commissioner Newman, one of the developers who hired you, before you do any grading in this area. Thank you."

She signed her name and positioned the note near the bottom of Grandfather Poplar's trunk held in place by a rock on either side.

"Grandpop, all I can do now is pray and ask my parents to help. I'll be here as soon as I can after school tomorrow. You can count on it."

"I always have," he said, "and you've never failed me. I will see you tomorrow."

After she left his side, Melissa felt anxiety overtake her as she ventured toward the nearby trails that led to the spot where the great twin cedars had lived. She didn't want to imagine much less view the damage that was done. As she approached, a suffocating fear expanded through her body.

A wave of pain struck her suddenly as she came upon the scene. Far into the distance she could see a blank and tortured canvas, a landscape bare of trees, only a few stumps remaining and lifeless tree bodies piled upon the ground, two bull dozers parked nearby. The panorama registered on her mind blankly for a moment. And then she experienced it all, felt the trees being cut down, their stumps being ripped from the ground, the frenzy of the four-legged and the winged ones who lived among them. Scenes of horror bombarded her senses, and she screamed aloud, her body doubling in pain as sobs contorted her frame.

She could not bear it. Running blindly in the direction of home, stumbling across the stream, tears poured down her face. Briars scratched her face and body as she ran clumsily where there were no trails. No time. No time. The full moon.

She arrived at her house with little strength or breath in her. Finding her parents in the family room, she fell to the floor and tried to speak without success. She hungered for breath like a drowning man.

"Honey, sit down. What is it?" her mother's voice spoke. "Catch your breath, sweetheart. Robert, will you get her some water?"

Her father was back quickly with a glass of water. "Here; drink this," he said, placing the glass in her hand and continuing to hold it with her.

She managed a sip as her breath began to come back. Kevin sat across the room looking wide-eyed and strange. Was the look on his face actually concern?

"What happened, Melissa," her father said. "Can you tell us yet?"

"The trees," she managed. "They've been working this weekend. It's horrible."

"Do you mean to say they're already on what used to be our land?" he asked.

"No, but they're close," she continued. "And they're really close to the hawk tree. I saw what they've done and it's...it's like nothing I've ever seen. The land is empty. It's empty." Although she felt like shrieking, her voice was barely a whisper.

"I really thought we'd made an impression on that *man*," her mother said. "I believed him."

"Politicians," her father said, his voice filled with rancor. Not a very trustworthy lot....

"Well, after the article in the paper, I doubt that they would take down your favorite tree. That would be really bad PR, and I guess I ought to know something about that. But I'll give a call first thing in the morning just to be sure.

"Don't worry, honey. We'll do whatever we can to save the old poplar. And I'll give the developers a piece of my mind about the clear-cutting of the trees they've already done. It may be we can stop them from doing any more with the help of the press. The TV station is going to be my second call."

"I need to call Arthur," Melissa said at last. "Is that okay?"

"Sure, honey. We can understand that you'd need to talk to a friend about this," her mother replied.

Communicating with Arthur helped alleviate her fears even more than her conversation with her parents. Grandfather Poplar had counseled her to channel fear into action to bring a change, and that was exactly what she intended to do.

"So that's the plan then," Arthur said. "I'll get my Pop to take me to the hardware store this afternoon. The big one over by the highway is open 'til 6:00. Hopefully, I'll have enough cash to buy the chains and padlock. If not, I'll ask Hannah—even she might be willing to help with this. Then I'll bring them to school tomorrow. Are you sure you don't want me to chain myself to the great poplar with you?" Arthur asked.

"I'd love that, but I don't think my Dad would," she replied, somehow managing a smile. "He'll be sore enough with just me doing it. Besides, I don't want you to get in trouble, and I think one person is enough to stop them from cutting him down."

Her plan was simple: Before her parents got home from work that Monday, she would gather some supplies, her sleeping bag, and the chains and padlock. She'd write a note explaining her decision as best she could and then set out for Grandfather Poplar's hillside. Her father liked to say, "It's easier to get forgiveness than permission," and she knew in this case that was almost certainly true. So she would say nothing of this to her family in advance.

Melissa had to force herself to eat dinner that evening. Even with a plan in action, she could barely stomach the anxiety and anger that seemed to ferment inside her. The scene she had viewed kept coming into her mind no matter how many times she pushed it away.

She went upstairs to her room not long after dinner, ostensibly to finish her homework, but the threat against her friends blocked out all else. So she turned off the light and looked outside. Sitting in silence by the window, she gazed out into the moon-drenched yard and the forest beyond. It all seemed so peaceful now—no way to detect the great disturbance and leveling of trees far in the distance. Cracking the window, she felt the coolness of the night rush in. Tears welled in her eyes again. With so many tree friends in view, she still felt terribly alone.

"You're not alone," a voice within her whispered ever so softly. "Never alone."

A part of her ached to reach out to that voice, to go inward and connect with the spirit of her ancestor and guide Adahy. But her mind was too clouded by pain and upheaval to still her anxious thoughts.

"Breathe," the voice within her urged. Yet, unmoved, she continued to ride the waves of inner chaos.

"I feel betrayed," she murmured. "I'm not exactly in a mood to listen now."

Even so, she thought she sensed a reassuring hand on the small of her back.

"I will be your strength," said that familiar voice that echoed within her. "I will stand with you."

Chapter 31:
The Three Stones

On the bus ride home that Monday afternoon, Melissa got some strange looks. Arthur had handed the heavy chains and padlock to her just as she got on the bus so that she wouldn't have to carry them as far. They completely filled and weighted down her backpack, which she kept empty of books for this task. Although she stuffed them into it as quickly as possible, the cumbersome and noisy load drew a lot of attention. She doubted that anyone among her school mates would imagine their purpose.

"What are you doing with *those*," Kevin said taking a seat beside her. "People are going to think you're nuts—that is if they don't already."

Melissa had often wished that Kevin went home earlier like the rest of his classmates at the middle school. But because he would have no one to look after him, he was forced to wait at the high school next door until she could leave each day. It was an arrangement neither of them relished under the best of circumstances, but today his questions and his presence were particularly irritating.

"It's really none of your business," Melissa retorted.

"Well, I'll bet it would be Mom and Dad's business. How about I call them when we get home?"

Melissa let out an exasperated sigh.

"If you must know I'm going to be an environmental activist."

"A what?"

"I'm going to chain myself to the huge poplar tree so that they can't cut him down," she said.

"Whew. You sure will be in for it."

"Just do me a favor," she said softly, an urgency in her voice. "And don't tell them before they get home."

"You know they'll have a fit, don't you," he asked, his tone sounding as if he cared at least a little. "You're *really* gonna get it."

"Yeah, I know. But I have to do this, so I'm willing to take whatever punishment comes."

"Okay, it's your funeral."

As the bus pulled to a stop in front of their home on High Ridge Road, Melissa's heart sank. Her plan hinged on neither of her parents being home, which was the case pretty much every day unless there was some emergency. But today her father's car was in the driveway. A sick feeling began to crawl up from Melissa's stomach.

"Well, you're gonna get it sooner instead of later it looks like," Kevin said as they started up the driveway, "unless you find some way of ditching those chains."

Melissa laid the chains and lock behind a bush by the house on her way in. Surely her father hadn't found out about the plan. Arthur would never have said anything. Maybe she could sneak out to the woods as soon as her father was out of the room.

As she came in the side door, she was greeted by an unusual sight. Her father sat solemnly at the kitchen table. *This can't be good*, she thought. She steeled herself as she entered.

"Have a seat, sweetheart," her father said. "I have something to tell you."

As she sat beside him at the table, he continued, "I have some bad news, Melissa....

"I called Commissioner Newman this morning just like I promised, and he said he'd already spoken to his brother about saving as many trees as possible. In fact, his brother's office had gotten a large number of phone calls over the weekend after the article in Saturday's paper. Their answering machine was full.

"So here's the thing, honey.... The commissioner's brother went to the site to talk to his foreman just after lunch about saving your favorite tree as well as quite a lot of the others on what was our land. He also wanted to see the tree causing all this commotion and planned to mark it among others to keep. But by the time he got there, it was too late."

IIis voice was thick and deep as he spoke. Melissa sat still and silent in disbelief.

"The commissioner called me back late this afternoon to tell me what happened, and I knew I'd better get home so I could break the news to you before you saw it for yourself.

"I'm so sorry, sweetheart. I know how much you loved that tree."

"You have no idea," she said, her tone hushed, barely audible. The tears came in silence, washing down her cheeks.

"I have to go to him," she said bolting up from the chair, which creaked against the floor as she shoved it aside.

"The workmen may still be there grading, Melissa. It's not a good idea to go out there alone. Besides, like I said, your tree is gone."

"I *have* to go," she said again, her voice cracking. "You can't stop me."

"No, I won't stop you. I'll go with you. Just let me grab my jacket."

She was out the door without a glance back, and her father had to run to catch up to her.

They walked wordlessly and swiftly through the forest. When they reached the creek by the hillside where Grandfather Poplar had lived, Melissa finally understood that she would never see him again. All that remained upon the hill were tree stumps, one larger than all the rest, the beginning of the twist in its trunk still discernible.

"Daddy, I need some time alone," she said emphatically.

"Of course. I'll wait here," he replied.

As she crossed the small stream and strode heavily up the hillside, Melissa heard a familiar screech from the sky. Red-tail. She looked up and saw him there, his life-long mate circling with him. They could have been looking for a juicy mouse, Melissa knew, but she believed they were saying good-bye to Grandfather Poplar, who had kept them safe and been their home for so long.

She walked over to the remains of Grandfather Poplar's trunk that was cut a few feet up from the ground. At least they hadn't pulled his stump away yet. But she knew that it too would be gone soon. The work crew had left for the day, their machines and saws silent.

Melissa sat on the stump and started to count the rings in the trunk of her old friend. She was only up to 14 when she started to cry again, this time deep sobs that echoed in her belly.

"Why did they have to take you away from me? Why you of all the trees in these woods, Grandpop?"

She thought she heard a whisper through her sniffles. *You must be going nuts*, she thought. *He's gone now, and he'll never come back.*

"But I'm not gone, little sapling," a familiar voice said weakly.

"Grandpop, is that you? I can hardly hear you. Am I going crazy? Are you really here?"

"Yes, I'm here," he whispered. "Put your heart close to what is left of me."

His voice was barely discernible, but she did as he asked. Leaning over the massive stump, she embraced him tightly.

"I drew in my life force when the saws came. I sank down deep into my roots so that I could wait for you. The pain is too great to stay for long, and it's taking all my last strength not to let you feel it. I don't have much time, and I have to ask something important."

Yet, Melissa felt his pain—only a trickle of what was surely a torrent—but she couldn't escape the blazing agony that permeated what remained of her friend. She fought through it and did her best to feed him strength and love through the torment.

"Even now, you keep fighting for me," he said. "No wonder I have always loved you. So little time left...."

"Look around you, little sapling," he said. "Do you see all the fruit on the ground?"

"I don't see any fruit. There aren't any fruit trees around here, Grandpop."

"But every tree bears fruit, Melissa. The fruit that carries my seed lies all around you. You've seen me wear it every autumn and shed it with my leaves."

Melissa looked down at the small, cone-like things on the ground. She'd seen them hundreds of times but never really thought of them as fruit."

"So few of them ever make it into the ground to grow and fewer still ever rise above the size of small seedlings before they're destroyed by weather or insects or careless walkers. Now, they'll have no chance at all with this development plowing them under the earth.

"But you can change that, sapling child. You can let me live on."

"I'd do anything to help you, Grandpop," she said, her words shaking with emotion. "You know I would."

"Yes, I know." His voice became lower and more distant with each moment. "Gather all the cones that you can, little one. Gather them and keep them safe, and then plant them under the richest soil you can find. Plant them in the sunshine where they won't have to fight each other for the nurturing light. And most of all, little sapling, give them your love and remember how to listen. Their voices may be quieter and different from my own, but hear them in your heart just as you've always heard me.

"And perhaps someday, when the ones who will live have grown old and lonely, a beautiful young girl will bring them hope and youth again.

"The last of my life will soon leave this place," he continued. "Even now I can feel my ancestors calling me to join them. But I'll never leave you, my sweet sapling. Not as long as you remember to listen to the voices of the forest."

"I'll never forget, Grandpop," she said, tears streaming down her cheeks. "I'll listen, and I'll love them—and you—as long as I live."

"Walk always in sunlight, little one," he said, his voice ebbing. Be nourished and be loved, my walker with the heart of a tree."

With those words, she felt him leave. The consciousness who had so long boomed through her veins, laughed into her heart, sung through her mind, was gone.

Trembling, tears spilling down her face onto the ground, Melissa took off her jacket and put it on the earth. She felt her way carefully along the ground and gently picked up the light brown cones and laid them on her coat. Her father walked across the rocks in the stream and up the hill toward her.

"What're you doing, honey?" he asked.

She explained that she wanted to gather the giant poplar's seedlings to plant.

"That's a great idea," he said. "We can plant them near the yard where you can tend them and watch them grow."

Her father began to help in the task, and together they collected every single yellow poplar fruit that was anywhere near Grandfather Poplar's trunk.

"I'll carry these back to the house," he said, picking up the bundle.

"You know, it's a funny thing, your attachment to this *particular* tree. It was my favorite too when I was young. I even used to imagine I could talk to it. Isn't that something? Just a child's fantasy, you know, sort of like an imaginary friend," he said smiling.

"It doesn't sound funny to me," she said.

"What do you mean?"

"I mean it was real, Daddy," she said, grief sharpening her voice. "I've been communicating with him since I was little," she said more softly. "And it was real. His name was Grandfather Poplar, and he was my very best friend in this whole world. I loved him more than my own life."

Her father was silent for a few moments as they began the walk back through the forest.

"I believe you, honey," he said at last. "I think maybe he was my friend too—a long, long time ago. So long ago I'd forgotten.

It seems almost like a dream now. But we carried on whole conversations, and I guess after I got older I just sort of thought it was something I made up."

She could hardly believe what she was hearing. As she had looked for a candidate who might hear the tree voices, her own household was the one place she didn't think to consider. She never imagined that her father might have been the very person she sought all along.

"I sure wish I'd known," she said quietly.

"Well, it isn't exactly the kind of thing that comes up in conversation. And like I said, I thought it was just imagination anyway. But now when I look in your eyes, I can see that it's true."

He carefully laid down the jacket full of poplar fruit and embraced her.

"I'm so sorry, Melissa. If I'd known the truth, yours and mine, I would never have sold the land, and I'd have done everything in my power to stop this from happening."

Grabbing the bundle with one hand, he strode the rest of the way with his arm around her.

"I guess sometimes when we grow up we don't necessarily grow wiser. I hope you don't ever lose what I lost along the way."

"So do I," she said. "I think I've lost enough already."

Her parents were unusually tender and consoling with her that night. After spending more than an hour on the phone, her father made certain that the Newman brothers would spare as many of the trees as possible on the land that had belonged to their family as well as on what remained to be cleared of the former Reynolds' land.

"I've already spoken with the TV station," she heard him say. "And they assure me that they'll be out tomorrow or Wednesday to do a story. They've gotten a lot of calls from folks in the area."

Her father knew how to work with the media from all his years in advertising. Melissa felt a keen sense of regret mingled with anger that she was trying to fight. She couldn't help thinking that if her father had helped sooner, as he had promised, Grandfather Poplar would still be alive.

The grief and anger welling up within her made it impossible to eat anything, and being with her family only amplified her anguish; so she retired to her room early for the second evening in a row. She longed to turn back the clock a day, to see the immediate danger more clearly and do something more to stop it.

"I don't understand why this had to happen," she screamed into her pillow. "Why didn't you warn me?" Her words flung venom at the air around her. She wanted to shriek to the heavens, to rend the very fabric of the universe, or at the very least shred everything within her sight. Instead she mindlessly pounded the pillow in her lap.

Adahy had often said he was always with her, but she had no sense of his presence now. She could feel only the unending well of grief that tortured her mind, her body, her very soul.

After sobbing and railing at length in the dark, Melissa fell asleep at last, spent and weak.

Into the realm of dreams she carried her sorrow, a sack heavily laden with rocks literally trailing behind her in her sleep journey. Adahy greeted her at the forest's edge just as he did so many times before, but this time he looked older, a grown man perhaps her father's age, yet still easily recognizable as her lifelong companion. His face appeared sad like a mirror for her own.

"What are you dragging?" he said quietly.

"Rocks," she replied. "I have to carry this with me now even here."

"Here. Let me help," he said.

He took hold of the heavy bag, and together they pulled it along behind them. Her load was lightened by more than half as he shared it with her.

"Thank you," she said.

They trudged together deep into the forest until they reached the stream flowing silently through the woodland.

"Lay down your burden here, Amadahy," he spoke softly. "And look up beyond the other side of the water."

There on the hill above the brook stood a great yellow poplar, its misshapen trunk etched with the rough furrowing of age, covered in the bright green leaves of springtime.

She gasped. "How can this be," she whispered.

"All that is remains, Amadahy. You have always known this. You just needed to remember."

"I don't understand," she said. "He's gone. I was with him as his life ended today. Nothing left now." Even in the dream state, her grief felt like a heavy stone upon the chest.

"Yes, his body is gone. But his spirit lives. Such is the truth of all things within the womb of beloved Mother Earth."

"I want to go to him," she said, starting to move forward toward the water, which shimmered in the moonlight.

"Not now, Amadahy," he said placing a hand upon her forearm. "He's making his journey into light. He requires a time of peace and stillness. But you will see him again.

"It's time to remove the stones from your bag—just as many as you're willing to let go."

Adahy pulled the sack of rocks to the water's edge. "It's up to you," he said.

Kneeling by the brook, she opened the bag and drew out one stone. It was small yet very weighty—much more than its size would have indicated—almost too heavy to bear for long. With all her might she tossed it into the sparkling water of the stream and, in so doing, noticed that she felt somehow lighter and a little more at peace. She repeated the action three more times. Each time the stones disappeared beneath the water. There were still three stones left, but she felt she didn't have the strength to heave them away just yet. Closing and tightening the sack, she looked up at Adahy, who was smiling broadly.

"I'm most pleased," he said. "You are farther along than you realize, my daughter."

She had no idea what he meant, but she felt better than she did when she arrived, and that was a blessing.

"Now cleanse your wounded spirit in the waters, dear child," he said. Lending his hand to help her stand, he waded into the crystal clear water with her. It was far deeper than the brook of her waking life. Adahy scooped a handful of water over her again and again, seven times pouring the refreshing liquid light over her head and shoulders. Oddly, even in the dream, she could feel the coolness and wetness wash down over her. A sensation of peace seemed to flow magically with each drop and an inner clarity stilled the turmoil within her heart and mind.

Adahy's face remained calm and emotionless, his dark eyes shining in the moonlight. At last, lifting her out of the stream, he embraced her tenderly as if she were a babe in his arms.

"There will still be pain, grief and anger," he said glancing down at the bag holding the last three stones and then back into her eyes. "But you will bear it more easily. And I'll be at your side."

"Why?" she said, the deep stab of sadness returning to her heart as she took hold of the sack once more. She looked across the brook at the friend she had lost, who still appeared to stand strong and beautiful upon the hillside of this dreamscape.

"Someday the Great One will answer all the questions within your heart, and you will understand and remember. Today know simply that all remains that ever was and that you are a part of it. You and your friend will be ever in oneness, Amadahy.

"The water that flows through the forest nourishes all life. The sunlight shines upon all."

Chapter 32:
The Choice of the Trees

Ever since he arrived home from school on Monday afternoon, Arthur had felt a great wave of inner turbulence. He sensed there was something terribly wrong with Melissa and wished he could do something to reach out to her. He knew that if he phoned their plan might be defeated or found out, and, if things had already gone awry as he suspected, his part in the scheme would no doubt evoke her parents' anger. So he was stuck in a fairly precarious position.

Arthur couldn't concentrate on his homework that night, and his sleep was fitful at best. He awakened a full two hours before the alarm, dressed quickly and went outside into the still, dark residue of night. A dog barked somewhere in the distance as he walked alone down the empty streets.

He had dashed off a quick note to his folks before sneaking out of the house. It read, "Gone to Melissa's house to ride to school with her. See you after school."

His folks were used to him being a little adventuresome, always one foot out the door to some place. He liked to go for runs in the early morning anyway. So they wouldn't be that surprised when greeted with the news that he had trekked all the way to his friend's house to share the ride to school.

He ran and walked at intervals along the way. Although he'd only been to her place a couple of times, Arthur had memorized the route. He had no idea of the street names and could never have given someone else directions, but every landmark along the way was clear in his mind. He started to sweat beneath his parka after a while, but he knew the body could chill easily when running; so he just let the perspiration trickle down his neck and back.

Almost an hour had passed by the time he reached High Ridge Road. He raced the rest of the way to the Kincaid house and caught his breath standing in the driveway. No lights were on yet in the front of the house; so he quietly walked around back and stood beneath the second-floor window Melissa had pointed to as her room when he visited on Friday. This too was dark as was the whole house. Early still, he thought.

He had a choice to make now. He could tramp through the woods in hopes of finding the great poplar. With his strong sense of direction, he felt certain he could. But would Melissa be there? The intense feeling of foreboding weighed on him. Somehow he was sure their plan had gone wrong. So he picked up a few pieces of gravel from the driveway and aimed carefully at Melissa's windowpane, doing his best to ensure the pitch was light enough not to break the glass and strong enough to hit the mark. After the third toss, he saw a light come on inside her room and sensed her unmistakable energy stirring within. A moment later she opened the window and looked outside.

Even in the dark, she was able to discern him. "Arthur, is that you?" she said in a kind of whisper yell.

"Yep. I've been worried about you. Can you come out?"

With the light behind her, he could see her nodding. After a few moments, the lamp inside went out and a couple of minutes later she exited stealthily out the side door of the house.

"Arthur," she whispered as she reached him. "I'm so glad you're here." Her voice sounded sleepy and strained. "How did you get here? How did you know?"

"I ran most of the way, walked some, all the way from my house," he replied. "I knew you needed me. I wasn't sure why. But your being in the house instead of chained to your tree friend answers part of it. What happened?"

But he didn't really require an explanation. Her grief emanated from every pore of her body. He reached out to her and pulled her against his chest, his arms around her back. His left shoulder muffled the sobs that followed as soon as his arms went around her.

"He's gone, isn't he?"

She nodded against him. "We were too late," she said, the words stuttering out between her sobs.

Since the moment he saw her in the cafeteria, since before he knew her name or even her face, he had imagined what it would be like to hold her. But not like this. The sensation of embracing her paled somewhat, but he couldn't help savoring the closeness even amidst the grief.

"I'm sorry," he said pulling away slightly to gaze into her eyes. "I was hoping my dream was wrong."

She stopped her sniffles as best she could and wiped her face against her jacket sleeve.

"What do you mean?" she said.

"Remember I told you about the warning dream I had last week? Well, I didn't tell you what I saw in the dream because it was so bad. I saw a forest obliterated—nothing but stumps and death.

"I heard you crying somewhere far off but couldn't find you for a long time. When I did, you said, 'He's gone. They're all gone,' but I told you it would be okay, that we'd build the world again.

"I guess I should have let you know the whole dream, but I didn't want to believe it, and I thought we could still change things. I'm sorry," he said. But he felt the words were small and useless.

She slipped her hand into his and started to walk toward the woods. "It's okay, Arthur. I don't think it would have changed things. We were already doing everything we could do.

"But what you saw in the dream is pretty much what happened. The hillside where Grandpop lived," she continued, her voice breaking, "and a whole bunch of the property that used to belong to Mrs. Reynolds has been clear cut. Grandfather Poplar and all his kin, so many of my friends, are gone."

As they reached the edge of the woods, she sat down in front of a tree, her back against the bark. He took a place beside her on the ground and held her hands in his. He didn't know what to say. He felt the tears still coming even though she seemed quieter.

"I remember you said the tree spirits will live on," she said, her voice trembling slightly. "I had one of those dream journeys tonight, last night, I guess now, and I think you're right."

"Do you want to tell me about it?"

"Not now. Maybe later," she said. "The thing is it turned out I was with Grandpop when he died. His stump was still there; so I guess he must have been one of the last trees they sawed down."

He could sense she was having trouble continuing. He moved over beside her and put his arm around her shoulders.

"So there was still a little life left in him, in his roots, when I found him. He asked me to pick up all his seeds around on the ground and plant them for him so his children could live on.

"And I got a chance to say good-bye."

She leaned against his shoulder, sobbing again. If he could take the pain away, he would. But instead he just shared it with her. He let down all his energy barriers and allowed her grief to envelop him and become his own. Tears flowed silently down his cheeks as their energies merged together.

"What just happened?" she asked suddenly. "I felt something kind of, I don't know, shift."

"I don't know exactly," he replied. "I guess I sort of decided to share your pain so you wouldn't have to hold it all. I should have asked you first. Ulisi would have my hide for not asking permission even for something like this. It just hurts to feel you suffer so much."

"I understand," she said sighing deeply. "But it's *my* pain and I just have to feel it. You can't save me from that any more than my parents can keep me from making the mistakes they did— although they sure do keep trying.

"I guess you'd better let me have it back," she added.

"You're right. I know," he said. "I'll let you bear it yourself then. But at least now I know how you're feeling in a *real* way, so I can be here for you better maybe."

"I think you probably would have done that anyway," she said, and she was right.

"Can I help you plant the seeds," Arthur asked. "The ground will be getting hard soon as it gets colder."

"I'd like that, and I think Grandpop would too. My Dad is planning to help, but who knows how long it will take for him to get around to it."

There was a hint of animosity in her voice.

"You're mad at him. How come?"

"Grandpop might have been here still if he had kept his promise and called the TV station when he said."

"Parents," Arthur said. "They're a mystery. I don't know where their heads go after they turn 30. Odd thing is, though, they seem to get back to their spirits long about the time they become grandparents. I know Ulisi sure understands me a lot more than my folks do."

Melissa was silent. He held her a little closer as a chilling wind rushed past them and whistled through the trees. The early morning birds were starting to warble and the sun would begin to stretch upward behind the distant hills soon.

"My parents will be waking up before long," Melissa said. "But I wish I could just stay here and capture this moment, pretend that yesterday never happened."

"Don't hold on to your grudge against your father," Arthur said. "I've seen what bad blood in a family can do, and I don't want that for you." He thought of the chasm between his grandmother and father, who had turned his back on his path so late in the training.

"I'll get over it," she assured him. "I just don't know how I'll ever get over losing Grandpop."

"He's still in here," Arthur said, thumping her hand lightly against his heart. "And he's still everywhere around us too."

"You sound like my ancestor. Adahy said something like that in my dream."

"I'd be proud to be compared to him," Arthur said sincerely. "We'll plant your Grandpop's seedlings and nourish them, and he'll live on that way too just as he wanted."

In the dimness he could see her face, a single tear streaking down her cheek. He wiped it with the back of his hand. The wetness felt warm against his cold skin.

"Sorry my hands are so cold," he said. "I guess maybe we'd better get inside if you think your parents will be okay with that. I could wait out here if you'd rather."

"No, that's okay. Right now I'm not too concerned about what they think anyway."

Arthur spat on the ground as he stood to go, giving thanks to the tree for the support its trunk had offered them. He continued to hold her hand as they strode side by side across the yard. A light came on in the left lower level of the house.

"Mom's up," Melissa said. "That's the master bathroom light. She'll be showering or doing her skin care for the day. She'd be less than thrilled if you saw her without her makeup; so you just wait in the kitchen while I let her know you're here. My dad will be dragging out of bed soon too."

Melissa put two cups of water in the microwave to make instant hot chocolate and then left Arthur in the kitchen, a large room that, except for the appliances, probably looked like it did more than three quarters of a century ago. A short time later Melissa came back.

"I didn't tell my mother how long ago you arrived. She assumed you just got here and I didn't say different. Just easier that way," she shrugged. "She said you're welcome for breakfast, but she's in a rush; so it's microwave instant oatmeal or cold cereal. Your pick."

"I'm mostly thirsty after the run."

"I'm sorry," she said. "I'm just not thinking this morning."

She grabbed a pitcher of filtered water from the refrigerator and a glass. Arthur drank the first glass down in one long gulp and then chased it with the hot chocolate, sipping more slowly this time.

He noticed Melissa looked tired and pale, dark circles under her eyes magnified by the overhead lights. Even so, to him she was beautiful, a face from his dreams, her dark auburn hair cascading down her back. He knew she considered herself anything but pretty, that she hated her braces and her thin frame, everything he found somehow just right.

Even though he was thankful for the warmth, he wished they were still outside sitting close to each other under the starlight. She had fastened on her secret skin when they came indoors, placing a wall around herself. He could sense it plain as the harsh kitchen lights. But he knew the spirit that breathed within those battlements, and he understood all too well the need for shielding against the world.

Before her family invaded the kitchen, he caught her hand and her eyes for a moment, a reminder of what they shared.

"Thank you for coming, Arthur," she said softly. "You don't know how much it helps." Her hand dropped to her side as they heard someone coming down the hall.

Her brother Kevin lit up when he saw Arthur sitting at the table.

"Hey, what're you doing here? Come to get your chains," he asked, a mischievous grin on his face.

At that moment Melissa's mother walked into the room.

"Chains? What on earth are you talking about, Kevin?"

Arthur took pains to explain that the tree chaining was his idea, something he'd heard activists did to save forests.

He figured Mrs. Kincaid was more likely to forgive him quickly since she wasn't his mother, and that proved to be right.

"Well, I think this is something we don't need to share with your father," she said to Melissa and more pointedly to Kevin. "Considering how things turned out, there's enough to stress about in this household.

"Mind you, Arthur. I think you're a very nice young man, but I hope you'll avoid putting any more plans like that into my daughter's head. She's got enough of them all on her own," Mrs. Kincaid said. "Anyway, if you hadn't thought it up, I'm sure she would have, or something equally foolhardy. I'm not sure where she gets it, but I suspect a little from me and a lot from her father."

She smiled at them and put a hand on Melissa's shoulder. "Truth is, if it would have saved her special tree, I might have done it myself."

Melissa looked surprised and skeptical at her mother's statement.

"Although I doubt I would have lasted long in the wilderness," her mother added honestly.

"I'd have done it," Kevin suddenly blurted. He looked at his older sister and then at Arthur.

"You know, bro, I bet you would have stayed even with the bulldozers staring you down," Arthur said genuinely.

"Thanks, Kev," Melissa murmured, somewhat stunned.

On the bus ride to school, Arthur sat beside her. He could feel their classmates' eyes on them and knew this might well be the talk of the school by midday. Speculation over why he was at their house so early would abound no doubt. But all that mattered to him was this moment sitting beside her, his hand holding hers, a reassuring smile to comfort her and help her feel less alone today.

As soon as they could, the two of them would find a quiet time to bless the spirit of the great poplar whose heart and mind had touched theirs. They would pray for his rebirth and honor his being. Come the weekend they would sow the seeds of this grandfather tree. Some would be planted in the Kincaid yard and some on his grandmother's land, where he and his ulisi would tend and bless them. He would treat them like his own kindred just as he knew Melissa would, because that was the truth of things. Arthur understood in this moment perhaps better than ever before what his grandmother had so often repeated: "All life is your kin, child," she would say. "Every plant, every animal, every person, every grain of sand or drop of water." With Melissa's hand in his, he felt this oneness.

Chapter 33:
Randy Red Maple
Meets Arthur

Melissa felt like the walking dead as she somnambulated through the beginning of school. The rawness of grief she had felt the night before, or even earlier in the morning as she wept on Arthur's shoulder, seemed to be replaced by a dull ache and an emptiness that she felt sure would never be filled. As soon as Arthur left her side to go to homeroom, the sensation of aloneness overtook all else.

Cheryl noticed instantly that something was wrong. Melissa was usually so good at keeping people out, except for Arthur and his grandmother, but today she could hide nothing. She imagined her face was as blank and empty as she felt. That in and of itself would catch her friend's attention.

"What's wrong with you?" Cheryl whispered to her as Mr. Brown took attendance. "You look like a zombie or something."

"He's gone. They're all gone."

"Who?" Cheryl asked.

"My favorite tree and acres and acres of others," Melissa said quietly, staring straight ahead rather than at her friend. She was certain that if she actually looked at Cheryl, the dull blanket covering her grief would disappear, and all the pain and anger would flood back again. She wanted to exist for a while in this strange limbo, a small respite from the utter anguish of her heart.

Cheryl reached out a hand and touched her arm. "I'm so sorry," she said. "I know how much you loved that tree."

Melissa gazed at her desk and tried to remain in the vacuum. But she could feel the edges of the void around and within her beginning to dissolve. She felt a tear run down her cheek and then another and another. She fought them back as best she could to no avail. In an instant the searing heartache returned.

"Melissa, what's wrong?" Mr. Brown asked in a concerned voice. "Can I help?"

She looked up at her teacher, her vision blurred for a moment by the well of tears in her eyes. Feeling every person's attention on her, she could say nothing.

"You know the tree we were trying to save," said Cheryl. "Well, they cut it down yesterday and lots more besides."

Mr. Brown shook his head, an angry frown etching his brow.

"This is such sad news," he said. "I'm really sorry to hear that, Melissa."

His sympathetic tone prompted more tears to fall, and it was all she could do to avoid breaking into sobs.

"Class, I think we'd better just have an independent study day today," he said. "Read Chapter 11 in your textbooks, and if you finish it answer the questions at the end. Whatever you don't complete in class, you can do for homework."

Mr. Brown walked over to Melissa and squatted beside her desk, placing a hand on her forearm.

"Melissa, I understand you're upset. Are you up to sharing a little more information with me?"

When she could find her voice, she explained in hushed tones what she had found when she visited the forest the previous afternoon. She tried to speak as calmly as she could, but emotion interrupted her words on several occasions.

"I see. But you say that the trees on what was your family's land haven't been touched yet?"

"Yes, that's right."

"At least that's something. I'll tell you what I'm going to do. During my free period, I'll call Hilary and a few of the other members of our chapter to mobilize the troops, and we'll start a phone-in campaign to save the rest of them. We'll hit radio and TV and we'll make so many calls to the development company that they'll think they're under siege."

"Thanks, Mr. Brown," she managed. "My father already talked to them last night, and they say they're going to mark and save a bunch of the trees that are left. He's contacted Channel 13 too."

"Good. Glad to hear it. But at this point, I can't say I trust them to honor that; so we'll still bombard them with phone calls and make sure we get them to do what they say."

His kindness and efforts on behalf of the trees provoked fresh tears when she thought they surely should be spent by now.

"I'll call 'em during lunch break," Cheryl said. "And see how many other people I can round up to do the same.

"Hey, before we're through with them, those guys will wish they'd never bought that land."

Cheryl was making a real effort to raise her spirits. Melissa realized that she might have done a disservice to her friend over the years by always keeping her at arm's length and hiding so much of herself. But there were deeper things to regret today.

"Thank you both," Melissa said.

"If you two can catch up on the assignment in a day or so," Mr. Brown said, "I'll excuse you from it so that you can work on this, dare I say, more important project. How does that sound?"

Melissa was truly grateful, and clearly Cheryl brightened at the prospect.

"No worries, Mr. Brown. We'll catch up," Cheryl said.

"But you do have to make it up. I'll expect the chapter read and the questions answered by Thursday. Got it?"

"Got it," Cheryl replied.

After her breakdown during first period, Melissa managed to get through the rest of the morning without making a spectacle of herself in any other classes. She sat out of P.E. thanks to a note from her mother, who had come through in ways that were unexpected of late.

At lunch Cheryl and Arthur helped Melissa look forward to the future a bit. After the three made phone calls to the development company, the newspaper and the TV station, they sat around the lunchroom table, their plans taking precedence over eating. Cheryl insisted on sowing one of Grandfather Poplar's seeds in her yard and promised to care for it without fail. Saturday would be their planting day in all three locations.

Once this discussion ended, the mood grew somber once again.

"Look," said Cheryl, "I'd say it's at least a good sign that the development company said they'd already gotten lots of calls and planned to remedy the situation."

"Not that they could remedy it," Melissa said. "It's too late to bring back my beloved hawk tree."

Her heart ached at the thought of him—the bass chuckle that thundered through her, the warm and humorous nature beneath the ornery exterior, the strength and the presence that she would never feel again.

"I know," Arthur said taking her hand and squeezing it gently. "I know."

That afternoon Arthur arranged with his family to have Melissa ride home with his sister Hannah and him so he could get what he needed. Hannah would take them both to Melissa's house after that, and the two of them would go to the spot where her dearest and oldest friend had spent his days to say a proper blessing for his renewal.

Melissa wondered what their classmates might think if they saw her riding home with Arthur after he had joined her on the way to school. In all likelihood, Bus 147 would be abuzz with rumors. But that mattered little to her now. As they left the high school, she sat beside Arthur in Hannah's old car, all three of them squeezing into the front seat. His nearness was a great comfort.

After arriving at her home, they had to wait and be certain Kevin got there safely. Even with stopping by Arthur's house, they easily beat the bus, which traveled a winding route through many neighborhoods and made numerous stops before reaching High Ridge Road. At last, with Kevin home, they got ready to head out toward the woods. Unfortunately, Kevin wanted to tag along.

"Kev," she said gently. "I don't know what we'll find out there or if the work crew is still around; so would you mind hanging out closer to home?"

Her younger brother's disappointment was easily visible on his face. She sensed that he was about to protest when Arthur spoke.

"I promise that you and I will check things out when I come back to help plant this weekend. Okay?"

"All right," he grumbled quietly.

There was a stillness to the woods as they walked together. The usual bird sounds seemed to be missing.

"Can we stop here a minute?" Melissa asked as they approached Randy Red Maple.

"Sure."

Lightly she embraced her favorite maple tree, a dear friend who had brightened her spirits on many occasions.

"Bright blessings to you, sunshine," he said, his voice lacking its usual enthusiasm and vitality.

"Do you know about Grandpop and Buddy, the twins and all the others?"

"No way not to know," he said softly. "But on days like these I wish there were. Oh, if only we trees could fly away from it all like a flock of starlings murmuring to and fro.

"Still, it's good to feel you with me," he said, a genuine love permeating the words as they cascaded through her being. "Just like the warmth of the sun on a chilly day."

"I don't feel too sunny today," she communicated to him.

"Nor do any of us.... But as long as we're still standing, today is a blessing."

"You're the blessing, Randy," she said.

"And who might be this handsome young buck, lithe and bronze as the stags that roam these hills? I seem to feel a difference in you, my favorite walker. Could it be that another has won your heart from me?" Randy's tone seemed as lilting as a leaf on the breeze despite his obvious sense of loss.

"This is Arthur," she said within her mind, a stream of images and feelings conveyed along with the thought so that Randy could know in an instant the spirit of the boy who stood beside her.

"Ah, I like him," he said after sifting through her thoughts. "It's the best medicine you could have to find one who understands you. I guess I'd be willing to share you with him."

A half smile passed her lips. "Only you, Randy, could bring me close to a grin today.

"Would you be willing to meet Arthur and let him know you?"

"It's only sporting to get to know my rival," he said, again trying to lift her from the sadness that seemed as expansive as the Earth herself.

As invited, Arthur placed one hand in hers and the other on Randy's trunk. Together they transmitted thought and feeling in communication with the tree who was so dear to Melissa.

"It's an honor," Arthur said.

"Lighten up, young walker. Meeting me may be a *joy*, I'll grant you. Meeting my elders would be an *honor*."

Arthur grinned. "I like you," he said. "I have a cousin Randy who's a joker too. You remind me of him except you're a lot taller and better looking."

The three of them shared a quiet laugh. For a moment Melissa felt almost guilty.

"Not so, my young friend," Randy said. "Joy and sorrow can live in the same moment. Be willing to take a little of the former with this large dose of the latter."

As Arthur and Randy both sent her the same internal message, Melissa allowed the twinge of remorse and self-judgment to pass.

After saying a deeply-felt farewell to Randy, she and Arthur continued until they reached the small stream separating the two pieces of land. She was thankful to see no more trees cut down along their journey. As they approached the hillside, they heard men talking a little farther ahead.

"What should we do?" she asked. "Should we wait and come back later?"

"No, I want to see what's happening. You should probably wait here and I'll check things out."

"I'm going," she said stepping on the first rock that made her passage across the water.

"Your Mom said you were hard-headed," he said in a teasing tone.

On the Reynolds' side of the stream, she noticed instantly that the remains of Grandfather Poplar's trunk no longer stood in the ground. A pang of sorrow cut deeply through the center of her chest.

Once they reached the top of the hill, she and Arthur saw a crane loading the long, now lifeless trunks of her friends onto a large truck. Two men were moving limbs, stumps and brush into a massive pile, and three others stood conversing loudly at a distance beside a vacant bulldozer that had obviously already done its work. Melissa recognized one of men, who wore a suit out of place amid the mud and upturned earth.

"I see him too," Arthur said. "The commissioner. I think we should see what he has to say for himself."

As they approached, conversation halted, and Melissa saw one of the men, cued by the commissioner, motion to the crane operator to stop what he was doing and turn off the engine.

"Good afternoon, Melissa," Commissioner Newman said.

She was surprised he remembered her name despite the length of time he was at their home. How much impact could she have made, after all, with results like these?

"Mr. Newman," she said between gritted teeth.

"Who's your friend?"

Strangely, the man sounded cordial, unperturbed by the unfriendly energy she directed toward him.

"Arthur Fox," he interjected, no doubt sensing her discomfort in the moment.

"Yes, I believe I recognize you from the meeting last week.

"This is my brother Don," he said placing a hand on the shoulder of the younger man next to him. "I'm afraid we owe you an apology," he added.

"Things just get so busy sometimes that even with all our modern forms of communication messages don't always get to the right party at the right time."

"Speaking of which," Don Newman broke in, "we got a whole slew of messages on our voicemail and emails over the weekend after that newspaper article. And if I'd gotten through to my foreman here a little sooner," he said pointing to the third man in the group, "we would have made sure that big old poplar was left standing.

"Now it looks like we'll never hear the end of it," he added looking into the distance. "Newspaper people, TV people, and crazy people calling constantly." He sounded bitter. "I can't believe what we're having to do just to stop all the ruckus."

The commissioner, who appeared somewhat disapproving of his brother's remarks, continued: "I've come over to look at the acreage that's not been graded yet and start marking trees that will stay. Can't have the whole community up in arms over this. Besides, I'll never hear the end of it myself otherwise since my wife and daughters have joined your cause." He smiled somewhat sheepishly although the level of his discomfort was apparent.

"How would you two like to help me mark the ones that will stay?"

For a moment, Melissa imagined what it would be like going to each of her companions and choosing who would live and who would die. A shiver ran down her spine, and she felt queasy.

"I don't think I can do that," she said quietly.

"Give us a minute," Arthur said pulling her away from the group of men.

He lowered his voice and spoke to her. "Don't you see what this means?" he asked. "Remember I told you when I had to cut down living trees, I asked them which were ready to leave this life? The ones that are ready always give me a sense of it. We've got a chance to do that now.

"I know you're afraid to choose and that it would be horrible for you. Believe me, I understand," he said taking her hand in his. "But we're the only people who can know the difference between the ones that are willing to pass from this life and the ones who want to remain. The *trees* will be making the choice, not us."

She knew what he said was true, but her heart felt as if it might be crushed all over again. Even if Grandpop had said he was ready, she could never have let him go.

"It's all right," Arthur said. "I'll help you. I'll stand beside you."

She turned and walked back to the group of men.

"All right, we'll help. If you promise to listen to us and leave the ones we say."

"Well, my guess is, young lady, that you'd leave every one of them, so I can't promise that. I can promise to leave as many as is feasible according to your requests and my own best judgment. Will that suffice?"

She knew it would have to do. The commissioner got several pieces of chalk and a bag full of orange plastic ties out of his truck and set out with Melissa and Arthur to the parts of the Reynolds' land where the trees still stood.

Her heart breaking a little more with each good-bye, Melissa became the voice for her tall, bark-covered companions.

"This one stays," she would say. "These will go." Arthur bolstered her beneath the arm as if she were a feeble old woman barely able to trudge through the forest. Indeed that was how she felt—as if her childhood grew more distant with each tree whose spirit would no longer grace the land along these ridges.

Their journey had to be in haste given the lateness of the day; so she was barely able to take the time to bid farewell to each beloved tree. But the communication that traveled between the standing trees made the work swifter. As soon as the first was told of the choice to be made, the word passed rapidly to all, and each one was ready with an answer and to share a last loving moment.

Annabeth Ash, Henry Hemlock, Julius Juniper, Harriet Hawthorne—these and countless more were willing to sacrifice themselves to save their friends. Hilda Hickory asked to stay as she'd grown rather attached to the squirrels who pranced upon her boughs in search of nuts. "It makes no sense," she said, "but the chattering critters have depended on me and kept me company for so long."

The sky was darkening as they walked back out to the clearing. Still so many of her beloved friends remained to be marked. They hadn't finished surveying the Reynolds' property much less crossed the creek to what had been her family's land for all those years.

"That's all we can do for today," said Commissioner Newman. "I have to say I would have gotten a lot less done without you two along. For someone so reluctant to help, you sure made swift work of it."

"These trees mean more to me than I could ever tell you in a letter or a speech," she declared. "It aches to have any of them go, but at least this way the ones that are strong and healthy enough to weather the years ahead will stay. I just wish I'd had more time to get to the rest."

The commissioner appeared thoughtful for a moment.

"Well, tell you what. The crew would be hard-pressed to get more done tomorrow than the areas we marked already; so if you want to meet my brother—or me if I can get away—back here tomorrow after school, I imagine we could continue then."

"Thank you," Melissa answered, genuinely grateful for this opportunity no matter how much it hurt. "I'll be here."

"That's just fine then.

"And by the way, I'll save this for your parents to tell, but I think when you get home you'll have some news that will lift your spirits a bit."

"What kind of news?"

"Just wait 'til you're home, which you'd better be getting to soon if you expect to find your way before it's too dark."

She didn't bother to say that she could have found her way blind-folded at midnight, and the full moon made it a picnic. The commissioner turned and walked toward his truck. His brother and the other workmen had left already. The machines silent now, the only noises she heard were the evening birds beginning to sing. Somehow the sounds seemed mournful to her. She expected everything would for a while.

"It's getting pretty late," Arthur said putting his arm around her shoulder. "We can bless the grandfather tree another time."

"No, I can lead us back just fine. We can wait a little longer, can't we?"

"Sure, if you think your parents won't be upset."

"Maybe. But I need to do this now."

Arthur had dropped his knapsack in the clearing before they went with Mr. Newman. Retrieving it, he and Melissa walked to the place where Grandfather Poplar had spent his days. Although all landmarks were gone, she could still sense the very spot where he had stood. He was gone completely now, she knew; yet, she could almost feel the energy of their long afternoons, the laughter and the longing, the wisdom and the foolishness, the essence of the moments they had shared—all this somehow remained.

"I feel it too," said Arthur. "Like a rainbow that ends here in just this spot. A wave of energy and love. You and your grandfather tree left your mark here."

"I'd like to think so," she murmured.

From his backpack he drew a large shell, a small bag and a book of matches and emptied the contents of the pouch into the shell.

"These are the blessing herbs," he said.

As he lit the dried leaves, he began to chant in Cherokee words her mind failed to grasp yet her spirit understood. Breathing deeply despite her sadness, she did her best to reach the still place at her center, and in so doing she felt the close presence of Adahy beside her as she knelt upon the ground, smoke from the herbs wafting around her.

Arthur continued to chant and in her mind she heard these words: "Great One who nourishes all, accept the spirit of our grandfather who has fallen. We honor the wisdom that he taught us and the shelter that he gave. We honor the heart of the sacred trees, our guardians, the givers of life. May the bosom of the Earth accept her child in grace and replenish his spirit. May he know rebirth in the heart of spring. May the Standing Trees live long and be blessed. May all who have fallen in this time be renewed."

His voice grew still at last, and the embers of the small pile of herbs burned to ash, a single strand of smoke rising beneath the moonlit sky.

Far off Melissa heard her father's voice calling her name and Arthur's. "Oh, gosh, I got caught up in the prayer," she said. "We'd better hurry back."

Arthur took a bottle of water from his backpack and washed the shell, sprinkling some on the ground where it had lain. To be sure no spark remained, he emptied the bottle.

Standing, he took hold of her hand and helped her rise. "Let's go," he said grabbing his pack. "Your Dad's voice is getting closer and sounding more anxious."

Hurriedly yet carefully making their way back through the dark woods, they came upon her father carrying a large flashlight about a quarter of the way back. She could tell he was not pleased.

"What in heaven's name have you two been doing out there? I couldn't get a straight answer out of your brother.

"Look, sweetheart," he added more gently, "I know you're having a rough time. But that doesn't make it okay for you to be traipsing around out here after dark with some boy."

A flash of anger swept through her tired and spent body.

"Arthur's not 'some boy,'" she said emphatically. "And if you want to know what we were doing, you could ask Commissioner Newman."

"What do you mean?"

Arthur calmly related the story of how they had helped choose which trees would be saved across the stream.

"After that we did a Cherokee blessing for the great poplar that your daughter loved so much. I'm real sorry we were so late doing it. That was the reason we went out to the site in the first place, and we didn't want to come back without doing the blessing."

She could feel her father's demeanor change as Arthur spoke. He was clearly a lot wiser about how to handle adults than she was.

"Well, that's all right then, I guess. But your mother and I were worried, Melissa. And all it would have taken was an explanation to your brother, a note, something. You just go off half-cocked without thinking....

"Still, I guess at your age I did the same thing. But promise me this won't happen again. All right?"

She promised half-heartedly.

Back at the house, her mother had held dinner for them. A look of genuine concern on her Mom's face made Melissa feel sorry that she hadn't at least left a note. She simply had no idea they would be gone so long.

Eating in silence for a while, Melissa's father spoke at last.

"I was so disturbed by you being missing that I had to calm down a little," he said. "But now seems like a good time to tell you this....

"We talked to the Newman brothers today. They've been getting downright lambasted since the article on Saturday; so they were way more open to our proposal than I would have thought.

"Your mother and I asked if we could buy back some of the land we sold them. They were reluctant at first, but with more bad publicity looming over them and a public outcry, they decided it might not be such a bad idea after all.

"So we're going to be able to buy back 42 acres that are closest to us plus a stretch that even goes down by the creek. What do you think of that?" He beamed as he gave them the news.

Melissa looked at her mother for confirmation, and a wide, toothy smile was her answer. She glanced at Kevin, chewing a mouthful of spaghetti with a grin, and then at Arthur, whose dark eyes met hers in silent joy.

"Wahoo," said Kevin, tomato sauce running down his chin.

"Melissa, don't you have anything to say," her mother asked.

Her eyes, already swollen from crying, filled once again with tears, and she felt as if her heart expanded all the way up into her throat.

"Just thank you," she croaked, a whirlwind of emotion making the words come out more air than substance.

"For myself and for all the trees I love who stand on those acres."

She longed to share the news with the one who would have most understood, the one whose voice would have resounded through the forest as he passed on the tidings. The Grandfather of her heart, the wonder of her life, the listener, the stubborn wit, the curmudgeon counselor, the best friend she'd ever known.

The END

About the Author

With a love of wordplay and drawing, much of Diana Henderson's life has focused on the pursuits of a powerful and gifted imagination. She began writing poetry at age nine and amassed quite a volume by the time she entered her teens. She loved storytelling as a child as well and never grew out of the joy she found creating worlds outside this reality.

Her writing background includes a B. A. degree in English, specialization in writing, from East Carolina University in 1980. She later went through the graduate school at UNCG for teaching certification. For years thereafter, she continued to exercise her passion by taking classes in writing. She remembers fondly her greatest teachers: Terry Davis, author of *Vision Quest* (made into a film), *Mysterious Ways*, and *If Rock and Roll Were a Machine*, and Orson Scott Card, award-winning author of *Ender's Game*, *Speaker for the Dead*, *Xenocide* and many more.

Diana has long been devoted to the woodlands and the Earth

and to this day finds the need to spend time walking the forest trails and breathing among the trees. Her inner child comes to life whenever she takes the time to wander those paths.

In *Grandfather Poplar*, she hopes to be a voice for the trees and the world of nature that she loves so dearly. This book truly flowed from her heart, and Diana hopes it will touch the hearts of others and awaken the inner youth that knows that the forest holds the keys to tomorrow, that in such pure places we can find ourselves and breathe freely of *life*.

In addition to being a writer, Diana works as an editor (creativetype.biz) and enjoys helping to polish the writing of fellow authors.

Afterword

If you wish to read traditional stories of the Cherokee, the Museum of the Cherokee recommends *History, Myths, and Sacred Formulas of the Cherokees* by James Mooney. To learn how to pronounce the Cherokee words in this book, you may find assistance in the book, *Let's Learn Cherokee Syllabary*, by Marc W. Case.

More information about herbs and their uses may be found in *The Cherokee Herbal: Native Plant Medicine from the Four Directions* by J. T. Garrett, a member of the Eastern Band of Cherokee.